H to
Remember

ALSO BY SUSANNE O'LEARY

The Road Trip

SUSANNE O'LEARY

A Holiday to Remember

Bookouture

Published by Bookouture in 2018

An imprint of StoryFire Ltd.

Carmelite House
50 Victoria Embankment
London EC4Y 0DZ

www.bookouture.com

ISBN: 978-1-78681-505-7
eBook ISBN: 978-1-78681-504-0

For my niece Sofie, who loves sailing as much as I do.

Chapter One

Portofino lay sparkling below them in the late afternoon sun. With its pastel houses clinging to the steep slopes all the way to the pretty harbour crammed with boats, it was an enchanting place. Leanne forgot all the stress of the long drive on the winding coast road from Nice. She looked at the breath-taking view of the town, the azure sea and cerulean skies and relaxed, leaning her sweaty back against the leather seat of the red Mercedes convertible.

'Stunning,' she sighed and pulled out her phone from the glove compartment. 'Perfect shot for the next blog post.'

She took a few photos and then paused, staring at the glorious view, trying to take in that they were here, at the start of the next leg of their journey. What a roller coaster ride it had been. Winning all that cash in the lottery and then taking off in a red convertible for a mad road trip was still like a fantasy to Leanne. The drive from Ireland, through Wales and England and on to Amsterdam, Paris and finally the French Riviera had taken a new, exciting twist with the travel blog they were writing for *Women Now* magazine. All those women who followed it, cheering them on, being inspired by their great adventure. She smiled and put her phone back.

'This is probably the most beautiful view of the whole trip,' she said. 'Don't you think?'

Maddy didn't move or speak. 'It's like a dream,' she finally mumbled. 'This town, this view… incredible.'

'A mirage,' Leanne said dreamily. 'A fairy tale. Or something from one of those 1960s movies with Marcello Mastroianni. I can imagine Sophia Loren sashaying down the street singing "That's Amore".'

'That was Dean Martin. And Sophia sashayed down the slums of Naples, not Portofino.'

'I know.' Leanne took a few more shots and put away her phone. 'Do you always have to be the teacher? Can't we take a break from our jobs for a while? It's such a treat not to have a whole class of teenage girls glaring at us, don't you think?'

'Yes, but I like to stick to facts.'

'Feck your facts. I like to dream a little. I'm sure Sophia sang "That's Amore" too while making her famous spaghetti sauce. Then she fed it to Marcello and he licked her fingers before they jumped into bed. Those two. So sexy. I used to watch those movies on rainy Sundays when I was a teenager.'

Maddy sighed. 'Oh yeah. Me too. There's been nobody like them ever since.'

'No.'

Maddy turned to Leanne. 'I'm glad we left France. Sorry if I rushed you. But it all seemed to happen so fast. All of it. You finding your dad after all these years, my marriage finally ending and me suddenly – single. And then your dad being so… attractive, his fantastic house in the hills above Nice and then…' She stopped.

'And then Dad and you falling for each other?' Leanne said softly. 'Yeah that was a bit of a surprise, I must say. Not that he's not very handsome and you such a hot chick, even at your age.' She glanced at Maddy, hoping to cheer her up with her teasing.

Maddy smiled. 'Thanks. I know anyone over forty is ancient to a thirty-two-year-old, but it seems the old libido is still alive and kicking.'

Leanne winked. 'I could tell.'

Maddy blushed. 'It's a very romantic place, up there above Nice.'

'It's fabulous. But a little too glitzy and glamorous maybe, not like the real world. Like one of those old TV series. *Dynasty* meets *Dallas* on a James Bond set.'

Maddy laughed. 'Yes, exactly. Overwhelming, I have to say. Sorry about being the teacher, bossy all the time. It's kind of hardwired into me after all these years.'

'I know.' Leanne touched Maddy's shoulder. 'That's okay. I didn't mean to snap. Must be the heat. Makes me a little bitchy. And you didn't rush me at all. I wanted to go too.' She gripped the steering wheel and looked at Maddy. 'We both needed to get away. From him. Dad, I mean. I know I could have spent more time to get to know him after all the years we've been apart, but I need some space now after all the drama. And so do you, right?'

Maddy sighed. 'Yes. It was getting a little too – hot.' She blushed. 'Sorry. Don't mean to embarrass you.'

'You're not.' Leanne took a bottle of water from the side pocket of the driver's seat. 'I could feel the vibes between you two.'

'It was more than vibes,' Maddy confessed. 'I think... Maybe... Given time, we could get together and build something. I felt very much in tune with him on so many levels. But it was too soon. We had this strong attraction to each other nearly from the first time we met. But it was only a little over a week ago! Too soon to start a relationship, even though the sparks between us were incredible. I never felt anything like it.' Maddy glanced at Leanne. 'I hope that doesn't make you feel uncomfortable.'

'Not really. I didn't want to be there when it was going on, that's all. But that's not why I wanted to leave. He was trying to get me to come and work with him and make me his top assistant. I had a feeling he wanted me to run the company so he could escape to somewhere and do his own thing.'

Maddy let out a laugh. 'Yes, that's about right. He's bought an old farm in Haute Provence that he wants to restore. And he's planning to breed goats and grow olives. Move there and live off the land.'

Leanne giggled, rolling her eyes. 'Yeah, right. The clichéd fantasy of the aging hippie. Middle-aged men, huh? Always trying to live the dream and clinging to the impossible idea of never-ending youth.'

'Who wants to grow old?'

Leanne shrugged. 'Nobody, I suppose. But my dad...' She paused. 'He's very determined to get what he wants and he always succeeds in the end. Me turning up on his doorstep after all those years was like a sudden windfall to him. There I was, all grown up, educated and perfectly capable to take over his empire. I even have "the nose", for feck's sake!'

Maddy laughed. 'That nose thing is a bit of a hoot. You both having this amazing sense of smell and him building a perfume business because of it.'

'Oh yes, I know. And he was delighted to find I had inherited this weird talent. And the icing on the cake was you – a woman to share his romantic getaway with. I bet he could imagine you in one of those floaty Provençal dresses, bare feet and a big Scarlett O'Hara straw hat feeding the goats. How perfect was that?'

Maddy smiled wistfully. 'You're probably right. Except for the goats.' She sighed and stretched. 'I needed some space too. I'm looking forward to the sailing trip.'

'Me too.' Leanne turned to look at their dog, asleep on the back seat. 'I'm sure Bridget's feeling the heat. Do you want me to put the top on and turn on the aircon? It's getting too hot to bask in the sun.'

'Yes, please.' Maddy turned to pat the little poodle. 'She's panting, poor thing. Maybe we should take her out to let her have drink?'

'We'll be at the hotel in a few minutes. Then we can let her walk in the shade.' Leanne pressed the switch and the roof came up behind them and settled with a soft click. She turned on the air-conditioning full blast and closed her eyes as the stream of cool air touched her face. It had been a tiring drive along the winding coast road from Nice on the first leg of the journey to the Adriatic coast of Italy where they would take the ferry to one of the Dalmatian islands. The road had been spectacular with hair-raising bends on the very edge of the cliffs, through long tunnels where enormous trucks thundered beside them, blaring their horns at cars that were in their way. And, as they emerged from the dark tunnels, the glimmering blue Mediterranean sea below them, sparkling under the hot sun, was sometimes too close for comfort. Leanne longed for the drive to end and the boat trip to begin.

The sailing trip had been just an idea at first. During a party at her father's villa she had met Carlo, a cute Italian marketing manager who worked for her dad. She had thought his talk about a cruise in Dalmatia was just idle chatter but the following day Carlo had called her and asked if she and Maddy would like to get in on hiring a sailing boat, joining the trip he had mentioned. At the same time, Leanne had spotted the growing attraction between Maddy and her father, noticing that Maddy had seemed both confused and tense about it. *Not surprising*, Leanne thought. Maddy had only just broken up with her husband, she didn't need to jump straight into a relationship, especially with someone like her dad. He was too impatient and driven. Maddy needed someone more gentle and relaxed, Leanne felt, not someone who expected everyone to march to his tune.

Having only just been reunited with him after twenty years, Leanne was as confused as Maddy. She had grown up with the conviction that her dad had abandoned her – that was the story her mum had told her – always feeling bitter and hurt about it. But when they met in France, she found that his side of the story was completely different. Instead of a selfish, irresponsible man, she discovered her father's kind heart and deep sadness of having lost his daughter through no fault of his own, which moved her deeply. She had felt incredibly sorry for him when he told her how her mother had refused to marry him and share his dream of running a perfume business in France. Discovering her father's considerable wealth and thriving perfume company had also been mind-blowing to her. She was still trying to get used to the idea of their reunion and future father-daughter relationship. He had talked about making her his heir and asked her to take over the business, and it frightened her. This wasn't the freedom she had craved when she left Ireland and her needy mother, who had, she discovered, blocked her father's every effort to keep in touch. It was beginning to dawn on her that her parents were oddly alike. Both strong and stubborn with a will of iron, unable to compromise and get on with each other. Domineering, controlling and – insecure. Maybe that was the source of the problem between them? Well, she wasn't going to get caught in the middle, or get stuck running her dad's business while he played farmers in the wilds of Haute Provence.

Leanne looked down the steep slope towards Portofino, where the road wound its way through olive groves and clumps of lemon trees and the fronds of palms swayed in the light breeze. She started the engine. 'Are you ready?' she asked Maddy.

Maddy's eyes sparkled. 'You bet!'

The car rolled down the hill. The next part of their adventure was about to begin.

Chapter Two

Dear friends, here we are in beautiful Portofino, which is just as romantic and picturesque as the photo I just took. We had gruelling drive along the coast from Nice, where the traffic was BRUTAL! But oh, what views we were treated to as we whizzed around the hairpin bends, while all around us mad Italian drivers did their best to kill us, or at least squash us to jelly. I felt like I was on the last leg of the Monte Carlo Rally. The only thing missing was Cary Grant in the passenger seat, like in 'To Catch a Thief'. (I'm into old movies, as you know by now.)

Anyhow, we're now relaxing in this gorgeous hotel over-looking the harbour where sailing boats and yachts lie side by side with colourful fishing boats and everyone is having drinks before dinner at the cute little restaurants. I'm getting peckish myself, so I'll say cheerio before jumping into the little black dress (with the emphasis on 'little') I bought in Nice on the way here. Maddy is wearing a white linen top with blue Capri pants, in case you were wondering. AND… we have a date with a hot Italian, the very man who invited us to sail around the Dalmatian Islands. We'll be discussing

boats and clothes and food and wine – ya know, the usual
stuff for cruises. Gotta go as the prosecco beckons (and the
cute Italian!). More later. Ciao bambini!

There. Done. Leanne closed the laptop and got up from the window seat in her hotel room where she had been sitting rather uncomfortably for the past half hour. Their blog on the *Women Now* website had become incredibly popular, growing from a couple of thousand followers to over a hundred thousand in the past few weeks. 'The Great Euroscape' blog was the go-to read for women all over Ireland and the UK, following Maddy and Leanne's adventure ever since they left Ireland after their Lotto win in the syndicate with the other teachers. It seemed like a hundred years since the day they had got into the red sports car and set off from Maddy's house, her grumpy (now ex-)husband waving them goodbye. Then there was a mad escapade in the Cotswolds, and the road trip winding through Europe all the way to Nice.

Leanne laughed and shook her head. You couldn't make it up. Gosh, it was exciting, especially finding Erik, her dad, who had left home when Leanne was only twelve, not heard of again until she discovered he had adopted a whole new identity and started a business in Nice that had taken off big time and earned him millions. Meeting him again after two decades had been laced with pain and sorrow, swiftly replaced by anger at her mother.

The bitterness she had felt all her adult life towards her father had disappeared as the story unfolded. After he left, Erik had desperately tried to contact Leanne only to be stopped by her mother, who had practically declared him dead, simply because she didn't want anyone to know he had just upped and left – she couldn't bear the shame. Their reunion had been emotional and tearful. But it wasn't all hugs and smiles. A good start, but that was all, Leanne reflected. It would take a long time before they had a solid relationship. He was still a stranger to her, someone she would have to learn about and get used to. And she was, no doubt, not the sweet little girl he had left behind, but a grown woman of thirty-two with a strong will and a need to be loved and accepted by her father.

Enough soul-searching. Leanne put the laptop into her suitcase and pulled the black dress out of the bag with the fancy logo from the boutique in Nice. Time to get dolled up for the dinner with Carlo. He was a 'hottie' as she had said in the blog post, and seemingly, much to Leanne's excitement, just friends with the delectable Italian beauty Lucilla, who she had met back in Nice. Or was he? Leanne had a feeling they were somehow connected, but then Carlo had made her forget her suspicions when they danced under the stars and a big full moon on the terrace of a little local restaurant in Vence. He had held her close and sung along to the songs in her ear and called her *bella* and *cara*… After that magical moment he had reassured her when she asked if he and Lucilla were together, saying 'no, no, we're friends and business partners, nothing more.' And then they danced, cheek to cheek all night, only pausing to drink champagne and look at the stunning view. Leanne smiled as she remembered his breath on her neck, his deep voice and the way he had looked at her. What a night it had been, even though he hadn't as much as kissed her when he drove her home, just stroked her cheek and said how much he had enjoyed dancing with her. That was class! Lucilla had left early and then been perfectly friendly the next day, so there was nothing to worry about, Leanne told herself. And Lucilla had driven on to Florence to spend a few days with her family, so Carlo would be on his own tonight. She couldn't wait.

She looked at the dress again. Was it a little too much? Very sexy, yes, but was it sending the wrong signals? Would it be better to be more subtle? She pulled out a pair of white jeans. Maybe team this with that little strappy top…

Maddy opened the door and peered in. 'Hi. Are you ready?'

'Not quite,' Leanne mumbled, eyeing the pile of clothes of the bed.

Maddy walked in and looked around. 'Holy mother, what happened here? A break-in?'

'No.' Leanne sighed and sank down on the bed. 'Just me trying to get the right look for the dinner tonight. Subtly sexy, I thought. Sedate with a hint of sultry, ya know?'

'No I don't.' Maddy let out a laugh. 'Jesus, woman, it's only going to be me and Carlo in a tiny restaurant. Why worry?' She stopped. 'Oooh. Okaayyy. I see. It's not me you want to be sultry and subtle for. Or was it subtle and sexy?'

'Stop laughing.' Leanne pouted. 'This is important to me.'

Maddy shook her head. 'Don't be so dramatic. Why do you need a "look" at all? Can't you just be yourself? Isn't that trouble enough for any man?'

'No… Yes…' Leanne sighed and buried her head in her hands. 'I feel so confused when I am with him. I *can't* be myself. I'm always worried he won't like it, so then I try to guess what kind of woman turns him on.'

Maddy sat down beside Leanne. 'Let's go through this stuff then and I'll pretend to be him.'

Leanne got up, laughing. 'Yeah, right, you're going to turn into a sexy Italian now?'

'Anything for you, darlin'. Go on, what are the options?'

Leanne went through the items one by one, while Maddy shook her head at nearly everything until Leanne held up her first choice; the black dress. 'Aha! That's perfect. I know, quite obviously sexy but it's gorgeous. Very chic. To me it says "confident woman who knows her assets but don't touch until I let you".'

'Really? Not like some jumped-up Dub, then?'

'A Dublin woman but proud of it.'

Leanne looked thoughtful. 'In that case, I'll wear it. With no jewellery or even earrings. It'll be just me and the dress.'

'Perfect.' Maddy got up. 'I'll go and get ready myself.'

'Okay. See you in the lobby in ten minutes.'

Hmmm, Leanne thought as she did a twirl in front of the mirror when Maddy had left. *Not bad for a Dub.* The dress skimmed her slim body and ended mid-thigh, showing off her bronzed legs. With her light-blonde hair and brown eyes, black was the perfect colour for a summer evening. The dress had a demure neckline but plunged sexily to her waist at the back. *Cheeky, like me,* Leanne thought and winked at herself. But it didn't calm her down. Butterflies twirled in her stomach as she closed the door to her room and ran down the stairs to meet Maddy in the lobby. She couldn't wait to see what the night would hold.

*

They found the restaurant on the harbour, after a short stroll from the hotel down a lane lined with old crumbling houses where washing hung from the windows and rapid Italian could be heard from open doors.

Carlo, wearing a navy polo shirt and white chino trousers, waited for them outside and flashed a brilliant smile their way as they approached. '*Buona sera, belle signore*,' he said and kissed their hands, sending sparks flying for Leanne.

Maddy laughed. 'You're a tonic, Carlo. But you can turn off the charm now. We're hungry and thirsty, and we're dying to eat, not indulge in flirting, you know.'

'Speak for yourself,' Leanne protested. 'I'm always up for a bit of flirting.'

Carlo laughed. 'You will forgive me if I show my appreciation. You both look lovely. I'm a very lucky man tonight, no?'

'And so are we,' Leanne retorted. 'You're the best arm candy two girls could wish for.' She looked around the terrace next to the small harbour, where colourful fishing boats rocked gently on the waves. The sun had just set and the sky was turning a deep shade of blue, with stars sparkling above them. The tables were crammed together, close to the edge of the water that lapped against the rocks. The restaurant was packed with people eating and chatting and there was a smell of fresh grilled fish, garlic and herbs in the air.

Most of the tables were occupied, but Leanne spotted one at the far side, near the wall. 'Is that our table?'

Carlo made a chivalrous gesture. 'After you, madame.'

'Thank you.' Leanne shot a look at him over her shoulder as she led the way. God, he was gorgeous. With his black hair, green eyes and golden skin, he would turn the head of any woman with a pulse. And the voice; slightly gravelly with that sensual Italian accent. She couldn't deny how attracted she was to him. She was so pleased that the sexy goddess Lucilla wasn't in the picture any more, which would have made her back off. But his smile and his warm hand on her back told her he was as smitten as she was.

'So, what's your story, Carlo?' Maddy asked as they dug into the antipasto, a colourful array of sweet prosciutto, spicy salami, big, juicy green olives, deep red tomatoes and tiny balls of creamy mozzarella.

Carlo swallowed his mouthful of prosciutto. 'My story?'

'Yeah, I mean how did you come to work for Jan Hovden, Erik's company?' Maddy asked.

'Oh.' Carlo nodded and passed a plate of olives to Leanne. 'Well, it's a long story. A lucky break for me. I met him when I was doing some modelling for a perfume advertisement and then there was a party for people in the business after the – how do you say – shot?'

'Shoot,' Leanne cut in and eyed his toned torso. 'Modelling, huh?' *That explains a thing or two*, she thought. 'So you met my dad after the shoot was over, at a party?'

Carlo nodded. 'Yes. I was saving up for a course in marketing in Nice. It's easy money, really. Modelling, I mean.' Carlo smoothed his hair. 'When I met Jan – or Erik, which is his real name, as you know – we started talking about some ideas I had and then he asked if I'd join his team as an intern. I said yes. I have my own marketing business now and he's my top client.' Carlo drew breath and smiled at Leanne. 'Not very interesting for a beautiful night like this.' He gestured at the dark sky with glimmering stars and a nearly full moon rising above the roofs of the town.

Leanne smiled back. 'I wouldn't say that. People's stories are always interesting.' She propped her chin with her hand and stared at him in the light of the candle the waiter had just lit for them. 'But what about the rest? Where are you from? Where did you get those green eyes?'

Carlo pulled back a little. 'Ah, well…' A phone rang. He jumped and pulled it out of his pocket, looking oddly relieved. 'Excuse me. It's Lucilla.' He got up and walked a little distance from the table, starting an animated conversation.

'Stop it,' Maddy mumbled, darting a stern look at Leanne.

'Stop what?' Leanne asked, trying to look innocent.

'You know. You're coming on to him like a ton of bricks. He's beginning to look uncomfortable.'

Leanne squirmed. Maybe Maddy was right? Possibly. She coloured slightly, feeling embarrassed and oddly caught out. 'Mind your own business,' she muttered, avoiding Maddy's gaze.

'Okay, sorry for butting in. I just thought… well, if he and Lucilla are an item, maybe it's not a good idea to egg him on? It could turn this boat trip into a very tense affair. '

'He told me they broke up a while ago.' Leanne tossed her head at Carlo, who was now gesticulating wildly and nearly shouting into the phone. 'Can't you tell they're having a row?'

'Italians always sound as if they're fighting,' Maddy remarked before Carlo made his way back to the table.

Leanne glanced at him and noticed he didn't meet her eyes. Maybe it would be better to cool it for a while. Play hard to get. She sighed and dug into the rest of the antipasto in the little dishes. 'What's next on the menu?' she asked to break the silence and the sudden chill in the air.

'A little spaghetti, then some fish,' Carlo replied. 'In Italy we eat pasta as a starter. Just a small helping before the main dish.'

Maddy nodded. 'Makes more sense than piling in all that carbohydrate as a main dish like we do in Ireland. No wonder all the Italian women are so slim.'

Leanne groaned. 'Oh, whatever! No one's going to get in the way of me and my carbs. I hope all is well with Lucilla?'

Carlo brightened. 'Oh yes, very well. She says she's looking forward to meeting up with you in Florence tomorrow. She will have beds for us all in her apartment. And she says her cousin will join us on the boat trip.'

'Sounds great.' Maddy drank some of the crisp Pinot Grigio. 'Looking forward to Florence and meeting Lucilla's cousin.'

Carlo nodded. 'Me too. He's half Irish, so you should feel very much at home with him. He's a doctor.'

'Oh,' Maddy said. 'Where does he practise?'

Carlo frowned. 'Practise? He doesn't have to. He's fully qualified.'

Leanne laughed. 'She means where does he work.'

'Oh.' Carlo smiled and shook his head. 'Sorry. English is a difficult language. Even after a few years in New York, I still make mistakes. Antonio has been working abroad. But now he's back here to rest and then he's taking up a job in an Irish hospital, I think. Very learned man, too. He's also a great historian.'

'Sounds fascinating,' Leanne remarked, making a face at Maddy.

Maddy's phone pinged. She looked at it and frowned. 'A text message. Do you mind if I reply?'

'Say hi to Dad from me,' Leanne drawled. 'If that doesn't break the romantic spell, of course.'

Maddy looked confused at the sarcasm in Leanne's voice. 'This is from Tom. My soon-to-be ex-husband,' she explained.

'I'm sorry,' Carlo said. 'Must be difficult.'

'Not at all, surprisingly,' Maddy laughed. 'We're having one of those amicable divorces. It's like we just found each other as friends. No more aggro or that hostile shite that was going on between us for years. We're both very happy to have sorted it out and to get on with our lives. It's nice to be free, you know.'

'I see,' Carlo replied, looking confused. 'That's not the way we do it in Italy. We scream and fight and throw things. Then there's the blackmail and threats of assault and murder. Can go on for years.'

Leanne burst out laughing. 'Just let it rip, eh? Sounds dangerous. But you Italians are always shouting at each other. Even when you're just discussing the weather.'

Carlo smiled. 'That's true. We like a little drama in our lives.'

'I've had enough of that to last a lifetime,' Leanne muttered. 'My mother is a real drama queen. I don't miss it at all.'

The waiter removed the antipasto dishes and served them each a steaming plate of pasta. Carlo dug into his plate of *al dente* spaghetti with juicy fresh clams. 'We have to make plans. I have a suggestion to make. About your car. Don't feel you have to do this but…'

'But what?' Leanne asked. 'You want to drive it? No way. It's ours and we don't let anyone—'

Carlo laughed. 'No, that wasn't what I meant. Driving it would be fun, but this is about where to park it during the sailing trip. Please listen while I explain. This was Lucilla's idea. Her house in Florence has a garage, where the car would be safer than in some public parking place in Ancona, where we will get on the ferry. She also has a big car – a people carrier, I think you call it. So we could all travel from Florence to Ancona in that together. It will be fun to get to know each other before we get on the boat, she thinks.'

Maddy and Leanne exchanged a look. 'That's a good idea,' Maddy said. 'Especially about the car. I've been thinking about that and been a bit worried about parking it in a public place.'

Leanne nodded. 'And this takes the pain out of finding our way to Ancona. It's a long drive, I gather.'

Carlo put down his fork. 'It's not that bad. We take the Autostrada A14 across the country. It takes a little over four hours.'

'Sounds easy. Except for the crazy Italian drivers. It'll be a relief not to have to drive.' Leanne tried not to slurp, but failed, as she sucked on the last of her spaghetti. 'Sorry. Eating this politely is an art I have yet to master.' She wiped her mouth. 'Great stuff, Carlo. And we can leave the luggage we don't need at Lucilla's.'

'Of course. You need to buy a few things for the boat,' Carlo suggested. 'Lucilla will give you a list and then you can get it all in Florence. We'll have time for a day or two there.'

'Great,' Leanne said as the waiter approached. 'Holy shit, here's more food. How come you stay so slim with all these delicious things thrown at you all the time?'

Carlo shrugged, smiling. 'I work it off. But I don't eat like this every day.'

Leanne looked at the grilled red mullet with herb butter she had just been served. She picked up a wedge of lemon and squeezed it over the aromatic fish. 'Well this doesn't look too fattening. If we don't have dessert and take a walk afterwards, it might not be so bad.'

Carlo's eyes were suddenly a lot more flirtatious. 'Why worry? You have a beautiful body. Tall and slim, like a ballerina.'

Leanne felt her face flush. 'Thank you. But I also have to work at it. We all do, don't we, Mads?'

Maddy looked up from her phone. 'What was that? Sorry, I was miles away.'

'Nothing important.' Leanne dug in her bag for her phone. 'Let's do a selfie now, will we? For the blog post,' she explained to Carlo.

'You have a blog?' Carlo asked.

Leanne turned on her phone. 'Yeah. It's a kind of travelogue about our European trip in this amazing car. For all the girls out there, who're stuck at home. It's for a magazine called *Women Now*.'

'Really?' Carlo asked.

'Yes. We post pictures and short pieces nearly every day, they've been getting thousands of likes and shares. And here we are in this cute little restaurant with the lights of the town all around us, and the glittering water and the boats. We just have to do one with you in it. Handsome men go down very well on the Internet. Nearly as well as cute cats. You're into marketing, so you must know this.'

Carlo looked excited. 'Of course. So how many followers do you have?'

'About a hundred thousand by now.'

Carlo's eyes sparkled. 'Wow. And you have some sponsors?'

'Quite a few. Some cosmetic brands and a designer. And my dad, as you might know, if you handle his marketing.'

'Ah, yes. I think I may have heard it mentioned in the office.' He looked apologetic. 'I'm sorry, I haven't studied this part of his account. I left it to my assistant. I had no idea how big it was.' He took the phone from Leanne. 'I'll be happy to be in this if it helps. I'll ask the waiter to take the photo. Then I'll look better.'

'You mean we'll both look good,' Leanne replied, trying not to laugh at his demeanour. He suddenly seemed a little full of himself, so anxious to be in the shot, looking his very best. *Sheesh, what a diva*, she thought as he smoothed his hair for the tenth time and put his arm around her when the waiter aimed the phone at them. But then... when he pulled her closer and looked into her eyes, she felt herself melt. It was only for the photo, but in the moment that hot look he gave her felt like a promise.

'*Bellissimo!*' the waiter shouted and took a second shot. 'A beautiful couple you make, yes?'

'Yes, they do,' Maddy agreed, turning off her phone.

Carlo laughed and let go of Leanne. 'You pose very well. Nearly like a model for Dolce & Gabbana. Have you ever tried?'

'Modelling? No, never,' Leanne replied. 'Hey, Maddy,' she exclaimed, 'you should be in a photo too.'

'Gosh, no,' Maddy said, laughing. 'You two make such a cute couple, it'll be great for the blog. Leave me out this time.'

'But you are very pretty,' Carlo protested. 'With your honey colour hair and the very blue eyes.'

'Thank you, Carlo,' Maddy replied. 'You're very sweet. But this time I feel I'd ruin the effect.'

'Okay, if that's what you want,' Leanne said. 'Anyway,' she breezed on. 'The people who run the website give us royalties and a cut of whatever they make on advertising. But we donate our own takings to charity. At the moment it's the homeless in Dublin, and Oxfam. But we can donate to one you'd like too.'

Carlo looked thoughtful. 'Nice. Okay, in that case, I'd like you to give some money to Doctors Without Borders. Lucilla supports them too. And her cousin Antonio.'

'Okay,' Maddy said. 'We'll add them to the list. We could rotate the charities and do different ones from time to time.'

'Good idea. Hey, this is really a great shot.' Leanne showed the photo to Carlo. 'What do you think?'

Carlo looked at the screen for a long time. 'This is very special, I think. Are you posting that on your blog?'

Leanne nodded. 'Yes. I promised them a hot Italian, so I have to deliver. You don't mind?'

'No,' he replied, if he was used to being called hot. 'Go ahead. I'll be interested in the reactions of your followers. I'll take a look at the comments later.'

Leanne glanced at Carlo wondering what was going on behind that smooth exterior.

He met her gaze, looking at her appraisingly. Then he smiled broadly and picked up his glass. 'A toast. To this night, to beautiful women from Ireland and to our future adventure. *Saluti*, as we say here.'

Maddy smiled and raised her glass. '*Saluti*, Carlo.' She finished her wine and got up. 'But now I think I'll turn in. It's been a long day and I want to walk Bridget before I go to bed.'

'Thanks, Mads,' Leanne said gratefully. 'I'll walk her in the morning, then.'

'Perfect. Goodnight, Carlo. Thanks for dinner.' Maddy leant over to kiss Leanne on the cheek. 'Don't do anything I wouldn't do,' she muttered in her ear.

'That'll give me a lot of scope,' Leanne whispered back, which made Maddy snort out a laugh.

Carlo turned to Leanne when Maddy had left. 'Nice woman.'

'Yes. My best friend.'

'It's good to have friends.' He took her hand gently. 'But you and I, we could be more than that.'

Leanne smiled, butterflies in her stomach. 'Maybe.'

'Oh, I'm very sure of that,' he said, bringing her hand to his mouth and kissing it. 'I'm so happy you're coming on the trip. Do you enjoy sailing?'

'Love it,' Leanne replied, her voice shaking slightly as he kept caressing her hand. 'My dad and I used to sail in Dublin bay when I was small. And when I was older, in Kerry, on the Atlan—'

'Ah, but that's not the Adriatic Sea. This trip will be something special.' He turned her hand and kissed the palm. 'But now I have to go, *cara mia*, Much to prepare and organise.'

'Oh, but…' Leanne started, glancing at the starry sky, the moon and the still water, reflecting it all. She had envisaged a romantic walk around the harbour and maybe a little smooching.

'And you have an early start tomorrow,' he said, pulling her up. 'But there'll be plenty of time for… friendship when we're on the trip,' he whispered as he held her tight for a moment, kissing her lightly on the mouth before letting her go.

Leanne smiled, reassured, her lips tingling from his gentle kiss. He was right. Tonight, despite the romantic setting, was not the right time for smooching. There would be plenty of opportunities when they were on the sailing boat. She couldn't wait.

Chapter Three

There were a lot of comments about the photograph the following morning. In bed in the little hotel, Leanne read through them just as the sun was rising on the harbour and the seagulls' plaintive cries began to fill the air. The photo looked even better on the blog; the contrast between Carlo's dark looks and Leanne's light-blonde hair and pale skin so striking. And the way they looked at each other was also quite revealing, especially his seductive smile in one of the shots. She smiled as she thought of that light kiss the night before. It had held a lot of promise. She looked at the screen again and laughed at the comments. She wasn't the only one to find Carlo divine.

'What a fab couple!' one of the followers wrote. 'A match made in Italy,' another said, followed by: 'these two are meant to have a sizzling love affair.' The comments from her Dublin friends made her laugh and cringe at the same time. Especially the one that said: 'that guy looks like a bit of a ride.'

Then there was an email from Brenda McIntosh, the editor of *Women Now*. *Fab photo. I see great potential for an online romance. Even if it's not really happening, if you see what I mean? Could you keep that going for a while? It could be huge…*

Leanne sighed. Brenda was so pushy. But to be fair to her, most of her suggestions had worked so far. This one was more challenging. Of course she was attracted to Carlo, who wouldn't be? But to fake a romance just for business seemed cold and calculating. And if the romance she hoped for actually happened, it would be a little cheap to make it public. And in any case, he probably wouldn't agree.

Leanne checked her watch and got out of bed. Time to get going if they were to arrive in Florence in time for lunch. Carlo had said it would take just under three hours, but they planned to see Pisa on the way, which might slow them down as it was a popular tourist attraction, bound to be busy.

Leanne pondered Brenda's email and the reams of comments as she pulled on linen shorts and a black t-shirt. A fictional romance with a man she fancied was, at first glance, a fun thing to do. But the more she considered it, the worse it seemed. She would have to act out her true feelings pretending they were fake and then appear cool and a little distant in real life. She would, she realised, have to pretend to pretend. The thought made her dizzy. No, she said to herself as she went downstairs to the terrace for breakfast. No, no, no. It wasn't going to happen if she had anything to do with it. But maybe they wouldn't have to pretend after all?

Maddy and Carlo were already at their table when Leanne arrived on the terrace. They were chatting and laughing while drinking bitter black coffee from large cups and eating fresh bread and apricot jam. Bridget had sought the shade under Maddy's chair and sat there panting. She wagged her tail when she spotted Leanne but didn't move from her spot.

'Good morning,' Carlo said and rose to pull out a chair for Leanne.

'Morning.' Leanne sat down and reached for the coffee pot.

Maddy pushed the bread basket to her. 'Sleep well?'

Leanne poured herself some coffee, inhaling the delicious scent as it filled her cup. 'Very well, thanks. How about you?'

Maddy shook her head. 'Not so good. It was too hot.'

'Was the air-conditioning on the blink?' Leanne asked.

'I switched it off. I hate aircon in the bedroom.'

'I'll drive today if you want,' Leanne offered. 'Then you can snooze on the way.'

'Thanks. Sure you don't mind? You drove all the way here yesterday.'

'It's an easy drive,' Carlo remarked. 'And you can stop on the way. You wanted to see Pisa, no?'

'If you think it's worth it,' Leanne said.

'Just for the tower, perhaps,' Carlo replied. 'But otherwise, not really. And you'll probably think it's small and a lot less spectacular than in the tourist brochures. Up to you, of course. I'll be going straight to Florence.'

'We'll think about it.' Maddy got up. 'I'm going back to my room for a little rest and to put my things together. Give me a shout when you want to leave.'

Leanne glanced at her watch. 'In about an hour at the latest, I think. It's already eight thirty.'

'Okay.' Maddy crouched to retrieve Bridget from under the chair. 'Come on, sweetheart. It's cooler in my room.' She gathered the little dog in her arms. 'See you later, lads.'

Carlo smiled at Leanne when Maddy walked away. '"Lads?" Is this Irish for "guys?"'

'That's right.' Leanne smeared the sweet, sticky jam on a warm roll. 'You'll be hearing a lot of Irish talk during the trip, so you'd better get used to it!'

'I like the sound of your accent. And the lilt in your voice.' Carlo's eyes were serious as he looked at her. 'I saw the blog post and the comments. Very flattering.'

Leanne managed to look back at him without blushing. God, he was even more gorgeous in the early morning light. 'I know. I'm sorry. I hope they didn't embarrass you.'

He laughed. 'No. It confirmed what I was feeling yesterday. About how we look together. But...' He paused. 'What does "a bit of a ride" mean in proper English?'

Leanne giggled, her cheeks hot. 'It's Irish girl-speak for "hunk".'

Carlo didn't even blink. 'I see. Good to know. The photo and the comments gave me an idea. I have talked to Lucilla about it and she's very enthusiastic.'

Leanne frowned. 'Enthusiastic? About me? I thought she might be still upset after your break-up?'

Carlo shrugged. 'No. She was the one who broke it off. But neither of us are upset. So much conflict and jealousy. Not good for us or our business. Now we're just friends, who happen to work together.'

'So definitely no romance between you, then?' They had looked quite close the first time she'd met them.

'Not any more.' He made a dismissive gesture. 'Forget romance. This is about a business proposition.'

Leanne's heart sank. 'What kind of business?' she asked, trying not to show her disappointment. He had been so romantic the night before.

'Fashion. We've just signed a contract to market a brand-new label. They're called Risorse Naturali.'

'Never heard of them.'

'That's because they haven't advertised much yet. They're launching a new concept in clothing. All made with biodegradable materials. The name means Natural Resources. Very stylish and at the same time good for the environment. Very in vogue. Plus, I think you'd like their style.'

'Oh. Okay, so what does this have to do with us? You and me, I mean.'

Carlo leaned forward and fixed Leanne with his green eyes. 'You and me, wearing the Risorse Naturali clothes in your blog posts. Can you imagine the marketing potential? I mean, as your blog is growing in popularity all the time, if there were more photos of us together wearing that brand and you mentioned it now and then, it could be a fantastic chance for greater visibility for this new designer.' Carlo's eyes softened. 'They are a young and talented couple and don't have much money. I want to help them get off the ground. I'm not going to charge them a fee, you understand. We have an agreement that we'll just get a cut of their profits, should there be any. If not, they don't owe us anything.'

Leanne blinked. 'I see. That seems incredibly generous.'

Carlo shrugged. 'Money isn't everything. I like to support people I believe in. Especially if they're young, poor and hardworking. The reward will be in seeing them succeed and begin to earn a living.'

'I see what you mean,' Leanne said, touched by the warmth in his eyes. 'I'll think about it. I have to talk to Maddy, too. And the *Women Now* people might not…' She stopped. What was she saying? Of course *Women Now* would love it, if it made money for them. And Carlo dressed in any kind of get-up would make women all over the world drool into their lattes. But… 'I'll let you know what we decide,' Leanne said, looking thoughtfully back at Carlo. 'And I'll have a look at their collection too.'

Carlo smiled and got up. 'I see. Okay. I'll send you a link to their website so you can take a look. It's a little… well, avant-garde. But now you have to excuse me. I have to make a few calls and then I'm going straight to Florence. Has Lucilla sent you directions to her flat?'

'Yes, she did. We had a long chat on the phone before we left and she sent me a map and full instructions.'

'Good.' He leant down and kissed her cheek. 'Ciao for now.'

'Oh, uh, ciao,' Leanne stammered, his light kiss still warm on her cheek as he walked away. She mulled over what he had just said. His suggestions seemed crazy, but at the same time, it could be fun and a great opportunity. Why was she hesitating? Posing with a drop-dead gorgeous guy in Italian designer clothes, what's not to like? Leanne let out a giggle. Her friends would be sick with envy. Especially those who had been swanning around boasting about their fabulous weddings, while she'd been single the whole time. It was worth it only for that.

Chapter Four

'So what do you think?' Leanne asked Maddy when they were driving on the autostrada, the roof closed and the air-conditioning going full blast.

Maddy woke up from her snooze. 'What? Oh, the… Could you tell me again? I wasn't really listening, sorry. Must have nodded off there.' She turned to the back seat as Bridget started to whine. 'I'll take her on my knee. She wants to look out the window.' Maddy hauled Bridget onto her lap, and the little dog settled happily, looking out the window and licking Maddy's hand now and then. 'She loves being part of the action. But go on, what was that you were saying?'

'Carlo wants us – him and me – to wear designer clothes in the photos I post on the blog. It's to market this new label he's handling for his firm. He thinks it has huge marketing potential. If you saw the reactions to the photos we posted last night, you'll know what I mean.'

'I see.' Maddy sat up. 'And where does this leave me? Don't get me wrong, I see the benefits for you. It's just that the blog was supposed to be our great escape and our amazing trip through Europe. How will you posing in some new fashion label with an Italian hunk tie in with that?'

Leanne glanced at Maddy, startled by her annoyed tone. 'Uh, well, it'll change things a little. But you weren't too hot on the blog in the first place. I still remember how angry you were when you found out about it.'

Maddy stared straight ahead. 'Yes, but that was also because you hadn't told me but went ahead without asking me first. And then I had to find out about it from that Brenda woman when she called me the very first day of our trip. But after a while I grew to like it. It's fun. I love reading the comments from all the women out there. How we're inspiring them. And some men too. People who're having vicarious fun through us.'

'I know. But won't the women love seeing me with Carlo? You saw the comments, didn't you?'

'I did. Maybe including Carlo in the posts would be a fun thing at first. But it could also become boring and then we'd lose followers.'

'Boring? Carlo?'

'Yeah. He's a little too into himself, don't you think? He might try to take over the whole thing if we're not careful. Why doesn't he start his own blog?'

Leanne shrugged. 'I suppose he could. But it takes a long time to get enough followers—'

'Hey, I have an idea,' Maddy interrupted. 'How many followers do you have on Instagram? Your own account, I mean.'

'I'm not sure.' Leanne thought while she stepped on the accelerator and changed lanes to overtake a red Fiat Bambino. 'Around fifty thousand or something.'

'That's a lot. How about using that account for your fashion fling with Carlo? You could mention it on the main blog and then those who want can follow you on Instagram if they want to drool over you and Carlo. Wouldn't take long for that to take off big time.'

Leanne glanced at Maddy, shooting her a big smile. 'You're a fecking genius, girl!'

'Sure I know,' Maddy said, flicking her hair back. 'But it'll mean extra work for you.'

Leanne let out a raucous laugh. 'Work? Smooching with that ride in designer clothes? That's the kind of work I like.'

'Stop calling him a "ride". I hate that word.'

'I know, but that's what gorgeous guys are called in Ireland right now. Your suggestion is a great idea though. This way we don't have to involve you, and the Euroscape blog will go on as always, keeping its universal appeal.'

'But you have to make some sort of agreement with Carlo and his firm,' Maddy said. 'This would mean free advertising for him otherwise. You don't want to be a pushover, do you? Even if you're madly in love with the guy.'

Leanne felt her face flush despite the air-conditioning. 'I'm not in love,' she protested. 'In any case, I think Lucilla still thinks she owns him, even if they broke up.'

'Yes, but she's been perfectly friendly to you, hasn't she?'

'Oh yes. And she was very enthusiastic when we talked about the sailing trip back at Dad's house that night of the party. And she invited us to her place in Florence and everything.'

'Seems okay, then,' Maddy remarked. 'Maybe it's all in your head – I wouldn't worry about it. She might just be a little sad about having broken up. She could still have feelings for him. But I'd say that's all.'

'I hope so,' Leanne sighed. 'I'm not sure I want to get involved in some kind of cat fight with her.'

Maddy laughed. 'Yeah, right. I can see that look in your eyes.'

'What look?'

'The one that means you won't give up until hell freezes over. I just hope you won't get hurt in the process.'

'Hurt? As long as I get laid, I won't complain,' Leanne said with more bravado than she felt.

'Is that all you're after?' Maddy studied Leanne intently. 'Just sex? Yeah, okay, he's drop-dead gorgeous and any woman's dream date. For a night. If that's all you want, fine. Can't blame you for being attracted.'

Leanne took her eyes off the road for a second and glanced back at Maddy. 'No, that's not all. There's a lot more to Carlo than a pretty face. Anybody can get laid, but love's a different matter. And I'll get it all, even if it takes forever.'

'With Carlo?'

'I've only known him for like five minutes,' Leanne replied. 'I need to test drive him first. Maybe he'll be the one – or not, who knows? Love is out there, though. Waiting for me.' She stepped on the accelerator and the car surged forward up the motorway towards Florence.

'Pisa,' Maddy said as they swept past a set of road signs. 'It's the next exit. We take the E76 and then go on the SS12, it says on the map. Doesn't look too far. And we've made really good time as you drive as if we're in a rally.'

'Pisa?' Leanne glanced at Maddy. 'You want to go there?'

'Sure, why not? Just a quick look to take few fun photos for the blog.'

'Okay.' Leanne nodded, indicating right at the next exit sign and driving up the slipway. 'The leaning tower had better be leaning.'

'It does. In fact, it seems to be leaning more and more each year, I've heard.'

'Then it's good to take a peek before it falls over,' Leanne remarked. 'Like my great-aunt Maureen when she's had one too many.'

Maddy laughed. 'She sounds like a lot of fun.'

'Fun? Not sure, but she never says no to a pint or two. Or five.'

'I don't believe you.'

'I swear. The women in County Clare know how to put away the booze. Worse than the men.'

'Scary.'

'You bet. My auntie Maureen has a hollow leg when it comes to drink.'

'How old is she?'

'Eighty-five. And she can still do a handstand when she's sober.'

'You're pulling my leg.'

Leanne grinned. 'Yes. Just about the handstands. But the rest is true. I swear.'

'I want to be like her when I grow up,' Maddy said, laughing.

'Oh, yeah, me too. I want to be wild like her if I get to live that long.'

'You're well on the way,' Maddy remarked. 'I was wondering where you got it.'

'Hehe, now you know,' Leanne chuckled. 'So where's this tower, then? Can't wait to see it.'

Maddy pointed ahead. 'I can see the tip of it, just there.'

'Oh yes.' Leanne focused on the view. 'There it is. Leaning like my auntie on a Saturday night…'

The famous leaning tower, standing on a patch of grass beside the cathedral, was much smaller than it looked in the pictures. But there was a great buzz in the air, as they got out of the car, with tourists milling about, chatting in all kinds of languages and buying ice cream and hot waffles, the sweet smell filling the air. They pushed through the throng and joined the happy crowd taking selfies in front of the tower, laughing, pretending to be drunk. Photos taken, they were about to leave when Leanne declared she simply had to have a plastic replica of the tower sold in the stalls near the tower, along with other souvenirs like gaudy scarves, straw hats and postcards.

'All made in China,' Maddy declared, while Bridget strained at the lead. 'But you go on, I'll take Bridget for a piddle in the little park over there.'

'Okay. Shouldn't take me long,' Leanne said and pushed through the throng of tourists to browse among the array of towers on the counter. She picked up one that was small enough to fit in her handbag. When she had paid for it, someone bumped into her so hard she dropped both the tower and her handbag, making the contents spill out. 'Feck!' she exclaimed, dropping to her knees to gather up her things, glaring at the culprit. She gasped as it dawned on her who it was. 'Jesus, if it isn't Assumpta O'Callaghan,' Leanne, almost shouted, staring at the short, chubby brunette.

The woman jumped and stared back at her. 'Leanne! Oh my God, I don't believe it.'

'Well, you'd better.' Leanne laughed, standing up. 'What the hell are you doing here?'

'I'm on my honeymoon,' Assumpta said and pulled at her bright yellow t-shirt with the Versace logo.

'But I thought...' Leanne paused. 'Weren't you going to the Bahamas? At least that's what you said in your Insta post about the wedding. Nice cake by the way. So big.'

'The Bahamas?' a voice cut in behind them. 'That must have been a typo. We were going to Benidorm, but the Ryanair flights were all fully booked. So we went on this bus tour instead. Five towns in a week.' The tall ruddy man held out his hand to Leanne. 'I'm Brendan, Assumpta's husband.'

Leanne shook his hand. 'Hi, I'm Leanne. Assumpta and I were in the same class in school.'

'Nice to meet ya,' Brendan said, smiling.

'Lovely,' Leanne replied with a fake smile in Assumpta's direction.

'Your blog is such fun,' Assumpta said as if it was nothing of the kind. 'But I'd appreciate if you didn't mention meeting me. We want to be... incognito during our honeymoon. Right, Brendan?'

'Fine with me,' Brendan replied. 'But hey, Assumpta, sweetheart, we have to go. The bus leaves in a few minutes.'

Assumpta nodded. 'Okay. I'll just pay for my stuff. Did you find the... what I asked you to buy?'

Brendan held up a supermarket bag. 'Yup. Got the prunes and some water. This should shift it. Bus tours, eh?' he said to Leanne. 'Bungs you up big time. Sitting for hours isn't good for the old digestion, is it?'

'I suppose not.' Leanne smiled at Assumpta and held out the plastic tower. 'Here. Have this as a wedding present. A memento of us meeting here. Hope you feel better soon.'

'Thanks,' Assumpta sniffed, shoving the tower into her handbag.

'Bye, Leanne,' Brendan said. 'Have a nice holiday.'

'Thanks. You too.' Leanne managed to keep a straight face until Assumpta and her new husband had left and then she burst out laughing. How ridiculous. And how revealing. All those blingy wedding photos were just a front. The truth was far less glamorous and she realised in a flash that her own life was probably a lot better and more fun. She didn't have to pretend, she *was* living the dream. She felt a dart of pure joy before she started to laugh again. She was still in stitches when Maddy caught up with her.

'What's the matter? What happened? Who was that?'

'Assumpta from school,' Leanne chuckled. 'One of the Bridezillas. Married a dentist and had this big splashy wedding. Boasted about it on Instagram and said they were going to the Bahamas on their honeymoon.'

'Why were they here, then?' Maddy asked, looking confused.

'Because she lied. They couldn't even get on a Ryanair flight to Benidorm so now poor old Assumpta is sitting on a bus for five days getting constipated. Her new husband had bought her a big bag of prunes. I bet that won't go on any Insta post.'

'Oh, God,' Maddy giggled. 'That's hilarious. Poor woman, though. She must be feeling awful.'

'She didn't seem that pleased to see me either,' Leanne remarked. 'I do wonder why?'

'Maybe she was worried you'd blow her cover? I mean if you even hinted at meeting her, it would make her look bad.'

Leanne shook her head. 'Tempting, of course. She was always so snooty to me at school. A real bully. I could pay her back for all those little jibes that made me feel so miserable. But I think I'll just let her sweat. I might hint at meeting someone, but...'

Maddy laughed. 'Sneaky, but brilliant. Much more subtle.'

'Revenge is a dish best served cold, they say. And this one is colder than ice cream on the North Pole.' Leanne bent down to pick up Bridget. 'How are you, my darling pooch? Ready for Florence? I bet you'll be a big hit there.'

Bridget licked Leanne's face and wagged her little tail, letting out a happy bark.

'She's ready,' Maddy declared. 'Let's go. Did you get your plastic tower?'

'I decided I didn't want it after all. I gave it to Assumpta as a wedding present.' Leanne's smile was wicked. 'But I got a much better souvenir.'

'What was that?'

'A glimpse behind the façade of Assumpta's so-called glamorous life. Priceless.'

They followed Lucilla's rather confusing directions through rolling green hills, past the vineyards of Tuscany, where beautiful old villas were surrounded by cypress trees and tightly clipped hedges. After a long frustrating drive around the middle of Florence, with its ancient houses and tiny squares, getting stuck in dead ends, they finally found the house. It wasn't quite the sleek apartment building they had imagined, but a magnificent crumbling sixteenth-century palazzo in a narrow street near the main square.

'Wow,' Leanne whispered, awestruck as she looked up at the pink stucco façade and the ornate windows. 'This is some pad.'

'Where's the garage?' Maddy shouted over the cacophony of hooting. 'Come on, we're blocking the traffic.'

Leanne stuck her head out the window. 'Shut up!' she yelled to the backlog of angry Italian drivers. 'We're trying to find the bloody garage. Give us chance!'

Maddy frowned, rolling her eyes. 'Stop shouting. It's around the corner, it says here at the bottom of the instructions she sent us. We have to put in a code and the gates will open.'

'Okay.' Leanne revved the engine, drove around the corner on two wheels, and slammed on the brakes in front of a set of tall black gates. 'Where's the code thingy?'

'I'll have a look.' Maddy jumped out, found the panel and punched in the numbers. The gates slowly slid open and they drove into a dark courtyard, parking between a Fiat and a battered Opel Zafira.

'I bet that's the people carrier we're taking to Ancona,' Leanne remarked. 'A bit of a come-down after our beautiful Merc.'

'Ah, come on,' Maddy laughed. 'You talk like a spoilt little rich bitch. It's far from luxury cars you were reared, my girl.'

Leanne stretched and smiled. 'Yeah, I know. But it doesn't take long to get used to money and style. What can I say?'

'You could have all of that if you took your dad's offer.'

Leanne snorted. 'Nah. I don't want him breathing down my neck for the rest of my life. I want to do my own thing and make my own mistakes. I love my dad but I wouldn't want to work with him. Too much, too soon, I think.'

'I know what you mean,' Maddy laughed. 'I'm not sure I'd want to work with him either.'

'There you go.' Leanne got out of the car and looked around. 'So this is where we leave our baby for a few weeks? Is it safe?'

'I'm sure it is. Look at the Lancia and the Audi over there on the other side.'

'Pretty fancy,' Leanne remarked as she clicked her fingers at Bridget. 'Out you come, sweetheart. Time to hobnob with the Italian aristocracy.'

Maddy got out and picked Bridget up. 'Aristocracy?'

'Yeah.' Leanne opened the boot. 'Lucilla's a countess or something. Do you want me to take out your suitcase?'

'Yes, please. We might as well take all our stuff with us. Then we can sort out what we're bringing and what we're leaving. Does Lucilla know we'll be taking a dog with us on the boat?'

'Yes. She said that was perfectly fine. One of her friends brought her little dog with her on a cruise like that last year. "*No problema*," she said.'

'Great.' Maddy let Bridget down and clipped the lead onto her collar. 'Give me my bag and we'll go.'

'Where?' Leanne asked, looking wildly around the courtyard. 'I don't see a door.'

'I think we have to go around the house and in through the main entrance,' Maddy suggested.

'Aha! Okay. I bet there is some scary concierge who'll ask us a load of questions before they let us in. These places always do,' Leanne said, as if she was constantly visiting grand palazzos in Italian cities. But it was only bravado. She felt very much out of her depth in this elegant environment. Wealth and class intimidated her, because of her mother's humble background and her childhood, where they'd struggled along. And this kind of class in a foreign environment was even more daunting. But Maddy charged ahead, carrying her suitcase in one hand, Bridget on the lead with the other, looking cool and confident. Leanne trotted after her with her own bag and Bridget's bed and water bowl.

The vast entrance door was opened by a surly woman in a blue dress and white apron. 'You are the guests of the contessa, yes?' she barked, glaring at them.

'Contessa?' Leanne asked. 'You mean Lucilla Fregene?'

'Contessa Fregene de Popolonia,' the woman corrected, looking annoyed. 'She waits you upstairs. Five floors.'

Maddy smiled at the woman. '*Grazie, signora.* Come on,' she hissed at Leanne. 'Get in the lift.'

Leanne followed Maddy across the shiny marble floor to the ancient-looking lift with its black iron gates. 'Jaysus, that looks lethal. Are you sure it's safe?'

'Of course it is.' Maddy put her suitcase down, pulled the iron doors open and stepped into the mahogany-panelled interior. 'It's old but posh.'

Leanne followed, darting frightened looks around the cabin and clanking the doors shut. Bridget shivered at their feet. 'Why are there so many mirrors? To make it look bigger?'

'Maybe to allow ladies to check their hair and make-up before they arrive?' Maddy suggested and pressed the button. The lift started to rise slowly, creaking through the building and as they got higher, they could see that every floor was home to two huge mahogany doors with brass plates, signalling two apartments. The lift creaked and groaned, and finally arrived at the fifth floor, which only had one door.

'She must have the whole top floor,' Leanne exclaimed. She heaved the door of the lift open and stepped onto the red carpet where she put down her suitcase. 'Red carpet, gee whizz. This place is fierce posh.' She looked up at the high ceiling, where cherubs floated among clouds. 'Will you look at that! A painted ceiling in an apartment block.'

Maddy pulled a reluctant Bridget onto the landing. 'It's not an apartment block, you twit, it's a palazzo. God, I wonder how they managed to get all the way up here before there was a lift. All those ladies in their rococo dresses.'

'Maybe this was the servants' floor?' Leanne suggested, eyeing the bell pull. 'If I pull this, will something happen do you think?'

'Try it and see.' Maddy gathered Bridget in her arms. 'Poor thing, she's shivering with nerves. I think she's scared of lifts.'

'She's never been in a – uh – *palazzo* before either.' Leanne raised her hand to the bell handle. But before she had a chance to pull it, the door swung open.

Chapter Five

'Here you are!' Lucilla, her generous curves poured into a slinky red dress, stood in the doorway. 'I was just going to give you a call. Lunch is ready and we have some family here who want to meet you.' With her flashing dark eyes and black curly hair, she was the epitome of a Italian beauty. But there was a friendly look in her eyes, which made Leanne feel more relaxed about her designs on Carlo. No aggro there. What a relief.

Lucilla stepped aside. 'Please come in. I see you brought your sweet dog as well.' She held out her arms. 'Give her to me. I want to cuddle her.'

Maddy handed Lucilla the little dog, who immediately started to lick the young woman's face. 'Oh, *carina*, so cute,' Lucilla cooed as she led the way into a vast entrance hall lined with marble statues and enormous mahogany cupboards the size of confessionals. The floor was covered in an Oriental carpet, its once vivid colours faded by sunlight and age. 'Put your bags here. I'll get Sofia to put them in your rooms. You need the – bathroom?'

'Yes,' Leanne said. 'I do need it, actually,'

'It's there.' Lucilla pointed at a door between two of the cupboards. 'We'll be in the *soggiorno* through there.' She pointed at a set of double doors through which voices and laughter could be heard. 'And lunch will be served on the terrace.'

Leanne stepped awestruck into the bathroom, which was bigger than the whole ground floor of her mother's house in Ireland. The floor was made up of black and white tiles and the toilet was the old-fashioned kind with a dark mahogany seat and a chain and pulley to flush. Enormous mirrors flanked a huge marble hand basin and the tall window was hung with a silk curtain with an opulent tropical motif. 'Holy God, this is elegant,' Leanne muttered to herself as she opened the loo cover and discovered the toilet bowl decorated with flowers and birds. It seemed nearly a sacrilege to use it.

Having flushed the toilet, Leanne glanced at herself in the mirror as she washed her hands and dried them on a soft linen towel. Her cheeks were pale and her eyes huge and frightened. What was wrong with her? These people were as normal as she was, only richer. No big deal. She applied an extra layer of mascara, pinched her cheeks and straightened her back, remembering her proud Norwegian grandmother. She would never have let plush surroundings or other people's money intimidate her. Leanne smiled, feeling restored. She nodded to herself and went out to join the guests in the living room.

The big room was empty, all the guests having gone out onto the terrace, seated at a long table that Leanne glimpsed through the French doors. She glanced around the room, muttering 'holy shit,' as she tiptoed across the marble floor covered in Venetian carpets, gazing at the walls crammed with oil paintings and tapestries and the windows swathed in faded red curtains tied back with thick silk ropes. The ceiling was decorated with frescoes of the same kind of cherubs as the entrance hall but with clouds, birds, grown men and women floating around. The furniture consisted of a mishmash of old and new pieces, which gave the room a comfortable, lived-in look. On closer inspection, Leanne noticed the worn upholstery of the sofas, the bald patches in the carpets and the cracks in the walls. Patina that spoke of former glory and wealth that hadn't lasted into this century. But it would probably cost a fortune to restore all of it.

Leanne squinted against the strong sunlight as she walked onto the terrace. She shaded her eyes with her hand, looked out over the edge and gasped. The view of Florence and the river Arno that snaked through the ancient city like a shiny blue ribbon was breathtaking. Beyond the terracotta roofs, the cupola of the Cathedral of Santa Maria del Fiore, otherwise known as the Duomo, rose majestically against a backdrop of the Tuscan hills and the Apennine Mountains in the far distance. 'How incredible,' she mumbled.

'Wonderful, no?' Carlo said as he rose to greet her. 'Welcome to Florence.' He kissed her on both cheeks, took her elbow and steered her to the table under the awning. 'It's hot. Please come and sit down beside me in the shade.'

'Thank you.' Flustered by the feel of his mouth on her cheek and the heady smell of his spicy aftershave, Leanne sank down onto a chair beside him. She looked around the table and smiled at the ten or so people busy eating, talking and laughing.

'Meet my family,' Lucilla called and spread her arms to encompass the people sitting around her. They all smiled and waved.

'And this is Leanne,' Carlo shouted over the din. 'The best blogger in the world.'

'*Benvenuto!*' someone shouted back.

Across the table, Maddy was deep in conversation with a red-headed man with tortoiseshell glasses. She turned to Leanne. 'Meet Antonio O'Grady, Lucilla's cousin.'

'Hi, Antonio,' Leanne said. 'Nice to meet you.'

'Hello, Leanne.' The man reached across the table and took Leanne's hand in a firm handshake. 'I've heard a lot about you from Maddy.'

Leanne laughed. 'That's a nice Cork accent you have there.'

He smiled, his hazel eyes glinting behind the glasses. 'Yes, I know. My dad's from Kinsale. I went to school there until I was ten. Then we moved to Florence, my mother's birthplace. After secondary school here, I went back to Ireland to do medicine at The College of Surgeons. The Cork accent stuck to me like glue. Yours is pure Dublin, though.'

'Sure I know,' Leanne chortled. 'You can never get away from your roots.' She turned to Carlo. 'Where are your roots? Right here, in Florence?'

No. A bit further south of Naples, actually. Not the posh part,' he added, looking a little unsure of himself.

'Oh, well we can't all be wealthy,' Leanne remarked. 'I'm not from the right part of town either.'

'Oh? But I thought your dad…'

'He made his millions when he ran away from home.' Leanne shrugged. 'Long story. Let's not go there right now, okay?'

'Of course. No need to share if you don't feel like it.' He smiled, suddenly oozing confidence again. 'I'm looking forward to working with you. Have you seen the clothes yet?'

Leanne fiddled with the heavy silver cutlery. 'No, I haven't had the time to look at them. I will later.'

'Good.' Carlo passed her a huge platter with sliced beef and shavings of parmesan on a bed of lettuce. 'Lunch. *Bistecca* from Florence.'

'Fabulous,' Leanne said and dug in.

'And of course, red wine,' Carlo continued and filled her glass. 'But,' he added, 'I would like to know if you can use that famous nose of yours and tell us if this one is good or bad.'

Leanne smiled, feeling all eyes on her. 'Okay,' she said with pretend confidence, raising her glass to her nose, taking a little sniff. 'Mmm… Yes. It's good. I get blackberry and raspberry with a touch of liquorice…' She took a small sip. 'Nice little hit of vanilla and perhaps just a hint of caramel.'

'Really?' Carlo said, looking intrigued. 'That's amazing.' He passed the bottle to Maddy. 'You have to taste this.'

'Wine at lunch time?' Maddy protested. 'But I'll be falling asleep.'

Antonio laughed beside her. 'Of course. That's why we have the siesta, so we can sleep it off. Especially in summer. It's too hot in the early afternoon to do anything but sleep.'

'Some people do other things during the siesta,' Carlo mumbled in Leanne's ear.

Leanne couldn't help laughing. 'I can imagine,' she replied. 'Hot weather can make you feel quite…' She giggled before stopping, noticing Antonio's eyes on her. He was looking at her intently, smiling warmly. He had kind eyes and a calm, self-contained air. Their eyes met for a second, and then he looked away when Maddy asked him a question. Interesting guy, Leanne thought. The quiet, conservative type. Not the kind of alpha male she'd normally go for but there was something about him she instinctively liked.

As they ate and chatted, Leanne noticed Lucilla looking at the door, then at her watch, then back to the door again. She exchanged a look with Antonio and shrugged. 'No idea. She said she'd be here for lunch.'

'Who are you talking about?' Leanne asked, intrigued. 'Is someone late for lunch?'

'My aunt Claudia,' Lucilla said with a sigh. 'Just arrived from New York. Fresh from her divorce. Recovering, she says. Needs a little r and r. We all know what that means, don't we?'

'It's time she retired,' Antonio remarked. 'Isn't she a little old for those shenanigans?'

Maddy put down her wineglass. 'What shenanigans?'

'Chasing men,' said a woman, who had been introduced as 'one of the cousins'. 'She marries men with a lot of—' The woman rubbed her fingers together, indicating money. 'Then she has a divorce and gets all his money.'

'Not all,' Lucilla corrected. 'You're exaggerating, Maria. This is only the second time. She's had bad luck with men. But she has a good lawyer.'

'And good legs,' Antonio said with a wink at Leanne. 'Good – everything. Especially when she was younger.'

'I'm not dead yet, Tony,' said a voice in an accent that was pure Park Avenue.

All heads swivelled towards the door to the terrace, where a tall, elegant woman in white linen pants and cerise silk top stood as if posing for *Vogue*. Her eyes were hidden by huge sunglasses and her shoulder length dark hair was held back by a scarf.

'Holy shit, Jackie Onassis has come back from the dead,' Maddy said under her breath to Leanne as everyone rushed to greet the woman – who must be the famous Claudia.

When the excitement of the late arrival had died down, introductions had been made and Claudia had been served what remained of the delicious beef, the lunch party continued in the living room, with Claudia holding court, sipping wine and nibbling on a tiny slice of tiramisu. When there was a lull in the conversation she fixed Lucilla with her startling turquoise eyes. 'So,' she drawled. 'What's this I hear about a sailing trip?'

'A few of us are hiring a sailing boat,' Lucilla replied from the depths of a sofa, where she was cuddling Bridget and drinking strong espresso from a tiny, elegant fine-bone china cup. 'And we're spending a week cruising in the Dalmatian islands.'

Claudia nodded. 'The new Riviera. I hear it's incredible.'

'Can't wait,' Lucilla said.

'Who's coming on this trip?' Claudia asked imperiously.

Lucilla suddenly looked trapped. 'Uh, just Carlo, me, Tony and our Irish friends, Maddy and Leanne. And their dear little dog, of course. Maddy and Leanne will be writing about the trip and taking pictures for their blog.'

Claudia's eyes widened. 'Really? What blog?'

'It's for *Women Now* magazine,' Leanne said. 'The blog is called "The Great Euroscape".'

'Oh. Haven't heard of that one. Must have a look.' Claudia picked up her phone. 'I've been a little out of touch with my social media platforms lately. Divorce is so tiring, you know.'

'No, I don't,' Leanne replied. 'But Maddy does. She's just broken up from her husband.'

Claudia's eyes softened as she looked at Maddy. 'Really? Sorry, darling. I know how tough that is. Have you got a good lawyer?'

'No, not yet.' Maddy shot an annoyed look at Leanne. 'In any case it's not going to be difficult. We've decided to stay friends. My husband doesn't want to start any rows.'

Claudia lifted an eyebrow. 'That's what they all say. Then they run to a lawyer and grab all your worldly goods before you have a chance to hide them. It hasn't happened to me, but many of my friends have been conned by the "let's stay friends" men.' She drew breath and turned to Lucilla. '*Cara*, your trip sounds fabulous. Any chance there is room for one more? It's exactly what I need right now.'

'Eh…' Lucilla squirmed. 'I'm afraid not. The boat we're hiring only has room for five, and that's with two people sharing the largest cabin.'

'So hire a bigger boat,' Claudia said. 'I'll pay the difference. What's the point of a holiday if it isn't comfortable?'

'If she comes, it won't be a holiday,' Carlo muttered in Leanne's ear. 'It'll be a torture in hell.'

'Why?' Leanne asked. 'She seems like a lot of fun. Old, yeah, but a lot of older women can be incredible company.'

Carlo rolled his eyes. 'Not Claudia. She is a pain in the behind. Excuse me, I have to talk to Lucilla.'

Leanne yawned. After the long drive and all the food and wine, a siesta would be heaven. She got up. 'I'm sorry, I feel so sleepy. If someone can please show me my room, I'll go and lie down for a bit, if that's OK.'

'Of course,' Lucilla replied.

'I'll be right behind you,' Maddy cut in, taking Bridget from Lucilla. 'And I'm sure our pooch will want a snooze too.'

'Okay.' Leanne started to walk across the vast room. 'So where…?'

'I'll show you where it is.' Antonio followed her and opened the door at the far end of the living room. 'Through here.'

'Thank you, Antonio.'

'Please, call me Tony,' he said, as he led the way through a long corridor lined with yet more ornate mahogany cupboards. 'Antonio sounds so formal. Everyone calls me Tony.'

'Okay, Tony. What on earth are in all these cupboards?'

He laughed. 'I have no idea. Old clothes and bedlinen from bygone days. The glory days, when they had an army of servants to run this house.' They reached a series of doors and he opened the first one. 'Here. This is your room. Maddy's is next door with a bathroom between you.'

'Thanks.' She paused in the doorway. 'Is Claudia really that bad?'

He shrugged. 'Yes, if you let her. But I bet you one thing; she'll be pulling out all the stops to come with us on the cruise. And she'll succeed.'

'Sounds like it's going to be an interesting holiday.'

'That's for sure.' He leant against the doorjamb, studying her. 'So… What's a girl from north Dublin doing in Florence? I mean, how did you get from there to here, if you know what I mean?'

'Oh, well…' She met his eyes and smiled. 'Long story. And a weird one.'

'I like weird stories. The weirder the better.'

Leanne laughed. 'In that case, you'll love this one. But I'll make it short because I could fall asleep any second.'

'That's fine. I'm a little sleepy myself,' he confessed. 'So, the short version, then?'

'Okay.' Leanne took a deep breath. 'In a nutshell; about a month ago, Maddy and I won a bit of money in the Lotto. More than a bit, actually, but whatever. We decided to take a break from teaching surly teenagers at an Irish girls' school and being there for other people the whole time and go on a trip of a lifetime in a red convertible.' She paused. 'But we both had issues and stories from our past that we've had to deal with along the way. I won't go into that right now though. Too much to tell.'

'Later perhaps?'

'Yes.' Leanne stifled a yawn. 'When there's more time and we're conscious. So, winding the story forward,' she continued, 'we met Lucilla and Carlo at my long-lost dad's house in Vence and they invited us to come on this cruise in Dalmatia.'

'I see.' Tony paused. 'I'm looking forward to the long version of this. I feel there is much more to what you've told me.'

'Oh, yes. Heaps.' Leanne supressed another yawn. 'But I need my siesta.'

'So do I.' He smiled sleepily. 'Just one thing before I go; what was that about your nose? And the wine?'

Leanne laughed. 'That's just a little party trick. I have a very keen sense of smell, just like my dad, who is a perfumer. But I was having you all on. It was just a very ordinary plonk, to be honest. All I could smell was red wine with a touch of vinegar.'

Tony burst out laughing. 'Thought so. But they all believed you, including me. Well done.'

'Thank you.'

'But you're tired, so I'll leave you. See you later. Sweet dreams,' Tony said, closing the door behind him.

Leanne took off her shoes, pulled the silk curtains across the tall windows and padded across the carpet to the ornate double bed with its carved bedhead and deep blue silk cover. She lay down and pulled her phone from her bag, intending to look at the clothes she and Carlo were supposed to wear in his marketing campaign – if she agreed to do it, that is. But her eyes wouldn't stay open and she reluctantly put away the phone. Sleep first, then work. Maddy was probably on her way to her room and would be asleep soon, too. They needed a rest before they went sightseeing.

Before she drifted off, Leanne thought about Carlo and his campaign. She knew she'd agree to do it. It was the best chance to get close to him.

A sharp knock on the door jolted her awake. 'Come in, Maddy,' she mumbled drowsily, 'I thought you'd be asleep by now.'

But the woman sliding into the room was not Maddy, but Claudia. 'Are you alone?' she whispered, looking around and closing the door softly behind her.

Leanne sat up. 'I think so. Haven't checked under the bed or in those massive wardrobes over there. They're big enough to hide half the Italian army so you never know.'

Claudia's smile was pale. 'Very funny.' She hovered in the middle of the floor, her slim form silhouetted against the dim light from the windows. She crept closer to the bed. 'I just want to ask you to do me a favour.'

'Okay,' Leanne said, feeling she'd agree to anything so she could go back to sleep. 'Go on, then. Shoot.'

Claudia jumped and looked behind her. 'What?'

'I mean, tell me what you want.' Leanne stared at Claudia, trying to figure out why she was so tense.

'Right. Okay… uh…' Claudia stood there, wringing her hands. 'It's about your blog. The Great Euroscape thing?'

'Yes? You want to be in it?' Leanne asked, confused.

'No!' Claudia hissed. 'Quite the opposite. I want… I need you to *never* mention my name or take any photos.'

'Oh. Okay,' Leanne sighed and lay down again, waves of exhaustion washing over her. 'No problem.'

Claudia fixed Leanne sternly with her turquoise eyes. 'You promise?'

'I swear on my grandmother's grave,' Leanne muttered and waved a limp hand at Claudia.

'Thank you so much.' Claudia breathed and tiptoed to the door. 'I'll let you sleep now.'

'No problem,' Leanne mumbled.

Claudia left, closing the door softly, leaving a whiff of fancy Acqua di Parma cologne behind her.

Peace at last. For now, Leanne thought, wondering who or what was haunting that strange woman. Was it her imagination or had the panic in Claudia's eyes been very real?

Chapter Six

Maddy was not sleeping. Lying on an identical bed next door with Bridget curled up at her feet, she was just about to drift off after having closed the curtains when her phone pinged. Another text from Erik. He had been messaging her since they parted with sweet messages, jokes and photos. It was nice to be courted like this – it had been so long. Maddy smiled and picked up her phone. She'd just look at it before she drifted off to sleep. But the message was not from Erik, it was from Sophie, her daughter, who at twenty-one was taking a gap year in Australia after finishing her degree at Trinity College in Dublin.

Suddenly wide awake, Maddy sat up and read the message. Sophie wanted to FaceTime with her. But what time was it over there? Must be the middle of the night. Something had to have happened. Imagining the worst, Sophie ill or injured, Maddy dialled her number with shaking hands. A fuzzy image of Sophie's sleepy face came into view.

'What's happened, Sophie?' Maddy exclaimed. 'Are you OK?'

Sophie smiled and yawned. 'Hi, Mum, I'm fine, honest. I just wanted to talk to you. I spoke to Dad earlier and he told me what's going on with you two and then I couldn't sleep afterwards.'

Maddy felt hot rage rising in her chest. 'He told you? But I was supposed to talk to you first. That's outrageous!' Her angry voice woke Bridget, who jumped up and started to bark.

Sophie sighed. 'Calm down, Mum. It's okay. I'm glad he told me. I had to know.'

Suddenly weak, Maddy lay down against the soft pillows, gathering Bridget in her arms. 'Of course. But I was going to call you tonight. When it's morning over there. And I was going to tell you my way. I want you to know all is well and that Tom and I are friends and that—'

'I know,' Sophie, interrupted. 'Stop feeling guilty.'

'How do you know how I feel?'

'I know you. You always take the blame for everything. Even when we were kids and we misbehaved or someone hurt us. But never mind all that. I was lying here, worrying about you. Wondering if you were okay. I've been following the blog and I love it! I love that you're finally having fun. I also love that you and Dad have finally realised that you're incompatible and that you're better off apart.'

'What?' Maddy nearly shouted. 'Incompatible? What do you mean?'

'Yeah, well I came to that conclusion a while back. You two haven't been having much fun together for years, have you? Especially you. I meant to talk to you about it before I left, but I didn't want to upset you. And now you've seen the light all by yourself. And that's a very good thing.' Sophie drew breath. 'You might think that I disapprove of my mum having fun and being famous, but I don't. You've earned it after all the years of looking after us, when Dad was off pursuing his career.'

Maddy shook her head and smiled, realising how much she missed her daughter. 'I know you have a degree in psychology, Soph, but I'm not sure you can do long-distance therapy like this. You can go to sleep now. I'm happy and having fun. There's no need for you to worry.'

'Great! So proud of you, Mum. You look so pretty in all the photos. Hey, how about coming out here for Christmas? Now that you're single, I mean. Perth is a fantastic town. I'd love to show you around and then you can meet Chris.'

'Christmas?' Maddy asked, feeling it was light years away. 'And who's Chris?'

Sophie laughed. 'I'll tell you later. I'm so glad you and Dad are friends. He said he was happy too and that when you've sorted out the property and asset stuff you'll be splitting everything in half. Even the cash you won, which I think is incredibly generous of you.'

'What?' Maddy exclaimed, shock rippling through her.

But the signal faded and the image of Sophie's face disappeared. 'Night, Mum,' she shouted. 'I'll email you with my own news.' She waggled her fingers. 'Say hi to the cute doggie.' The screen went blank.

Rigid with shock and outrage, Maddy lay against the plump pillows and stared blankly at the ceiling. What that woman – Claudia – had just said popped into her mind. 'They grab all your assets before you have a chance to hide them.' She hadn't given the question of divorce proceedings a thought, even after her meeting with Tom in Nice. They had parted friends, dear, close friends, even, with a lot of history and a promise to make the divorce as amicable as possible, and not to rush it. But now Tom had mentioned her money to Sophie. Was it true? Could he grab half of it? And what about her other account? And the furniture, some of which had belonged to her mother… Hide it, Claudia had said.

There was only one thing to do. Spend as much of it as she could.

Later that afternoon, when Leanne and Maddy were about to set off for their sightseeing tour of Florence, they heard loud voices coming from the living room.

'They're fighting again,' Leanne remarked. 'Or discussing the weather.'

'Let's just go out,' Maddy suggested. 'Must be some kind of family thing. None of our business.'

Leanne pricked her ears and listened. 'It's Claudia,' she whispered. 'She's speaking English. They're discussing the cruise.'

Maddy walked toward the hall. 'Why not let them sort it out?'

'But it concerns us too.' Leanne opened the door to the living room and peeked in. 'Hi,' she said. 'We're off to see the town. We'll be back for dinner.'

Lucilla looked up from her laptop on the big coffee table around which Claudia, Tony and Carlo were gathered. 'Could you please come here for a minute and help us settle this? We can't agree.'

'About what?' Maddy asked, as she walked closer.

'The size of the boat we're hiring – or the type,' Tony explained. 'Motorboat or sailing boat? Now that we've agreed to include Claudia, we need a bigger one than we planned before, which will cost a lot more. Claudia has picked a motorboat—'

'A yacht,' Claudia interrupted. 'Boats are small and uncomfortable. Yachts are not. I'm not into camping either.'

Lucilla tapped the screen with a picture of a big sailing boat. 'You call this camping?'

'Six people and two bathrooms? Yes,' Claudia snapped. 'And sailing? Not sure I like the idea. Sailing boats, even if they're big, *lean* too much.'

Lucilla, Carlo and Tony exchanged exasperated looks. 'But the boat – I mean yacht – you picked costs twenty thousand euros for a week,' Carlo argued. 'That's a lot more than we agreed to spend.'

'Hell, yes,' Leanne cut in. 'That's way over our budget.'

'I'll put in half of that,' Claudia said. 'I'm prepared to pay for comfort.'

'*Si*, but the other half is still ten thousand,' Lucilla said. 'Even that is too much for us.'

Maddy looked at the picture of the yacht. 'It looks lovely, though,' she said wistfully.

Leanne leant down to have a look. The yacht was truly fabulous. Bright white, gleaming in the sun. Like something straight out of the movies. 'It's spectacular,' she sighed.

Tony nodded. 'Of course, but—'

'I'll pay the other half,' Maddy interrupted.

Leanne's jaw dropped. 'What? Are you mad? I know we won a fair bit of money, but to blow ten thousand just like that…' She stared at Maddy and noticed a determined look in her friend's eyes. Something was going on.

'Are you serious?' Tony asked, looking concerned. 'Very generous, of course.'

Claudia smiled and winked at Maddy. 'I think I know. Spend it before he does, right?'

'Something like that,' Maddy replied.

'Come on, Maddy,' Leanne pleaded. 'You can't mean you'd fork out that amount for this trip?'

'I'm serious,' Maddy said with a steely expression. 'Take it or leave it.' She pulled at Leanne's arm. 'Come on. I want to see Florence.'

'So we'll book this then?' Carlo asked, looking confused. 'This yacht with eight berths and a crew of four and…'

'I think we can manage without a crew, as long as we have a skipper,' Claudia cut in. 'That'll make it a bit cheaper too. We can clean our own cabins and cook. The galley, or whatever you call a kitchen, is top-notch. It'll be fun to go to the markets,' she said, sounding like a little girl. 'Staff, even if you call them crew, are such a nuisance.'

'Oh yes,' Leanne agreed, with a cheeky smile. 'I try to manage with as little staff as I can at all times.'

Carlo laughed and exchanged a look with Tony. 'I think we have a problem, Tony.'

'Yes,' Tony agreed. 'We do. Carlo and I were looking forward to sailing. We're both good sailors and the Dalmatians offer some very challenging waters. But then we have to consider everyone's wishes. But…' He hesitated. 'I have a suggestion that might solve everything. How about hiring two boats? One for those who want to sail and a motor – ahem – yacht for those who don't.'

There was silence around the coffee table while they considered the idea.

'Bit extravagant, but not a bad idea,' Leanne said, trying to hide her disappointment. She had dreamed of being on the same boat as Carlo. But as she considered the option, she realised that being together all the time might not be a good thing. Better to keep a little distance at times. 'I love sailing too,' she remarked, 'but not all the time. So how about you guys hire a sailing boat and the girls hire a smaller, less expensive motor-thingy and we can travel in a kind of convoy. We'll all meet every evening at some appointed island and have dinner on the motorboat.' She drew breath.

Maddy nodded. 'I like it. As you know I had a little queasiness on the North Sea when we came over from England. A motor yacht seems more my kind of thing.'

'A little queasiness?' Leanne snorted. 'You puked your guts out all night.'

Maddy sighed. 'Yeah, okay. Not something I want to dwell on, thank you. So let's do what Tony suggested. I'll still want to pay half for our boat – yacht or whatever, though, just to get something comfortable. Thank you for suggesting it.'

'Fabulous idea, Tony,' Claudia agreed. 'And Leanne too. This way we don't have to share a tiny sailing boat with men who'll snore and pee all over the bathroom.'

'I don't snore,' Carlo protested.

'Of course you do,' Claudia fired back. 'All men snore. Just ask the woman they sleep with.' She winked at Lucilla. 'Isn't that true, Lucilla?'

Lucilla shrugged and looked at her nails. 'I wouldn't know if Carlo snores. We didn't do much actual sleeping when we were in bed.'

Claudia laughed. 'I can imagine.'

Tony's mouth quivered. 'Let's not delve further into that one.'

'Good idea,' Leanne muttered under her breath, trying to push away the image of those two in bed. Thank God their relationship was over.

Tony shot her a look. 'So this is okay for everyone?' he breezed on. 'Lucilla?'

'Yes. I like it,' Lucilla said after a moment's consideration. 'And we can take turns to sail with the men, if we want. Then all we need to do is find a suitable motor yacht. With a skipper. You boys can pick your own vessel.'

'Let me pick the yacht for us girls.' Claudia turned the laptop towards herself. 'I'll find something cute and comfortable. How about a budget of around ten thousand, Maddy? Five each.'

'Great,' Maddy replied. 'You can tell us what you picked when we get back. Come on, Leanne, I want to go to the Duomo before it gets dark.' She smiled at Lucilla. 'Bridget is still having her siesta in my room. Could you please check on her in a while?'

Lucilla nodded. '*Certo*. I'll give her water and see if she wants a walk.'

'Thank you.'

Carlo caught up with Leanne in the hall. 'Have you looked at the designs yet?'

Leanne clapped her hand to her mouth. 'Oh no, I forgot. I'll look at them when we're taking a break from the sights. Promise.'

'How about I meet you for a drink? There's a nice bar on Piazza Degli Strozza. Near the Uffizi museum. I'll wait for you outside. Seven o'clock?'

Leanne nodded.

Before she closed the door, Leanne spotted someone behind Carlo. Lucilla. Looking at her with such animosity it made her shiver.

This holiday might not turn out to be as blissful as she had thought.

Chapter Seven

Florence turned out to be as magical as the guidebooks promised. The late afternoon sun gave the old city a golden glow and the air smelled of sweet flowers and newly brewed coffee. The heat had abated and there was a cool breeze from the river Arno as they walked across Ponte Vecchio, the oldest bridge in Florence, which spans the river at its narrowest point. They looked at the artefacts, jewellery and fashion for sale at the little stalls lining the bridge and admired the craftmanship.

Leanne stopped at the old wall under the arch and looked out over the calm river and a single scull breaking the pristine surface of the water. She picked up her phone and took a shot of it. 'So beautiful. Like an old painting,' she said.

'Gorgeous.' Maddy flicked through the guide book and started walking. 'We have to go and see the Duomo now, and all the other amazing buildings.'

Leanne tore herself away from the view and fell into step with Maddy. 'I want to see that art museum too.'

'The Uffizi Gallery? Then there's the Basilica di Santa Maria Novella, the…' Maddy stopped. 'There is so much to see. Too much, really.'

'Let's just do the Duomo and the Uffizi,' Leanne suggested. 'Or we'll be exhausted. In any case, I'm meeting Carlo at seven for a drink and a kind of business meeting. We're going to look at the designs and work out some kind of agreement.'

'Have you seen the clothes yet?' Maddy asked.

'No. Forgot to look. Hang on, I might as well take a peep right now.' Leanne leaned against the parapet of the bridge and took out her phone, while Maddy snapped a few more photos.

'I think these will be great for the Florence blogpost,' she said. 'I got a nice shot of the fabulous hand-made jewellery. Did you see the necklaces? Beautiful semi-precious stones. Especially the rose quartz set in silver and the amethysts.'

Leanne nodded, her eyes on the screen of her phone. 'Here we are, the website. Risorse Naturali… Here's the collection.' She stared at the picture on her screen and gasped. 'Whaaa…? I don't believe it. Holy shit!'

Maddy nearly dropped her phone. 'What's going on? Are you sick?'

'Yes,' Leanne groaned. 'After seeing this. Just look.'

Maddy peered over her shoulder. 'Holy mother, what are those? Sacks?'

'Yes, and bandages and rags,' Leanne moaned, staring at the models on the website wearing shapeless bits of cloth and strips of material, all either in black or white. Like something straight off a catwalk. 'Is this some kind of sick joke?'

Maddy studied the picture on the screen. 'Switch to the next page, the one that says beach wear.'

Leanne clicked and another page came up. She stared at the skinny models dressed in more of what she had first seen. 'It's the same stuff.' She stared at Maddy with huge, frightened eyes. 'Is this the collection I'm going to wear on Instagram?'

'If you agree to do it, yes.'

'Maybe they'll look better on a boat?' Leanne suggested.

Maddy giggled. 'They'd look better on a horse.'

'Please. It's not funny.'

'I think it's hilarious.' Maddy couldn't stop laughing. 'Typical arty-farty shite. Come on, Leanne. You can't wear those rags.'

'But… but the designers are Carlo's friends. A young couple who are just starting off in the fashion business.'

'I think they should stop right there and do something else. Like design tea cosies or something.'

Leanne failed to see the funny side. 'He said the clothes were avant-garde,' she sobbed. 'Now I know what he meant. Oh, Christ, Italians are so weird. I mean yeah, their fashion designs are often way ahead of the times. It's as if they throw everything at the wall just to see what sticks.'

'Have you read what is says?' Maddy asked, pointing at the text at the bottom of the screen. "All materials are recyclable or compostable. Fashion for the environment." It's so mad I bet this will actually take off.'

'You think?' Leanne clicked and more clothes in the same vein appeared. 'Look, these binbag thingies are t-shirts. Completely biodegradable. You can buy three in a pack and then throw them on the compost heap when you don't want them any more. Kind of practical, if it didn't look so awful.'

'It's an interesting concept, even though the designs are crazy.' Maddy glanced at the photos and then looked at Leanne. 'Are you going to say no to Carlo?'

Leanne felt panic rise in her chest. 'I don't know,' she moaned and put her phone away. 'You tell me. What am I going to do?'

Maddy frowned and looked down, a strange sound coming from her throat.

'You're still laughing!' Leanne exclaimed.

Maddy let out a giggle. 'Sorry. But I can't help it. Come on, Leanne, admit it's a bit of a hoot.'

Leanne looked annoyed. 'If it was you I'd be splitting my sides. But it's me and I'm not laughing. Jesus, what a con job. I bet it's some kind of joke he and Lucilla made up. They're probably laughing their heads off right now.'

'I wouldn't say that. How could they make up a whole website just to fool you? And you know what? That concept is kind of genius when you think about it. Fashion these days is all about new looks practically every month, so most people throw away their clothes all the time. Can't be good for the planet to have all that stuff piling up in landfill sites, not to mention the amount of energy used to manufacture them.'

'I suppose. But couldn't they have made stuff that was actually nice while they were at it?' Still feeling glum, Leanne put her phone into her bag.

Maddy put her arm through Leanne's. 'Well, it's certainly unusual.'

'I still don't know what to do,' Leanne muttered, wondering how she was going to tell Carlo the deal was off. She desperately wanted to please him and if she said no, he was bound to be annoyed.

'Let's drop it for the moment and enjoy our sightseeing tour,' Maddy suggested. 'The Duomo is supposed to be incredible. I'm dying to see it.'

Leanne let herself be pulled along with Maddy, her spirits lifting a little as she walked down the quay and across the street toward the cathedral, the rounded cupola of which rose over the terracotta roofs of the city. You simply couldn't be cross on such a glorious afternoon in such a beautiful city. Leanne shrugged off her worries and turned her mind to the pleasures ahead.

As they drew closer, they could see the breathtaking pink, white and green marble façade and graceful bell tower of the cathedral that must have dominated the town and the surrounding landscape in mediaeval times.

'I took nearly a hundred and fifty years to complete,' Maddy read from the guidebook. 'Imagine, those who started it never saw it finished.'

They stepped inside and were immediately enchanted by the stained-glass windows and the beautiful frescoes, even if the vast space was more Spartan than they had expected. The guidebook told them that a lot of the artefacts had been removed, some of them now held in museums. But the still vivid frescoes by Giorgio Vasari of the *Last Judgment*, and intricate wood panelling were truly wonderful.

'It smells of incense and prayers,' Leanne whispered.

'Five hundred years of worship by millions,' Maddy said in a reverent voice. She walked to a statue of the Virgin Mary where rows of candles flickered, spreading a warm light through the dim cathedral. She put a coin in the slot and lit a candle, pausing for a moment, her head bent. Leanne stepped away to give her some space, as she was probably saying a prayer and thinking of her mother. She knew they had been close, and even though she knew her mother had died when Maddy was in her early twenties, Leanne felt a jolt of envy. How lovely it must have been to grow up so close to your mother. That was something Leanne had not experienced, her own childhood and teenage years having been full of conflicts and animosity. Would she ever be able to talk to her mother as a friend? Probably not. Her heart sank at the thought. How could she ever forgive what her mother had done? Hiding the truth about her father all these years. It was too much to forgive – or even accept.

After the cathedral, they walked to the Uffizi Gallery, which proved to be an enormous museum packed with art from different eras. The collection had been gifted to the city by the Medici family in the eighteenth century. Too much to tackle in one day, Maddy said, having consulted the guidebook before they set off. She led the way to the most famous paintings, starting with the portrait of Eleanor of Toledo and her son by the Italian artist Agnolo di Cosimo, painted in around 1545.

Leanne gazed at the painting and the face of the young woman. 'Beautiful. So calm and peaceful, nearly as if she were dead.'

'She is,' Maddy quipped. 'That was painted like five hundred years ago.'

Leanne gave her a push with her elbow. 'Duh, I know. I meant at that time… When she was sitting there… You know? And the little boy looks like a doll.' Her gaze returned to the face of the woman. 'She's looking at us. Hmm, her eyes are half-closed. And that little smile on her lips… There's something happening there. Maybe she had a thing going with the artist?'

'She was probably just falling asleep,' Maddy suggested. 'I mean just look at that dress, of heavy brocade. I'd say it was very uncomfortable.'

'It'd be a killer to have to wear it all day long.' Leanne looked at the woman's face again. 'Imagine. Five hundred years, and it's still so alive.'

They continued on to admire a few key paintings and then emerged into the street, where the setting sun cast a final few rays on the roofs before sliding behind the green hills of Tuscany, transforming the sky into a soft dark blue with just a few wispy clouds tinged with pink.

'That was fabulous,' Leanne sighed as they stood on the street corner. 'But now I have to go and tell Carlo—' She stopped, all her confusion rushing back. 'What'll I tell him?'

'What do you want to do?'

Leanne bit her lip. 'I want to make him like me.'

'Like you or just – lust after you?' Maddy asked in a stern voice.

'I don't know,' Leanne whimpered. 'A bit of both, I suppose.'

'You want to please him, in other words?'

'Something like that,' Leanne replied, with a feeling that Maddy had hit the nail on the head. She did want to please Carlo, but she didn't want to appear to chase him. The clothes were awful, but was that the whole problem?

Maddy sighed and hitched her bag higher on her shoulder. 'This is where I should say it's all up to you and you're an adult and I have enough of my own problems. But this is not like you, Leanne. You're usually so sure of yourself. But now you're standing here, dithering.'

'I know.' Leanne put her hand on Maddy's arm. 'Please give me your gut feeling, here, even if it's something negative.'

Maddy frowned and looked at Leanne in silence for a moment. 'Here's my take: first of all, you and Carlo do look great together in the photos. You'd look good in bin liners, the two of you. So yeah, it could be a success. Or it could totally bomb and you'd end up looking a bit of a twit with a crush, all for the wrong reasons. So have a good think about what it would do for you and don't get fooled into doing something you'd regret.'

'Oh,' Leanne said, completely taken aback. 'Never thought of it that way. I've been thinking about my blogging, you see. It might turn into something more than just a bit of fun.'

Maddy nodded. 'It could. You're so good at it. Those posts have shown your talent for writing. So you might take that into account too. But hey, is this really such a big deal? Couldn't you just wear those things now and then in those Insta pictures and do a few hashtags? Not make it into something big, just a casual thing. Add a few jokes, see what happens.'

Leanne brightened. 'Oh yes, that's a great idea! That way it'll be a little less important and nobody will really notice.'

'Except those who like the concept.' Maddy pushed at Leanne. 'Go on, tell that hunk you're doing it your way or not at all. Show you have a bit of that famous Irish chutzpa.'

'That's not Irish.'

'I know but it's such a great expression.' Maddy fixed Leanne with her eyes. 'Are we agreed?'

Leanne laughed and gave Maddy a shove. 'Sure we are, girl.'

'That's the spirit. See you later, and then I want to see a smile on your face.'

'I promise,' Leanne said, walking down the street to meet Carlo, vowing to show him who was boss.

Chapter Eight

Maddy arrived back at Lucilla's spectacular apartment, where she found Claudia on the terrace having a drink and looking out over the floodlit city. She looked up when Maddy stepped through the open French doors.

'*Buona sera*. I'm having a Campari and orange. Help yourself. The drinks are on the table over there.'

'Thank you. I've never tried Campari before. But it looks nice.' Maddy poured a little of the bright red liquor into a tall glass, topping it with orange juice and a few ice cubes. She sat down on the bench beside Claudia and sipped the drink. 'Mm, this is really gorgeous. So refreshing, sweet and sour at the same time. Lovely.'

'One of my favourite evening drinks,' Claudia said. 'Much nicer than champagne.'

'Especially in hot weather.' Maddy gazed out across the moonlit city which had taken on a fairy-tale quality, with the old stones of the buildings bathed in a golden light, and the dark velvety sky dotted with stars.

'The city is lovely, don't you think?' Claudia said after a moment's silence.

'Fabulous,' Maddy breathed. 'It's like a dream to be sitting here on this terrace.'

'I love it too. I always missed it during my years in New York.'

'Ah, but you must have had an amazing life there, too.'

'Of course.' Claudia passed Maddy a bowl of big, juicy green olives. 'It was fun. Most of it anyway. My first husband was very wealthy. We had an apartment in Park Avenue, and a summer house in the Hamptons. We spent January and February in Palm Beach.'

'Wow, really?' Maddy said, confused by the flat tone in Claudia's voice. 'Must have been wonderful.'

'Yes. For about three months.' Claudia laughed. 'Don't look so shocked. I was joking. I was quite happy for many years with my first husband. He was property developer, much older than me. I was his third wife.'

'How did you meet him?' Maddy asked, intrigued.

Claudia drained her glass. 'We met here in Florence nearly forty years ago. I was working as a tour guide during the summer. He was here on holiday just after his divorce from wife number two. He was rich, handsome and very sad. I cheered him up and then we fell in love.'

'Sounds like a fairy tale.'

Claudia laughed and shook her head. 'If I was to tell it like a story from a book it would go like this: Once upon a time there was a young Italian girl called Claudia who met a handsome, rich, heartbroken man. They got married and he brought her to New York to live in his beautiful ten-room apartment. Claudia was very happy at first, but then she met her two nasty step-daughters who did everything to make her leave. Claudia carried on regardless and gave her husband the one thing his other wives hadn't; a son.'

'How lovely,' Maddy said, sighing. 'Apart from the nasty step-daughters.'

Claudia got up to make herself another drink. 'It would have been if that was the end, but it wasn't. The step-daughters won in the end by telling their dad Claudia was carrying on with other men and that she was just a tart. The handsome husband believed their lies and left the lovely Italian wife. Divorce proceedings started and there was even a custody battle for the son, who was now a teenager. But… Fate – or our Lord in heaven – intervened and the husband died suddenly of a heart attack in a hotel room in Florida while, ahem, cavorting with a girl from an escort service.'

'Oh, no!' Maddy exclaimed. 'How awful.'

Claudia grinned. 'Yes. Of course. Horrible. But what happened next was truly amazing.'

Maddy stared at her. 'And…? Come on, Claudia, I'm dying to know.'

Claudia sat down again with her drink. 'As we had signed a prenup, I thought I would end up with only the clothes on my back. But a newly written will was found in the safe of his lawyer. He left me the Park Avenue apartment and ten million dollars. The step-daughters got the rest. And there was a codicil saying anyone who contested the will would end up with nothing. All signed by witnesses so the whole thing was airtight. The end.'

'Fantastic,' Maddy laughed.

'That story was,' Claudia remarked. 'The next one wasn't quite as lovely. More like a horror story really. Not something you'd like to hear on a beautiful evening like this.'

'Maybe not,' Maddy agreed, sensing it was a touchy subject, but disappointed she couldn't find out what had happened next.

'Enough about me.' Claudia stood up and put her glass on the table. 'Ah, Florence. What magical city this is. I'm so happy to be back.'

'It's truly wonderful.' Maddy checked her watch. 'It's nearly nine. Where are Leanne and Carlo?'

'Probably gone straight to the restaurant. We're all meeting at this new Neapolitan pizzeria later. I'm really looking forward to it. Rome and Naples are the only two places in Italy where you get a decent pizza. And now, like Mohammed and the mountain, a little bit of Naples has arrived here in Florence.'

'Sounds great.' Maddy got up. 'I'd better change, then. What does one wear to a pizzeria?'

Claudia shrugged. 'Anything, really. It'll be casual but chic. That kind of thing.'

Maddy laughed. 'That's the hardest look to achieve.'

'We'll just have to do our best. Let's walk to the restaurant together. It's only a few blocks, as they say in New York.'

'Okay. I'll meet you in the hall in about twenty minutes?'

'Perfect,' Claudia said, disappearing into the cavernous living room.

Maddy stood on the terrace for a moment, staring out at the glittering city, worrying about Leanne. She felt Leanne needed a guiding hand, someone to look out for her. Leanne was rough and tough on the outside but inside there was a hurt little girl who had to put up with a lot of heartache as she grew up. And now she seemed to be attracted to a man she had only just met and agreeing to something that might ruin her chances of developing her blogging into a career… Not that Carlo was in any way bad, but he was probably spoilt and used to women throwing themselves at him. And then there was Lucilla, a lovely bubbly woman who might turn into a tigress if someone threatened to steal the man she loved, even if they were no longer a couple. Maddy suspected there was a lot going on below the surface. She just hoped it wouldn't ruin their holiday…

Leanne found Carlo at a table outside the bar in the quiet little square just a street away from the museum. It was a peaceful oasis, away from noise of traffic and crowds of tourists, with planters full of roses and a lime tree in the middle, where a dove was cooing softly. Piano music could be heard streaming from an open window.

He rose as she approached and pulled out a chair. '*Buona sera*,' he said, kissing her on both cheeks in the Italian way. 'Did you have a nice afternoon?'

'Wonderful.' Leanne sank down on the chair. 'My feet are sore though. We only managed the Duomo and the Uffizi. So much to see and so little time.'

'That's true.' Carlo sat down and snapped his fingers at a waiter. 'What do you want?'

'I have no idea. A cold beer, maybe.'

'Good choice. Is Peroni all right? It's an Italian beer.'

'Lovely.' Leanne eased her sandals off under the table. 'The Uffizi is amazing. I never knew renaissance art could be so fabulous.'

'What kind of art do you like?' Carlo asked, looking intently at her.

'I could say Picasso but that would be a lie. In fact,' Leanne confessed, 'I don't know much about art. This is the first time I've been
in museums and seen paintings in real life. I mean, the paintings in
their original...' She stopped and laughed. 'Oh shite, I don't know
what I'm saying. Hey, I wasn't brought up to appreciate art and music
and things like that. The nearest I ever came to a concert was an Irish
music session in a pub. And art? Well, we had a few framed prints of
hunting scenes because my mam thought it was posh.' Leanne laughed
again, feeling both excited and flustered as he directed his luminous
green eyes at her. Why did he have to be so bloody gorgeous?

Their beers arrived and Leanne took a huge gulp from her bottle
to cover her nervousness. The cool liquid slid down her throat like
an ice-cold stream. She burped discreetly and smiled at Carlo,
blushing. 'Lovely'.

'Cold beer on a hot day is always nice.' Carlo took a few sips
from his bottle, wiped his mouth and smiled. 'So... you have seen
the clothes?'

Leanne coughed. 'Clothes? I wouldn't call them that. More like...
weird garments. Are you sure there isn't a mistake and those things
were meant to be costumes for a zombie movie?'

Carlo threw his head back and laughed. 'I know what you mean.
The designs are a little unusual. I was shocked myself when I saw
them. But it's very new and very daring.'

'You can say that again.' Leanne took another, more careful sip
of her beer.

'I know it's not like anything you'd wear,' Carlo said. 'But I think
we can do a great job marketing them on your blog. The photos
would be eye-catching and...'

'Not the blog though,' Leanne interrupted. 'Maddy doesn't want us to post the photos there. It'll have to be on my own Instagram account. I already have fifty thousand followers, and I'm sure it'll grow if…' She stopped. 'Honestly, I don't think your idea will work. I've thought of a different approach that'll be less work and more fun and won't make us look stupid if it fails.'

He looked intrigued. 'Go on.'

'Marketing by stealth,' Leanne said. 'Like product placement in movies.'

'Oh.' He thought for a moment. 'You mean we'll wear some of the items in fun photos and then just mention the brand here and there?'

Leanne beamed at him. 'Exactly! And this way, we'll have covered our behinds in case the stuff doesn't attract any attention. Or we could say we wore the stuff for a bet.'

Carlo nodded while he considered her idea. 'I like it. You're a very smart woman.'

'Thank you,' Leanne said, smiling. 'I'm glad you like it.'

'It's perfect. I'm so glad you've agreed to help me with this. Thank you, *cara mia*.'

She sighed, unable resist his lovely green eyes. 'You're welcome. But I'm only doing it because of the planet, you understand.'

'The planet? Which one?'

'The one we're on, of course!' Leanne drank the rest of her beer. 'The clothes are all biodegradable. The manufacturing is done without harming the environment, unlike most of the clothes we wear today. It's sheer genius. If it takes off, that fashion brand will probably be the hottest thing in clothing.' She wiped the foam from her lips with a napkin. 'So that's the deal. My way or no way, okay?'

Carlo's face broke into a brilliant smile. '*Fantastico*,' he exclaimed, his perfect teeth glimmering in the dim light. He kissed her cheek. 'Thank you, Leanne, you're *un tesoro*.'

'A what?'

'A treasure!'

'Ah sure, I know,' Leanne said, blushing furiously. 'I'm so glad you agreed. No hard work, just a bit of fun and a little cheeky plugging, if you see what I mean.'

He nodded. 'It's a very good start. And if you just give us a mention or two on the main blog, we'll get more exposure. We'll work together and put this company on the map.'

'God, I hope so. Or it'll bomb, but this way nobody will notice.'

Carlo took her hand. 'Nothing I've ever done has bombed.' He pulled her up. 'Come on, we have to meet the others in the pizzeria. I'll tell Lucilla you have agreed and we have to contact the firm and get them to deliver the stuff. I'm going to ask them to send it to Trogir. That's the harbour town near Split, where the boats are moored.'

'Good idea.'

'And now I'm ready for that pizza.' Carlo kissed his fingers, his eyes gleaming. 'Real pizza from Napoli. Delicious!'

'Sounds great,' Leanne replied, wishing he'd look at her with the same desire.

Chapter Nine

In the cosy little restaurant overlooking the Arno, Leanne instantly understood Carlo's delight when she took the first bite of her Pizza Napolitano. The base, which looked thick and heavy, was the exact opposite; light as a feather and melt-in-the-mouth. The topping had a depth of flavour she had never tasted before; thick tomato sauce fragrant with oregano, anchovies with just the right amount of salt, and mozzarella, both soft and chewy and deliciously creamy. Unable to stop herself, she had soon devoured the big pizza that had been put in front of her and thought she'd be unable to finish, washing it down with a glass of a sparkling Italian red wine called Lambrusco. She wiped her mouth, feeling full, and glanced around, a little embarrassed at having wolfed down so much in such a short time. But everyone else was either still eating the last bite or sitting back looking at an empty plate with a satisfied smile on their faces.

'Wonderful,' Claudia sighed. 'I haven't had a pizza like that since I was a child.' She discreetly undid the stylish Hermès belt on her designer jeans. 'Must move the decimal point a notch. I'll be fasting for days after this. But it was worth it.'

'That wine is really good with it,' Maddy remarked. 'I never tasted a sparkling red before. Unusual but nice. Especially with this amazing pizza.'

Carlo wiped his mouth and nodded. '*Molto delizioso*, I agree.'

'It's the tomato,' Lucilla declared and dabbed his chin with her napkin. 'You eat like a little boy.'

Leanne smiled, pretending she found it funny, but the gesture grated on her.

'What's so special about the tomato?' Maddy asked. 'It had an unusually deep flavour.'

'It's the San Marzano tomatoes,' Tony explained. 'They are grown in the volcanic soil near Mount Vesuvius. And the mozzarella has to be Mozzarella di Bufalo Campana, or it's not an authentic Neapolitan pizza.'

'Oh,' Leanne said, awestruck. 'I knew it was something special. I'll never eat any other kind of pizza again, that's for sure.'

'Better than…' Maddy stopped. 'I don't know what it's better than, to be honest.'

'Please don't say it's better than sex,' Claudia snapped. 'Because that wouldn't be true.'

'Absolutely,' Lucilla said with feeling, taking Carlo's hand. 'Isn't that right, Carlo?'

He pulled it away, throwing her an annoyed look. 'Depends,' he said. 'On the pizza, I mean.'

Leanne glanced at the two of them as they sat there, not really looking at each other. Lucilla appeared as if she felt she owned Carlo and he went along with it because it suited him. Apparently they were business partners but no longer in a relationship, even though the chemistry between them was obvious. How could that possibly work? Leanne tried to get her mind around it but failed. Italians were clearly strange about sex and love and relationships. Feeling someone looking at her, she turned her head and met Tony's gaze. She smiled and picked up the menu. 'Funny, after all that food I still feel like eating a little more. Is there dessert? What's this thing called Mont Blanc?'

'Oh, no,' Claudia groaned. 'Not Mont Blanc! It's loaded with fat and sugar. At least five hundred calories.'

'My favourite,' Carlo declared and clicked his fingers at a passing waiter. 'Mont Blanc *per tutti*,' he ordered.

'Not for me,' Claudia protested.

But nobody listened and before they knew it, six portions of sweet meringue topped with ice cream, whipped cream and chestnut puree appeared at the table. 'I love this,' Lucilla said as she dug in. 'It's pure sin.'

'I've sinned enough,' Claudia declared and pushed away her plate after taking a few bites.

'Like an Italian pavlova,' Maddy declared through a mouthful. 'The chestnut puree is too good to be true.' She closed her eyes. 'I'm going to do a Leanne and say the flavour is smooth and nutty with a hint of vanilla and sugar.'

Tony laughed. 'Excellent. But not quite Leanne's expertise, of course.'

'I'm just a happy amateur,' Maddy laughed.

'What's this, Leanne?' Claudia asked.

'It about my nose,' Leanne replied. 'Or my sense of smell, actually. I inherited it from my dad. I can smell thing other people can't. Like you wearing Iris Nobile by Acqua di Parma.'

'Oh.' Claudia looked impressed. 'That's interesting. I thought your nose was a little on the big side. But very straight,' she added.

Leanne stifled a laugh. 'Thank you. I'm going to have to go to confession after this,' she said, licking her fingers. 'It has to be a mortal sin to eat something as divine like this.'

Carlo burst out laughing. 'I love your humour. I'm so looking forward working with you.'

Lucilla directed her dark flashing eyes at Leanne. 'So you said yes? Nobody told me this. And it's my account.' She turned to Carlo and let out a stream of rapid Italian, none of which sounded remotely friendly. Her diatribe was accompanied by wide gestures and angry expressions.

'Jaysus, she'll murder him next,' Maddy hissed to Leanne. 'Maybe we should leave?'

'No,' Leanne hissed back. 'I want to watch. It's like a drama in a movie with Sophia Loren and Mastroianni. Never knew it was the same in real life.'

'I know. Exactly like one of those melodramas,' Tony remarked under his breath beside Leanne. 'But the storm will pass and they'll kiss and make up. Again.' He looked serious but there was laughter in his hazel eyes behind his glasses.

'You sure?' Leanne asked, wondering if he was having her on or laughing at her. 'It sounds like the next World War is breaking out.'

'And he hasn't even replied yet,' Maddy said. 'Maybe he'll just sit there and take it?'

'He'll start screaming when she pauses for breath,' Tony said as if he was an expert on Italian dramas. And he probably was, Leanne thought, wondering if he had grown up with this sort of thing going on between his parents.

Right on cue, when Lucilla took a deep breath, Carlo opened his mouth and shouted: '*Basta!*' Then he grabbed Lucilla by the hand

and dragged her outside, where they could be seen gesturing and shouting without the sound effects.

'Oh my God, such passion,' Claudia sighed and applied a fresh coat of bright red lipstick. 'So tiring. That's why I never married an Italian. Had enough of that with my parents.'

'Oh,' Leanne said. 'Did they have problems?'

Claudia laughed. 'No, they were just typical Italians. Fought about everything and made up in spectacular fashion. It's the way we do things.'

'Maybe that's better than ice-cold silence and indifference,' Leanne remarked, thinking of her own parents, who had barely spoken to each other during the last tension-filled time before her dad had walked out. It had been frightening for a twelve-year-old girl to witness what felt like pure hatred between her parents. And then the echoing silence when Erik was no longer there. She pushed the thought aside, not wanting to think about that troubling time.

'Could be, but the shouting isn't nice either.' Claudia shrugged. 'I got used to it but I didn't want that kind of relationship. So I married an American who ended up cheating on me. And an English writer who tried to steal all my money. Go figure.'

'Your second husband was English?' Maddy asked.

'Yes.' Claudia put her lipstick into her Dior clutch. 'But enough about me. Have you seen the yacht I picked? Small but perfectly formed. Four cabins, each with a little shower and toilet. I hired a skipper too. So we're all set if the boys have organised their sailing boat.'

'I've booked it,' Tony replied. 'Nice eleven meter Bavaria thirty-seven. Very fast and just perfect for Carlo and me. I'll tell him as soon as he—'

Maddy glanced out the window. 'They're hugging.'

Everybody in the restaurant was looking out of the window at Carlo and Lucilla, starting to applaud and laugh. After a moment Carlo ushered Lucilla inside and they returned to the table, smiling and waving.

'What a performance,' Maddy said to Leanne, laughing.

Leanne nodded. 'Yes. Quite ridiculous.'

'Silly, really,' Maddy agreed. 'By the way, did you take a shot of those amazing pizzas?'

Crestfallen, Leanne put her hand to her mouth. 'Nooo. I forgot. It was so delicious I just gulped it all down in record time. I only have one of you with cream on your nose, but no pizza. Feck!'

Tony showed his phone to her, with a cheeky smile. 'But I did. Couldn't resist taking a shot of you with that pizza.'

Leanne stared in horror at the photo of herself taking a huge bite of pizza, her mouth smeared with tomato sauce, and strings of cheese hanging from her chin. 'Jesus, I look a fright! Delete it or I'll kill you.'

Maddy looked at it and laughed so loudly everyone stared. 'It's a scream! Come on, Leanne, it's too good to waste. We have to have that.'

'Yes, I think it's fun,' Tony agreed. 'Is your blog all prissy and well-behaved? Would this not make you look normal?'

'Who wants to look normal?' Leanne grumbled.

Carlo took Tony's phone and started to laugh. 'It's fun and cute. Kind of sexy, *cara*. Why not make those women laugh? And drool over the best pizza in the world?'

Leanne met his eyes and felt her face flush. He called her *cara* – darling in Italian. And he said she was sexy… She took Tony's phone and looked at the photo again. It *was* funny, even if she looked a total mess. But why not? Did she want to be the perfect, prissy all-made-up model, or the fun girl on an adventure? There was only one answer to that question. She beamed at Carlo. 'Yeah, you're right. It's perfect. Send it to my phone, Tony and I'll post it with my next blogpost. I'll call it "my date with a Neapolitan".'

Carlo laughed even louder. 'That's funny. Because I'm a Neapolitan too.'

'Double jackpot, then,' Leanne quipped, directing a cheeky look at Lucilla.

Lucilla smiled back. 'Sorry about the little upset. I was just annoyed at not being informed. That always makes me explode. What can I say, I'm a control freak.'

Leanne beamed her a smile. 'But of course. That'd upset me too, big time. So,' she continued, 'am I right to think this is new fashion label is your client?'

Lucilla nodded and picked up her wineglass. 'Yes, that's right.'

'Oh, great. So then Carlo has explained my idea?'

'Yes, he did. I was disappointed at first that you didn't agree to a full advertising campaign. That's why I was angry with him. I thought he had blown it. But then he explained—'

'When you stopped shouting,' Carlo cut in.

Lucilla waved at him. 'Yes, all right. I got excited. But now that I've thought about it, I think it's…' She paused and leaned forward, fixing Leanne with her dark eyes. 'You, my friend, are a genius!'

Leanne sat back. 'What? Why?'

'Because you know the power of the word of mouth. That is the most difficult, nearly impossible thing to get rolling. And your subtle approach might just do that.'

'Oh, eh…' Leanne blushed. 'It wasn't me really. It was Maddy. She said I shouldn't be too easy… I mean shouldn't get involved, I mean…' Leanne shot a look at Maddy, silently praying for help.

'I just thought the subtle approach would be better,' Maddy explained. 'No screaming and shouting, just a little tease here and there. Make it mysterious, make everyone want it, but don't push it in anyone's face.'

'Oh.' Lucilla looked awestruck. 'You Irish women. So smart.'

'Ah sure, it's easy,' Leanne said and winked. 'We just go with the flow, ya know?' She smiled sweetly at Lucilla, knowing she had won the battle. But… had she won the war?

Chapter Ten

Our date with a Neapolitan in Florence.

As you can see by the mess on my face, we enjoyed a real pizza from Napoli (aka Naples in the lingo of your country) last night. How can I describe it? The crust, all puffed up, was light and fluffy with a hint of burnt edge and salt. The topping – oh what a delight. Tomatoes grown in volcanic soil, fresh oregano, succulent little anchovies and cheese from buffalo grazing on the plains near Naples. That combo was enough the make me drool and gobble it all up in seconds. I could have managed another one, but I didn't want to look like a pig (as you can see, I failed spectacularly). Besides, there was the dessert to top all desserts. It's called 'Mont Blanc' and consists of a messy, delicious pile of meringue, ice cream, whipped cream and a huge dollop of chestnut puree on top. Finger-licking good! I took a shot of Maddy eating it before it disappeared. Such a greedy-guts!

But let's wind the clock back a bit to earlier and our wonderful lunch on top of an old palazzo overlooking this beautiful city (see second photo). Then our tour of the gorgeous town centre, which included a visit to the glorious Duomo and the amazing art museum called the Uffizi. The renaissance paintings are stunning. I couldn't take my eyes off the faces and the costumes still so vivid today. Must say, though, I'm glad I don't have to wear those clothes all day – tons of corsets and brocade would kind of cramp my style. Our walk across Ponte Vecchio was pretty good too, with views of the lovely river Arno and then those little stalls that sell all kinds of gorgeous fashion accessories. Maddy took the photo of the stunning jewellery. The photo of the single scull rowboat on the river was by moi.

And then… I had a hot date with my new partner. Strictly business, you understand, even if he is drop-dead gorgeous, as Neapolitan as the pizza I just mentioned and just as delicious! The business, you ask? Well it's a secret for now, but all will be revealed on my Instagram account very soon. Do follow me there, if you aren't already. What an amazing day we had!

Today, a little early morning shopping and then off to the Adriatic coast with the new recruits for our cruise (introductions later) where we'll catch the ferry to Split. Ciao for now, belezze!

Leanne read through the post and pressed 'publish'. She closed the laptop and climbed out of bed, knocking on the door to the bathroom she shared with Maddy. 'Are you in there?'

Maddy opened the door, clutching a fluffy towel around her. 'Yes. Just had a shower. Breakfast will be served on the terrace, and then—'

'Shopping!' Leanne filled in. 'Can't wait to hit those little boutiques.'

'Claudia has promised to guide us. She knows the best ones.'

'She's a riot for an old bird,' Leanne remarked. 'How old do you think she is?'

'Lucilla told me she's sixty-two.'

'Gosh, she looks years younger than that.'

'Or maybe that's what sixty-two should look like,' Maddy suggested. 'I'm finished here. I'll see you outside in a while.'

'Okay, catch you out there.'

Leanne jumped into the shower for a quick wash, then put on white linen trousers and a pink t-shirt and walked onto the terrace in the golden light of the early morning sun. 'Morning,' she said to Claudia, who, dressed in a classic beige linen shift and large designer glasses, was surfing on her phone. 'Fabulous weather again.'

Claudia looked up. 'It's always fabulous this time of year.'

Leanne helped herself to orange juice. 'Of course. Unlike Ireland, where a fabulous day gets huge headlines.'

Maddy cut up a fresh, juicy peach and poured herself some coffee. 'I could get used to this,' she said, taking a sip.

Leanne sighed and looked up at the bright blue sky. 'Me too.'

Claudia put away her phone. 'Your blogpost is fun, Leanne. Great photos.'

'Thank you. Even the pizza one is great.'

'Especially that one,' Maddy said. 'We must remember to take some good shots from our shopping trip. Some more funny ones.'

'Yeah we need to funk it up a little,' Leanne agreed.

'But I would like to remind you not to include my name or any photos of me,' Claudia said. 'If you don't mind.'

Leanne shrugged. 'Yes, sure. No big deal. You're travelling incognito?'

'Something like that.' Claudia checked her watch. 'It's early. We'll have time to pop into the beauty salon beforehand.'

'Uh... what?' Leanne said. 'Beauty salon? I've never been inside one, to be honest.'

Claudia stared at her. 'You've never had a facial?' she asked incredulously.

Leanne shrugged. 'No, never, so shoot me. What about you, Mads?'

'Same here,' Maddy laughed. 'I do the occasional exfoliating myself and maybe a facemask at Christmas, but that's it really.'

'Are you serious?' Claudia asked, looking as if they had confessed to doing their own dental treatments.

Leanne nodded. 'Yeah, we are. Is this a big deal?'

Claudia didn't reply. With a determined look she picked up her phone and dialled a number. After short conversation, she hung up and looked from Maddy to Leanne. 'All fixed. I got Tina to look after you. She had a cancellation. She said she'll do a quick fix-up this morning, cleanse, tone and moisturize. All we have time for right now, but it's better than nothing.'

'A first-aid job for wrecks like us?' Leanne asked, teasing.

'Something like that,' Claudia agreed. 'We need to get primed before we go on the cruise. Especially Leanne, if you're going to do fashion shoots with Carlo.'

'Not real fashion shoots,' Leanne protested, 'just fun shots of us.'

'In that case it's even more important,' Claudia argued. 'If it's going to be amateurish, then you need your skin to look good. You need to be positively glowing.'

'Nah, count me out,' Leanne retorted. 'You go on though. We could meet for the shopping trip later.'

'This a lot more important than shopping,' Claudia said sternly. 'In fact, I think I could get you into my very exclusive spa. Incredible place. You should be jumping at the chance. We could all do it together. My treat. I'll cancel Tina and get you into this one.' She picked up her phone without waiting for a reply while Maddy and Leanne exchanged a look.

'We should do it,' Maddy said. 'Can't hurt, can it?'

Leanne shrugged. 'Yeah. Sure. Why not? And it could be a fun blog post too.'

'I've booked for me too,' Claudia announced when she had hung up. 'So I'll take you there and we'll get looked after together. Massage, facial and waxing. Then a moment of relaxation to recover and we'll be ready for the trip.'

Leanne nodded. 'Okay, sounds painful, but we'll try not to scream too much. Then we'll have to hit the road in the late afternoon.'

'All in the same car,' Claudia said with a shudder. 'But we'll have our own cabins on the ferry, I take it.'

'No cabins,' Maddy said.

'What?' Claudia's eyebrows rose in alarm.

Maddy shrugged apologetically. 'They were all booked. But we'll be in Split just after midnight and then in our hotel in Trogir. Tony has organised it all.'

'Oh that was nice of him.' Leanne picked up her phone and got up. 'I'm going out to do a bit of shopping. See you later, lads.'

'But the beauty salon,' Claudia protested. 'We need to wax. And exfoliate.'

'Jaysus, I forgot,' Leanne squealed. 'Okay. I'll just go and ask Lucilla about the clothes for the fashion pictures and go and get my bag. See you in the hall in a minute.'

As she left she bumped into Tony, who had just stepped out onto the terrace.

'Good morning, Leanne,' he said. 'Where are you rushing off to?'

'Morning,' Leanne muttered, her eyes glued to her phone. 'Got to go and see Lucilla. And then Claudia is taking us to a spa to cleanse and exfoliate.'

'Sounds scary.'

'You bet. But she says it'll be worth it. I'll introduce you to the new me afterwards.'

Tony laughed. 'Looking forward to it.'

'Not sure I am,' Leanne muttered.

As she walked to her room she thought about Tony. At first, she had put him in the over forties age group, but this morning, with his cheeky grin, he had looked a lot younger. In fact, Leanne reflected, he had a young face with lines and grooves, etched into it not from age but from something stressful he must have been through. She knew he was a doctor and that he had worked abroad, but that was all. Where had he been? And what had he been through? She suddenly looked forward to knowing him better and to hearing his story, whatever it was. She had a feeling it would be interesting.

*

The spa was situated in a modern building only ten minutes' walk from Lucilla's apartment. There was no sign outside or anything that indicated that there was any such thing as a spa behind the heavy metal door with an intercom and a CCTV camera. Maddy and Leanne gathered beside Claudia while she pressed the buzzer and a tinny voice replied, asking who they were.

'Claudia Fregene with guests for the appointment,' she said, after having glanced up and down the street.

There was a buzzing sound from the door and Claudia pushed it open and walked inside, gesturing for them to follow her. The door closed behind them with a discreet click and they followed Claudia across a vast marble hall to the lift that took them silently to the top floor.

'What kind of spa is this?' Leanne asked. 'I didn't see a sign or a plaque outside the door downstairs.'

'It's private,' Claudia explained. 'With a very select clientele.'

'Like the mafia?' Leanne whispered to Maddy.

The lift came to a stop and they emerged straight into a luxuriously carpeted lounge where a blonde in a white coat was standing behind a counter.

She looked up as they approached. 'Ah, here you are. Everything is ready.'

'Ready for what?' Leanne whispered in Maddy's ear. 'Maybe they're going to drug us and remove our brains or something.'

Maddy giggled. 'Yeah, this looks like something from a sci-fi movie,' she whispered back.

'What are you whispering about?' Claudia demanded. 'Come on, let's get started.'

They were ushered into the changing rooms where they got into matching pink robes before being marched to the treatment room where, lying side by side on massage tables, they were pounded on and pummelled by three enthusiastic young women who spoke to them in broken English.

'Ouch,' Leanne groaned as her masseuse worked on her back. 'This is not as soothing as I thought.'

'You're very steef,' the woman said. 'Please relax.'

'I'm trying,' Leanne said. 'How are you doing, Mads?'

'It's bloody murder,' Maddy grunted, as her thighs were rubbed by strong hands. 'But I'm sure this is the easy bit.'

'Can't wait for the bikini wax,' Leanne muttered as she turned over.

'Facials first,' Claudia interrupted, sitting up when her massage was finished. 'Then leg and bikini wax and then, if we have time, manicure and pedicure.'

'I can cut my own toenails,' Leanne offered. 'Just give me a nail scissors and—'

'Irina will see you now,' the masseuse interrupted.

'Uh, great,' Leanne grunted and got off the massage table.

'Through that door,' the masseuse said. 'And Tina will do your friend.'

'Good luck,' Maddy called after Leanne as she left.

'Thanks,' Leanne muttered as she entered the treatment room, where a tall brunette greeted her with a cheery 'hello' and invited her to take off her robe and lie down on the treatment table. 'My name is Irina,' she said, tucking a towel around Leanne's torso, and giving her a headband. 'Please put this on to keep your hair off your face.'

'Are you from here?' Leanne asked, trying to make conversation.

'No. I'm from Russia. But please be quiet while I look at your skin,' she said, shutting Leanne up. She turned off the overhead light when Leanne was lying down on the treatment table, switched on a spotlight and proceeded to examine her face. 'What is this... stuff?' Irina asked, scraping at Leanne's face with a spatula. 'Some kind of self-tan?'

'It's a real suntan,' Leanne said, feeling like she had just confessed to a deadly sin. 'I spend a lot of time outdoors, swimming and walking and so on.'

'A suntan?' Irina exclaimed with a shudder. 'Have you never heard of sunblock?'

'Yes, of course,' Leanne replied. 'I do put it on but, well, it could be that it comes off with sweat and water.'

'Uh, okay,' Irina mumbled. 'You seem to have quite sallow skin, despite your fair hair. This is very strange.'

Leanne was tempted to joke that she was an alien from outer space but, being slightly nervous of Russians wielding spatulas, she changed her mind. 'I'm half Scandinavian,' she said instead. 'Scandinavians usually have quite dark skin despite their fair hair.'

Irina was not impressed. 'Scandinavian?' she said as if it was an affliction. 'That explains your colouring.' She studied Leanne's face again. 'I'm going to peel off the dead skin,' she announced, 'and then I will put on a hydrating mask and apply a very strong Vitamin C lotion that will boost your cell renewal. That's all the skin treatment we have time for today. Then I'm afraid we'll have to do a little waxing.'

'Okay,' Leanne said, squeezing her eyes shut. 'Go for it.'

What followed was an excruciating half hour of peeling and squeezing, which Leanne endured, somehow managing not to scream. The waxing was a different matter, however. Leanne couldn't help letting out a few yelps and moans as the hair was mercilessly yanked off. But after the suffering came the reward; the hydrating mask on her face that smelled of lavender and a soothing, cooling lotion on her bikini line. Then Irina dimmed the lights, played some classical music, covered Leanne with a soft blanket and left the room, telling her to relax for twenty minutes.

The moment the door closed, Leanne felt her body slump in a kind of after-shock. Not exactly falling asleep, she went into some kind of meditation mode, breathing in the scent of lavender while her mind drifted, feeling as if she was floating, reliving everything that had happened during the past crazy month. Winning the lottery. Her friendship with Maddy. Reuniting with her father. Meeting Carlo and that instant attraction, but most importantly, the discovery of her talent for writing. This, she realised, she wanted to develop into something more permanent – a whole new career, perhaps.

As the last notes of the Nocturne by Chopin faded away, she slowly woke up from her trance, feeling not only physically cleansed but mentally spring-cleaned, ready to start afresh.

When Irina returned and finished off the treatment, Leanne got off the table, ready to head out and face the world again.

'Don't forget to exfoliate regularly,' Irina ordered, as Leanne walked out, her face glowing and her spirits soaring.

'Promise,' Leanne said, feeling suddenly very fond of this woman. She met Maddy in the changing room and beamed at her. 'Fabulous, wasn't it?'

'Incredible,' Maddy said. 'I feel reborn.'

'Would you do it again?' Leanne asked.

'You mean will I spend what it would cost to have dinner in an expensive restaurant scraping dead skin off my face? And have my hair ripped off delicate parts of my body? Definitely.'

'Me too. It's totally addictive.' Leanne looked around the changing room. 'But where's Claudia? Her clothes are gone too.'

'That's strange. She must have left early? Let's go back and pop into that cute shop on the way,' Maddy suggested. 'We might find some stuff for the cruise.'

They walked slowly back, popping into the boutique on the way, where they browsed the summer collections. The shop was stocked with designer clothes and they succeeded in buying a lovely cotton sarong for Maddy, two swimsuits and two ankle length linen dresses, one deep blue and the other one a shocking pink for Leanne. On an impulse, Maddy added a gorgeous handbag she couldn't resist to the pile. As they paid the bill, Maddy declared them ready to depart for the cruise.

Packing only the essentials and leaving the rest in Lucilla's apartment, they gave Bridget a final walk in a little park nearby, before joining the others in the courtyard to pile into Lucilla's battered people carrier.

'Dalmatia, here we come!' Leanne exclaimed as she got into the back seat beside Maddy.

'Can't wait,' Maddy laughed, pulling a new guide book from the Gucci handbag she had bought earlier as part of her new plan to spend a lot of money before Tom could get his hands on it. 'Just look at all there is to see and do.'

Tony started the car. 'All aboard?'

'Yes,' Lucilla said from the seat at the very rear. 'I'm a little squashed here, but I will be looking after Bridget. Everyone's here and we have all our luggage.'

'Let's go!' Claudia suddenly shouted, making everyone jump.

'Okay,' Tony said and drove the car slowly through the entrance gates. 'No need to shout. We're off.'

Leanne glanced at Claudia, whose eyes were hidden behind her huge sunglasses. 'What's the matter with her?' she whispered in Maddy's ear. 'She looks frightened.'

'By what?' Maddy whispered back. 'Maybe she didn't get a chance to have a bikini wax?'

Leanne giggled. But when she looked at Claudia again, she felt there was more to it than a furry bikini line...

Chapter Eleven

The Ancona to Split ferry ride took a gruelling nine hours in a huge, noisy vessel packed with tourists. All the cabins were fully booked, so they had to find seats wherever they could. Claudia, still wearing her huge sunglasses and her hair wrapped in a colourful silk scarf, sat at one of the tables staring glumly out the window. She nibbled on a ham sandwich Tony had bought for her, muttering about standards and quality and how they should have gone by plane instead of this 'gypsy' way of travelling. She waved away Lucilla's explanations that they had decided on the cruise too late to find seats on any of the flights. 'Bad planning,' she muttered, glaring at a family with two screaming children at the opposite side of the table. 'I've never had to travel like this before.'

'Maybe it's time you saw how the other half live,' Tony suggested.

'Why?' Claudia asked. She sighed and finished the sandwich despite it being 'packed with carbs' and did her best to drink beer straight out of the bottle, before failing and asking for a glass. Then she leant back, announcing she was going to sleep and asking them to wake her up when they docked. Maddy and Leanne left her with Tony, and with Bridget in Maddy's arms, went to find somewhere to sit. After climbing the stairs to the less crowded upper deck, they managed to buy sandwiches and water and found two free window seats opposite each other. Maddy fell asleep at once while Leanne stayed awake, taking Bridget, who curled up in her lap and drifted off.

A voice startled her. 'You found a good place,' Tony said, handing her a paper cup. 'I got some tea for you both.'

Leanne took the cup. 'Thanks. But Maddy's asleep. I doubt she'll wake up.'

Tony reached over and patted Bridget on the head. 'Here's another one fast asleep.'

Leanne smiled. 'Yes. She trotted around for a bit and got a lot of attention from all the children, but then she got tired. She's behaved beautifully, considering how unsettling it must be for her not to have a proper home.'

'Yes, but she seems to love you both. She's happy to be wherever you are. That's the way it is with dogs.'

'I wouldn't know. This is the first time I've had one.'

Tony placed the other paper cup on the table and sat down on the edge of the bench beside Leanne, who moved closer to the window to give him more room. 'You never had a dog?'

'Never had as much as a budgie. My mam didn't like animals in the house.'

'Oh, that's a pity. My parents thought it was good for kids to have a pet to look after.' He laughed. 'Not that we did a lot of the looking after, though. It was mostly my mamma who took the dogs for walks and fed the gerbils and hamsters and other critters we insisted on having. They let us get whatever we wanted, within reason. Except for white mice after mine escaped and ended up inside the sleeve of her dressing gown, giving her a fright early one morning. Her screams would have woken the dead.' Tony laughed at the memory.

'You were very lucky. Sounds like you had a very happy childhood.'

'Mostly yes. Normal I suppose. I have a sister and a younger brother who's studying medicine in Dublin.'

'Like you.'

'Sort of. But he has no wish to go to third world countries like I did.'

Leanne turned and stared at him. 'Third world countries? Where did you go?'

'Africa.' His eyes darkened. 'It was… hard.'

'I can imagine. Do you want to talk about it?'

'You wouldn't enjoy it. Not a very pleasant subject to bring up on a summer holiday.' He got up. 'I'd better check on Claudia. Being up close and personal with members of the public is traumatic for her. I'd better make sure she doesn't have a nervous breakdown if she has to queue to go to the loo or something. I just came to see if you were all right. Lucilla said to tell you she has booked a minivan at the harbour so we can get to the hotel quickly.'

'Oh. Great. I saw she got a seat on the lower deck.'

'Yes. And Carlo is crammed in with a bunch of soccer players from Belgrade. They're still discussing some match or other. Not really my bag, but he seems happy.'

'I was wondering where he'd got to,' Leanne said, slightly miffed he hadn't been the slightest concerned about her. Unlike Tony, who had been checking on them.

Tony touched her shoulder. 'I'd love to stay and discuss the meaning of life with you, but there's plenty of time for that. See you later. Try to sleep if you can.'

'I will. Thanks for the tea.' She drank the tepid liquid when he left, watching him push through the throng and disappear down the stairs to the lower deck. What a decent man. Why couldn't she fall for someone like him? But he was too nice, and he didn't have Carlo's film star looks or sex appeal. Not her type, but a good man all the same.

Love, she thought, as she sat on a hard seat, staring out over the starlit Adriatic. *What is love, really?* She had never quite understood it, or experienced it. The 'I love yous' in movies and on TV didn't seem to fit her idea of what love was all about. Having grown up in a dysfunctional family, with her father leaving when she was only twelve, there hadn't been much love or affection in her life during her teenage years. Her mother, suddenly abandoned and raising a child on her own, had been affectionate from time and time and seemed to try her best, but without much conviction. She had mostly tried to make Leanne understand that she had to be strong and independent, to manage on her own, and to never, ever trust men. There had always been her mother's hand in the small of her back, pushing her forward, urging her to perform well, to be the best at everything. As a result, Leanne had been at the top of her class in all subjects, the president of the students' union and the captain of both the swimming team and the girls' hockey team, and just for the hell of it, the editor of the school magazine. And when she became head girl, her mother's eyes were bright with pride. Not that Leanne had worked hard to achieve those things for her own sake, but simply to earn her mother's love. Because love had to be earned, Leanne had learned at an early age.

As she grew into a young woman and ventured out into life she still felt that hand in the small of her back, pushing her forward, those disapproving eyes on her as she came home from parties and the odd date. Had she done her best? Had she been strong and independent? Had she resisted men's advances? those eyes seemed to silently ask. She pretended and avoided and lied her way through her late teens and early twenties, only to finally try her best to do the exact opposite to what her mother wanted, hoping she'd be asked to move out of the house they shared – because she felt too guilty to leave her mum of her own accord. So Leanne changed her look and suddenly bristled with piercings, cut her hair short, swore like a trooper and stayed out until the early hours. But it was no use. Her mother, although visibly shocked by this new Leanne, clung to her, growing needier than ever and using emotional blackmail. That, combined with the rising property prices in Dublin, made it impossible for Leanne to get her own place. But now, with all the money she had won in the lottery and her recent reunion with her father, things were slowly shifting in her life.

But men… Leanne sighed. That was a different story. Her edgy looks had attracted attention both at college and in her professional life. She'd been flirted with, harassed, asked out on dates, all of which she'd handled with a cool confidence that hid her inner fears and doubts, planted by her mother. Plus, her father's sudden departure was her first experience of rejection, a hurt that never healed. Nobody was going to do that to her ever again.

Her relationships had always been brief, usually ending with Leanne walking out as soon as she noticed his focus on her drifting away. It could be anything; a glance at a phone during a conversation, looking over her shoulder at another woman in a restaurant. Little things she had learned were the first signs of him wanting to break free. *Better to end it before he does*, she thought, always trying to prevent rejection, unable to bear any more hurt. So she always broke it off, time and time again.

She had never dared to truly love someone. In her mind, giving her heart away was the worst thing a woman could do, her mother being a prime example. In order to beat men at their own game, she learned to act like one, taking, rather than giving, having fun for as long as it lasted and often leaving heartbroken men in her wake. But... Leanne sighed. It also left her sad and lonely. And her friends beginning to drift into permanent relationships and getting engaged and married contributed to her feelings of loneliness and being left out. Not that she yearned for a big wedding or wanted to flaunt a big engagement ring on her finger, she just wanted someone to love her enough to want to commit.

Assumpta and her husband suddenly popped into Leanne's thoughts. She wondered if Assumpta knew that true love was not about a fancy wedding or a honeymoon in the Bahamas. It was rushing to a supermarket in a foreign country to buy prunes. One day, Leanne thought, she'd find someone who would truly love her, and stay with her for the rest of her life. And buy her prunes if she needed them. But so far she hadn't been that lucky. Until she met Carlo.

There was so much about him that appealed to her. His sweet expression and his liquid green eyes had pierced a tiny hole in her cast-iron heart. And when he'd said he wanted to help that young couple get started with their business, she'd seen a kind, considerate side to him. That, combined with his divine good looks and the way he actually seemed to like her and listened to what she had to say made him all the more attractive. Once they started working together they would get closer and closer. After all, love had to be earned, and she was going to work hard to earn it this time.

They arrived long after midnight, following a bumpy ride in a rickety minivan from the ferry port in Split, and so they didn't see Trogir until the following morning. But when Leanne stepped out onto the terrace of the hotel, she was immediately struck by the charm and beauty of the little town. She put on her sunglasses and stood there, mesmerised by the view of the ancient buildings with their red roofs and the glittering Adriatic Sea beyond. 'Wow,' she breathed.

'Beautiful, no?' Carlo said beside her.

'Stunning,' Leanne whispered. 'I know Italy is lovely, but this—'

'I know. So special. I've never been here before. I didn't know it was like this. The colours and the air…' He sniffed. 'It smells of the sea.'

'I can smell seashells and seaweed. And breakfast,' Leanne added with a laugh. 'Freshly baked bread, peaches and apricots, some kind of pastry – and coffee.'

'Looks like you're right.' He laughed and took her by the arm. 'There's a table over there – I booked it for all of us. Let's go and eat.'

'Good idea,' Leanne agreed, and let him lead her to a table set for six under two huge umbrellas, shading them. He pulled out a chair and she sat down, squinting up at him. 'Thank you.'

'*Prego*,' he said and sat down opposite her. He dabbed at his forehead with the paper napkin. 'It's very warm this morning.'

Leanne only then noticed how hot it was. It hadn't struck her as she stood admiring the view, as there was a cooling breeze from the sea. But here, in the shelter of the high walls, the heat was more intense, even in the shade of the umbrella. 'You're right. It's boiling. Much hotter than Florence yesterday.'

'They're having a heatwave,' Maddy said behind them. She sank down beside Leanne and fanned herself. 'It's already thirty-two degrees. I saw it on the thermometer outside the reception area.'

Claudia and Tony arrived shortly afterwards, both complaining about the heat. There was no sign of Lucilla, but Carlo explained she had gone to the marina to inspect the boats and arrange for the skipper. 'She wants us to join her there as soon as possible so we can get going,' he said. 'It'll be cooler at sea.'

'Thank God for that,' Claudia panted. 'And also for an air-conditioned boat.' Dressed in a white linen shift, a big hat and sunglasses, she still looked tense, her eyes darting around the terrace.

'What's the matter, Claudia?' Maddy asked. 'You look a little nervous.'

Claudia let out a brittle laugh. 'Nervous? It's just that I didn't sleep so well. It was too hot even with the aircon.' She eyed the assorted dishes on the table. 'What a wonderful breakfast. All this fruit and fresh bread. Not that I'm going to touch the carbs, of course. But I enjoy the smell,' she said wistfully.

'Amazing,' Maddy agreed and reached for a big bowl of pomegranate seeds. 'I didn't realise that food would be this good here in Dalmatia.'

'Looks nearly too pretty to eat,' Leanne said, admiring the display. 'Like a still life.'

'But we should eat it.' Tony handed her a plump peach. 'Here, try this.'

Leanne bit into it, the sweet juice dribbling down her chin. 'Mmm, lovely,' she mumbled as the rich flavour hit her taste buds.

Maddy picked up her phone. 'Lovely shot,' she exclaimed.

'I'll look like a pig,' Leanne said, laughing.

'Perfect,' Maddy said. 'Our fans will love it. You look totally disgusting.'

'I don't care. This peach is worth it.'

Tony bit into an apricot. 'This is delicious. I had heard how good the food is here. It wasn't great during the communist era, because everyone had to supply the markets in Belgrade in some kind of cooperative. Now the farmers can sell where they want, so the local markets are full of whatever grows here.'

'Fantastic,' Leanne said, busily taking shots of the fruit and bread with her phone. 'And look, honey too. Must be local.'

'Do we have time for a little sightseeing?' Maddy asked, gazing out over the town as she ate. 'There's so much to see here.'

'We don't, I'm afraid,' Tony replied. 'But we'll be visiting a lot of little towns and villages on the trip, all packed with ancient sites and buildings. This area is full of history, all the way from the Greeks to modern times. Dalmatia has been invaded so many times through the years. The Greeks, the Romans, the Venetians… This is the first time they're truly independent.'

'That's right,' Maddy agreed. 'That's what's so fascinating. And so much of the old architecture was left untouched.'

'I just love the view from here. I can't wait to see the other islands and to swim in the sea,' Leanne said, looking longingly at the azure water, sparkling under the sun.

'We'll stop in the first bay,' Tony promised. 'Then we can swim. But first, we must shop for food and get settled on the boats.' He drained his coffee cup and got up. 'Come on, gang, let's get going.'

As they walked the short distance to the marina, Carlo drew Leanne aside. 'The clothes we'll be wearing are already on the yacht. Please try them on when you have the time. We have to do a few shots tomorrow morning, before it gets too hot. Just to see how they look in photos.'

'Oh.' Leanne nodded. 'Great. Okay. I'll try them on and let you know if they fit.'

Carlo shrugged. 'Fit? They probably won't. But you have to see what you can do to make the stuff look good, that's all.'

'Feck, you're right.' Leanne admired Carlo's toned body. 'But draped all over you, it'll look stunning. On me? Not so much.'

'You'll look beautiful in anything.' Carlo pulled her closer. 'Together we'll make it work,' he whispered in her ear and let his lips brush her neck briefly. 'I'm so glad you agreed. You'll see, it'll be a hit.'

'I hope you're right,' Leanne said, smiling into his eyes.

'Of course I am.' He touched her cheek and then took her hand and led her across the bridge to the marina.

Despite the heat and their sweaty hands, Leanne felt a pull of joy as they walked hand-in-hand, feeling a sense of belonging to this handsome Italian. As they caught up with the rest of the group, Carlo let go of her hand. Nobody seemed to have noticed them. Except Tony, who shot Leanne a glance she couldn't quite decipher.

But she ignored him and looked back at Carlo, feeling suddenly confident about their plan. Not only that. It would also make her girlfriends at home sick with envy. The two of them flirting on yacht in Dalmatia had to top a wedding at some hotel in Killarney, even with twelve bridesmaids in matching designer dresses and a wedding cake the size of Mount Brandon.

Chapter Twelve

The yacht Claudia had picked out was called *Yolanda* and it was lovely. With a sun deck in the fore and a dining deck with a blue awning in the rear, there was also a saloon and galley kitchen in the middle. The bridge where the skipper would be piloting the boat was above the sun deck and would be a great place to look out over the sea and islands during the journey. The cabins were small but comfortable, each with a wide bed and a little en-suite shower and toilet. 'So cute,' Maddy exclaimed. 'Like a doll's house.'

'Yes, but we're not dolls,' Claudia remarked drily after inspecting her quarters. 'But it'll do. Comfortable for one, not so much for two.'

Leanne rolled her eyes. 'It must be such a pain to be used to luxury. This cabin is way nicer than my bedroom at home.'

Claudia stared at her, appalled. 'You're joking, of course.'

'Nope,' Leanne said and bounced on the bed. 'This is heaven compared to my IKEA bed. Still has a Barbie duvet cover too. Pathetic, don't you think?'

'Ugh,' Claudia grunted with a shudder.

'The living room is nice,' Maddy remarked.

'It's called a saloon on a yacht,' Claudia corrected.

'Thank God you're here, Claudia,' Maddy laughed. 'Otherwise we wouldn't have a clue.'

'Yeah,' Leanne agreed. 'I wouldn't know about saloons and stuff. But I know the toilet on a boat is called "the head", which always made me laugh.'

'Possibly on a small sailing boat. But not on a yacht,' Claudia sniffed.

'Let's get organised,' Maddy interrupted. 'We can snipe at each other later over the champagne the yacht club gifted us,' she said, pointing at an ice bucket on the table of the dining deck.

As there was no sign of the skipper, they quickly put their things in their cabins and walked the short distance to the supermarket to buy supplies. They met Lucilla there, who was pushing a trolley full of canned food and bottled water.

'Hello,' she said. 'I'm glad you're here. I got the basics; tuna, sardines, all kinds of tinned beans and tomatoes. What else do you think we should buy?'

'Nothing with lactose or gluten,' Claudia ordered.

Lucilla snorted. 'What about that pizza you had in Florence? Must have been packed with gluten.'

'I make an exception for Italian food,' Claudia declared.

'We'll buy a mix of things,' Maddy said. 'Coffee, tea, jam or honey or whatever for breakfast. Bread maybe and then some fresh fruit and veg?'

Lucilla nodded. 'Yes. You'll find a little market around the corner. And there's a fish shop. But only buy fish for tonight. All the villages on the islands have markets and fish stalls. And bakeries.'

'And restaurants?' Leanne asked, wanting to eat out and sample the local cuisine.

Lucilla smiled. 'Yes. There are little restaurants everywhere. Very simple, fresh fish, home grown vegetables and anything they can grow themselves. Even wine.'

Claudia lifted an eyebrow. 'Wine? From here? Is there nothing Italian? Or even French?'

'The local wine's very good, I've heard,' Lucilla said. 'Please, Claudia, this is a boat trip, not a cruise in the Caribbean.'

'No room for snobs,' Leanne said, with a glint in her eye.

'I'm not a snob, I have *standards*,' Claudia drawled.

'You'd do better to park your fecking *standards* right here,' Leanne quipped. 'Or this holiday will be torture for you. And us,' she added under her breath, meeting Claudia's haughty stare with a steely look of her own. This woman was beginning to be a real pain.

'Claudia, please come with me. I need you to help me with this stuff.' Lucilla wheeled the trolley around and started to walk to the checkout. 'Maddy, could you please get the rest of the things and we'll sort out the bills later?'

'Just a minute. Hey, everyone stand by the trolley and say cheese,' Leanne ordered and picked up her phone. 'I need a shot of reality before we get going.'

'No,' Claudia exclaimed and backed away, her eyes wild. 'What did I tell you? I'm not going to be in any photo of any kind.' With that, she turned and walked swiftly towards the checkout, her hat flapping.

'What?' Leanne lowered her phone and stared at Lucilla and Maddy. 'What the hell is eating her?'

'She's been like that since yesterday,' Maddy said. 'What's going on with her?'

Lucilla shrugged. 'Who knows? Maybe she's worried about looking old? In New York she was like a real… how do you say, social case?'

'Socialite,' Maddy corrected. 'If you mean someone who's important in society, not someone who's poor and needs free food and shelter.'

Lucilla laughed. '*Si*, that's what I meant. She was married to a famous writer, and they were always in the newspapers.'

'Famous?' Leanne asked. 'How famous?'

'Very,' Lucilla said. '*Molto importante*. He writes for TV and movies in Hollywood. Was nominated for Oscar last year.'

'What's his name?'

'His name…' Lucilla thought for a moment. 'Oliver something.'

'Oliver Wilde?' Maddy asked.

Lucilla nodded. 'Yes. That's his name.'

'Oh my God,' Leanne whispered, her eyes on stalks. 'Oliver Wilde? The one who writes horror books and movies? And gory thrillers?'

Lucilla sighed. '*Si*, horrible.'

'She was married to Oliver Wilde?!' Maddy exclaimed. 'Why didn't she say?'

Lucilla shrugged. 'I don't know. She left New York in a rush. Then she says she doesn't want to talk about it. She's changing her name back to her old one too.'

'Aha,' Leanne said. 'That's why she wants to be incognito. Because of the divorce, I mean. If there are complications and gossip or something. Media interest maybe?'

'Or her husband wants to murder her,' Maddy whispered, her eyes wide. 'Then he'll get all her money, if the divorce hasn't gone through.'

'Aren't we overacting a tad?' Leanne said with a wink. 'Thank God your divorce is amicable, or we'd be looking over our shoulders for Tom wielding an axe.'

Maddy burst out laughing. 'I think he'd be more likely to bludgeon me with a niblick or whatever one of those golf clubs are called. But I'm sure that's not what Claudia is worried about.'

Lucilla shook her head. 'No, I think she just wants to disappear for a while. I don't think she's afraid of Oliver at all.'

'He must be super rich himself, though. But it's all very mysterious,' Leanne mumbled, deciding to Google Oliver Wilde as soon as she had the chance.

Lucilla straightened up as if forcing herself back to business. 'Okay, we'll talk about that later,' she said, pushing the trolley. 'Don't forget to buy dog food, Maddy.'

They resumed their shopping, getting everything they needed in the supermarket and arranging to have it delivered to the marina. They bought fresh mullet to grill for dinner in the fish shop, and big, plump peaches, ripe apricots, juicy apples, crisp lettuce and deep red tomatoes in the stall beside it. Shopping done, they went to organise the supplies and to see if the skipper had arrived. Then they would cast off and sail to the first little bay for lunch and a swim. *Heaven*, Leanne thought, wiping the sweat off her brow as she lugged the shopping onto the yacht. Everything was falling into place. But when they had put the supplies away and Carlo and Tony had left on their sailing boat, there was still no sign of the skipper.

As they sat on the rear deck drinking lime ice tea, Lucilla phoned the charter company complaining loudly, listening to the excuses and explanations at the other end. She finally said goodbye and hung up. 'He's on the way,' she announced. 'I think they made a mistake and thought we didn't want a skipper. They're organising some kind of reserve.'

Claudia peered out under the awning. 'I see someone running this way,' she announced. 'A man dressed in white with a captain's hat, carrying a big bag. Must be him.'

Leanne followed her gaze and spotted a tall deeply tanned man with greying short hair and beard running towards them. 'Looks like it.'

'Not bad looking,' Claudia remarked.

The man came to a stop by the gangplank. He looked at the name of the yacht painted on the rear, wiped his forehead with a large handkerchief, holding his duffle bag in a tight grip. 'Hello,' he called when he saw them under the awning. 'I'm Nico, your skipper. Sorry about the delay, there was some mix-up at the office.'

'Hi, Nico,' Leanne called back. 'Please come aboard.'

Nico boarded the boat in two easy strides up the gangplank. He saluted, shook their hands and beamed them a brilliant white grin. 'Nice to meet you, ladies,' he said in accented but good English. 'I've skippered this yacht before, so I know where everything is. I'll just put my stuff in the cabin and then we'll be off.'

'Fabulous,' Leanne sighed. 'We can finally leave.'

'Very nice man,' Claudia whispered when Nico had gone to put his bag away. She smoothed her hair and straightened her hat. 'Wonderful manners.'

Nico reappeared and climbed up the steps to the bridge. 'Where will I take you?'

'Anywhere you like,' Claudia said with a flirty smile, all her earlier tension gone.

Lucilla frowned at Claudia. 'Nico, we have an arrangement with our friends to meet up at Dvenik… something. The islands just outside Trogir. We'll have lunch and a swim in the bay and then we have to get going to our evening spot. I'll show you on the chart later and we can map out the journey for tomorrow as well.'

Nico made a sign to the yacht club staff on the marina to undo the dock lines and started the engines. 'Okay,' he called over the noise when they were pulling out. 'We'll be there in half an hour.'

Leanne put up her thumb. The yacht gathered speed and they were soon travelling fast, the water in their wake foaming, the wind whipping the women's hair and cooling their hot faces. As they left the rocky coast of the mainland, they gradually approached the little islands sticking up out of the blue sea.

Leanne felt a surge of excitement as the speed increased and the little town disappeared in the distance. This was the best part of their adventure, she mused. Whatever happened now she would always remember this moment, when the boat took off and headed into the vast unknown.

The sailing boat was already anchored in the bay and they could see Carlo and Tony swimming around it. As soon as Nico killed the engine, Leanne nipped into her cabin and put on her bikini, a blue paisley patterned one she had bought in Florence. She ran out on the sun deck and dived straight into the crystal clear water. This was a dream, she thought as she emerged and floated on her back, her eyes closed. The cool, clear water on her body was like a soothing balm after the hot rays of the sun. Swimming had always been her favourite sport and she could outswim them all, being a champion long-distance swimmer. She gave a start as Tony's head appeared beside her.

'You're a real water baby, I see,' he remarked, floating beside her.

'Yes,' Leanne said, her eyes half-closed. 'I love the water. I used to swim with my dad on holidays in Kerry. And sail too. Lots of sailing.'

Tony floated on his back beside her. 'Ah, Kerry. Lovely county. The water is warm there in the summertime too.'

'Mmm,' Leanne mumbled. 'And in Norway. My dad's from Norway, you know.'

'I know. Maddy told me. But I knew the moment I saw you there was Viking blood there. Apart from your lovely Irish eyes, of course.'

'I'm a mongrel.' Leanne turned to look at Tony. Without his glasses he looked younger and a little vulnerable. It moved her in a strange way, seeing him like that, despite all his teasing.

'Me too,' Tony said, meeting her eyes. 'Italy and Ireland meet in my body.'

Leanne smiled. 'Yeah, red hair but dark skin. Hazel eyes with black lashes. And then you have freckles too. It looks nice though.'

'Thank you.' Tony turned on his stomach. 'I have to get back. Carlo's fixing one of the riggings that seems to be a little wonky. Then lunch on your yacht.'

'Fab,' Leanne mumbled and resumed floating, closing her eyes to the sun as Tony left her, swimming away with a practised crawl. *A sweet but somehow troubled man*, she reflected, judging by the expression in his eyes. She tried to figure out what it was as she slowly floated back to the boat, where she could see Lucilla and Maddy laying the table on the rear deck. There was no sign of

Claudia, but Nico was still on the bridge consulting a chart. As she lay back, soaking up the peaceful scene and the gentle voices floating across the water, she reflected on what a close-knit group they were becoming, all connected to each other in some way or other. How strange that people from so many different backgrounds could bond like this. It must be the beautiful setting, the sunshine and the general holiday mood. Except… she was certain there were tensions and troubles brewing under the glossy surface. Would some of that come to a head and suddenly explode?

Chapter Thirteen

Life's a beach!

Hey there, lovely fans! We're now on the ocean blue, living the life of castaways on this rather snazzy little yacht. As the girls are not into camping or getting seasick in tiny sailing boats, we decided to split up. The girls opted for a cute little yacht. She's (all boats are a 'she') called Yolanda *and she's fabulous, with a cabin for each one of us and a tiny shower and bathroom all to myself. The group consist of Maddy and me, Lucilla (fabulous Sophia Loren look-alike) and ML (Mystery Lady, as she wants to keep a low profile), plus hunky Captain Nico on the yacht, and Tony (cute Irish-Italian doctor) with HI (Hot Italian) on the sailing boat (which is called* The Happy Adventure *for some reason). Photos of all (except ML) to follow, but here's one of my cabin and the gorgeous rear deck, where we take our meals and generally sit around chatting in the evenings. The boat has a living room (which, as you may not know, is a saloon on a yacht), but it's too lovely outside to sit indoors. The galley kitchen is top-notch and I thought I'd have a go as it's my turn to cook today. (Or I'll chicken out and take everyone*

to a restaurant!) But right now it's time for breakfast, and
then I'll slip into something more comfortable… Stay tuned!

Leanne uploaded the post on the blog and got up to join the others for breakfast. She laughed as she thought of the scene last night when Claudia had pulled a face because Nico was joining them for dinner. 'But he's *staff*,' she had whispered to Leanne.

'And who are you? Lady Muck?' Leanne had whispered back. 'He has to eat and he's nice and we want him to join us. If that's not okay with you, go and have your dinner in your cabin.'

Claudia had pinched her lips at this but demurred and ended up being charming and, after a few glasses of Croatian rosé, had turned even more flirtatious than before.

There was something still a little odd about her though. What could it be that had her so on edge? And why had she been so anxious to join them on this boat trip? It struck Leanne that she hadn't Googled her husband's name to find out the latest gossip about him. She sat down on her bed again and quickly searched for Oliver Wilde.

At first, she could only find his professional details and there was a Wikipedia page all about his early life. He was born in a small town in Yorkshire fifty-nine years ago. Went to university in London, where he studied journalism, etc. Then he had published his first book in the horror genre, which had become a bestseller. No Stephen King, he was nevertheless successful, two of his books having been bought by Hollywood and done well as movies. His latest screenplay had been nominated for an Oscar two years earlier.

Leanne scrolled to his personal life. Two previous marriages before he met Claudia Jones, widow of property tycoon Blake Jones and married her in Los Angeles eight years ago.

Okay. That was the biography. Leanne clicked back to Google and turned to the society pages. Lots of glam shots in various magazines of the two of them in fancy gear at premieres and swish parties. They had homes in Manhattan, the Hamptons and LA and commuted between them, preferring their villa in the Hamptons in the warmer months. Not much other gossip and no candid shots of Oliver with other women or any kind of rumour of that nature, even in the tabloids. He was quite handsome in a rough way, with thinning fair hair, a square jaw, a large nose and piercing grey eyes. Someone who took no prisoners, Leanne thought with a shiver, and tucked her phone into the pocket of her shorts. Time for breakfast and a little photo shoot with Carlo. They had spent the night at the marina of one of the many yacht clubs that dotted the islands, but were about to cast off and get going to their next destination, a quiet inlet on one of the outer islands. Carlo and Tony had already taken off, as the winds were favourable but might drop later.

Leanne put together the items they would use in the shoot. The garments were shapeless and drab, but with a nice natural feel to them once she put them on. She had been surprised how soft and comfortable the fabric felt, nearly like a second skin. If the designs had been better they would have no trouble marketing them. But she was determined to do her very best to make them sell. If only to impress Carlo.

*

Maddy decided to give Tom a call before breakfast. Sophie's remark about the money had rattled her and she needed to hear from Tom if what she had said was true. Being an early riser, she knew he'd be up and already having breakfast before hitting the golf course.

He picked up at the first ring. 'Maddy? What's up?'

'Nothing much. Just thought I'd call and see how things… are progressing.'

'Things?' he asked. 'What things?'

'Our separation, I mean. I was talking to Sophie recently and… she…' Maddy paused, suddenly feeling angry. 'You told her about us splitting up although I wanted to speak to her first as we agreed.'

'Yeah, well… I just thought she should know. I haven't told Darren yet. He's on a camping trip somewhere in Donegal. But I'll let you talk to him when he gets back.'

'Thank you so much,' Maddy said, her voice laced with irony. She knew the talk with her son might be awkward. He was very close to his father. 'About what you told Sophie and our assets and all that…'

'Yes?'

'She said you thought I'd share everything with you. But…' Maddy swallowed, wondering how to put it without looking greedy.

'You're worried I'll grab your fun money?' Tom said with a laugh. 'All that lovely cash you won?'

'Well…'

'Don't worry, pet,' Tom soothed. 'I have no designs on that. You've been very generous already. I'm so grateful. Do whatever you want with the rest. Blow it on shoes and handbags for all I care. But maybe you could put a little aside for a rainy day and for the kids if they decided to do something crazy, like buying property or getting married.'

'Oh,' Maddy said, taken aback by his warm tone. 'Thank you. That's very kind of you.'

'You're welcome, sweetheart. In any case, Claire tells me that divorce takes a long time in this country. We have to live apart for four years before we can even start. So that gives you plenty of time to live it up.'

'Claire?' Maddy asked.

'Yes. You might remember her? She's the secretary of the golf club in Lahinch. She's a lawyer as well. We're… dating.'

'I see.' Claire, Maddy thought, that was the woman Tom had been smooching with while away on a golf trip. Jacinta, her sister-in-law, had posted a photo of them on Facebook out of spite. Maddy couldn't believe it when she'd seen it. It had been the final nail in the coffin of their marriage. 'Great,' she managed. 'I'm glad you're happy. Thanks for clearing things up.'

'No problem. Was there anything else? We need to talk about the house and everything but that can wait.'

'Yes,' Maddy whispered, tears welling up. 'Bye for now.' She hung up without waiting for a reply and wiped her eyes with the edge of her t-shirt. No need to feel sad. They were both happier apart than together. But the word 'divorce' had triggered memories of their time together. More than twenty years and two lovely children. Lots of happy memories of being a family, bringing the children up and struggling to make ends meet. Maddy sighed and got up from the bed. She had to put it all behind her. She had so much to be happy about. *Look forward*, she told herself. *This is the start of the rest of my life. And I'm the only one who can make it work.*

*

The rocky shore of the little island looked like something from a *Star Wars* set, Leanne thought as she sat in the dinghy approaching the beach. White boulders with jagged edges rose from the beach strewn with sharp pebbles, and a few pine trees and dry shrubs provided the only greenery. High above them the sun shone from a cloudless blue sky, reflected in the still water, turning it turquoise near the shore.

Dressed in a shapeless white top with slashes down the front that threatened to expose her breasts, and her own shorts, she jumped out as soon as the water was knee-high.

'Ouch,' she yelped, as she stepped on a sharp stone. 'The bottom is really rough here.'

'I told you to put on the rubber shoes,' Lucilla said. 'But you thought they weren't pretty enough. I brought them anyway.' She handed Leanne a pair of black rubber bathing shoes.

'Thanks. You were right,' Leanne admitted, putting on the shoes while holding onto the edge of the dinghy. 'I can see a sea urchin down there,' she added, peering into the clear water. 'So yeah, shoes it is, even if they look like toads.'

'I have mine on already,' Carlo announced, alighting from the dinghy. 'Lucilla, please give me the bag with the clothes and get your camera ready. We have to take about five shots of each item and then pick the best one later. Okay, Leanne?'

Leanne nodded and waded ashore, stepping carefully on the sharp rocks that threatened to slice her rubber shoes in half. 'Jaysus, this is lethal,' she exclaimed. 'How are we going to take shots here?'

'I was thinking over there,' Lucilla said, when she had pulled the dinghy onto the beach, pointing to a smooth rock further away. 'Look at how it hangs over the blue water and the reflection. It'll make a beautiful photo.'

Leanne followed her gaze and immediately saw what Lucilla meant. The rock was flat on top and would be the perfect platform for them to pose on. The screen of pine trees would provide a stunning background, and the deep blue water would offset the black and white clothes perfectly. Leanne dabbed her face with a paper towel, hoping it wouldn't be too shiny. She didn't bother wearing foundation as there would have been little point in the searing heat, it would just melt right off her. But Claudia had helped make up her eyes with a sexy smoky look, and they appeared even bigger and darker, a startling contrast to her almost white hair and golden skin.

They climbed up on the rock, Lucilla behind them. Carlo helped Leanne and Lucilla up the steepest part.

'Okay,' Lucilla called, her camera ready on a tripod. 'I know what we should do. Leanne, sit with your legs over the edge and lean back slightly.'

'Okay.' Leanne sat down, her heart hammering as her legs dangled over the sharp edge of the cliff. She looked down at the water far below. 'Gosh that's a bit steep.' She leaned back. 'Like this?'

'Yes, perfect,' Lucilla said. 'Carlo, sit behind her and bend your leg with your foot just off her back, so it looks like you're about to kick her over the edge.'

Carlo laughed and sat down. 'Like this?'

'*Ecco!*' Lucilla called and snapped away. 'Looks good!'

Leanne relaxed. 'Well, thank the Lord for that.' She moved back a little but stayed there, looking down into the water below and laughed at herself and how she had ended up here. *Secondary school teacher living with dreary mother in a North Dublin semi ends up modelling with sexy hunks in the Adriatic*, she thought. What a surreal change of careers. But hey, it was just the summer holidays. She'd be back teaching before she knew it. Or... She looked at Carlo as he reached out his hand to help her up and Lucilla took another shot of them. Leanne felt sure the Instagram posts would be a hit. She was also writing a blogpost in her head – this was so much fun and she didn't want it to stop. Deep in thought, she let Carlo pull her up.

'That's it,' Lucilla called. 'I think we have enough for the first few photos. After this, we'll just take normal holiday snaps.'

Leanne smiled at Carlo. 'Flirty shots,' she whispered in his ear. 'Can you manage that?'

'I'll do my best,' he whispered back and nibbled her earlobe.

'I said stop,' Lucilla protested. 'No more posing. But I got that one. Cute shot.'

'Thanks,' Leanne said with a chuckle. 'Funny how photos turn out best when you're not actually posing.'

Lucilla didn't reply but gathered up her things and climbed down from the rock. They returned to the yacht in silence, Lucilla at the oars, dropping Carlo off at the sailing boat on the way.

Leanne watched as he climbed on board. 'Nice butt,' she said without thinking.

'But what?' Lucilla asked, as she pushed away from the sailing boat.

'But it was very hot,' Leanne replied, relieved her remark had been misunderstood. 'Very hot indeed,' she added, as Carlo's trim behind disappeared over the railing. 'And getting hotter.'

Lucilla stopped rowing and looked at Leanne with growing suspicion. 'Take care, my dear. Remember what happened to Icarus.'

'The guy who flew too close to the sun?'

'Yes.'

Leanne met Lucilla's gaze. 'Was that a warning of some kind?'

Lucilla smiled sweetly. 'No, just a bit of advice. In case you were becoming too dazzled – by the sunlight.'

Maddy was on the rear deck in her red bikini when they came back. 'How about a swim?' she asked. 'You look like you need cooling off.'

'In more ways than one,' Leanne said with a laugh. 'But yeah, a swim would be great. And why not up the fun a little? I saw snorkelling masks and flippers in a cupboard in the saloon. Maybe we could spot some marine wildlife in this little bay?'

'Brilliant idea,' Maddy said. 'And Lucilla could take some shots for the blog.'

'Yes!' Leanne went to change into her bikini, picking a green one with a pattern of tiny fish. She reappeared minutes later as Maddy emerged from the saloon with two sets of snorkelling masks and flippers.

They donned the masks and Leanne handed her phone to Lucilla.

'Okay,' Lucilla said, aiming it at them. 'Put the masks on your heads and then stand by the railing with your arms around each other.' She stopped and lowered the phone. 'Leanne, that's a very small bikini. You'll look nearly naked in the shot.'

'So what?' Leanne shot back. 'Haven't you heard? Naked is the new black.'

Lucilla laughed. 'I know, but you have to consider your followers. They might not approve.'

'Why wouldn't they?' Leanne asked. 'I don't think there are any nuns among our fans.'

'How do we know?' Maddy enquired. 'There could be all kinds of people with high moral standards watching us.'

'Yeah, sure. Maybe. And all kinds of pervs too.' Leanne pulled up the bottoms of the bikini and adjusted the top across her bust to make it look less skimpy. 'Better?'

'Yes,' Maddy replied. 'Much better.'

Lucilla took the photos and they climbed down the ladder, sitting on the small deck at the rear to put on the flippers. Then they sank into the crystal-clear sea and swam off until they were nearer the shore where they put their heads underneath the water, floating and watching the shoals of rainbow-coloured fish swimming around the underwater rocks. Leanne was amazed at the beautiful sights in this silent, blue world. Yellow, blue and stripy fish of all shapes and sizes milled around the rocks and seaweed. Sometimes they swam up to investigate, peering at her through the mask or even nibbling at her fingers. She felt she could float there forever, weightless, lost in this soundless world of colour and light.

She stayed there, mesmerised, until Maddy tapped her on the shoulder. 'Wow,' she exclaimed as they came up, pushing their masks onto the top of their heads. 'How utterly beautiful.'

'I had no idea it was this wonderful down there,' Leanne panted. 'We must do this again.'

'Absolutely. I wish I had an underwater camera. Then we could take shots of each other snorkelling.'

'Would be nice, but I'll paint a picture with my words, don't worry,' Leanne promised.

'You will. You're a very good writer,' Maddy agreed. 'But now my stomach is rumbling. I need food and maybe a siesta. This sleeping after lunch is growing on me.'

'You'd better not make that a habit. It'd be a little awkward if you dropped off after the ham sambo at work in front of all the girls.'

'Work,' Maddy groaned. 'Please don't mention it. I don't know how I'm going to get my brain back into teaching mode again after living the champagne lifestyle.'

Leanne floated on her back. 'You could always quit, of course. And then move in with Dad and the goats up in the mountains. While I take over the business and run it into the ground in six months.'

Maddy glanced at Leanne as they swam leisurely back to the yacht. 'Run it into the ground? Why would you do that?'

'Because I'm lousy at maths and money. That's one little detail my dear old dad hasn't thought of. I'd be the worst thing that ever happened to his firm.'

'Why don't you tell him?'

'I will next time he tries to arm wrestle me into taking over.'

'You should.' Maddy ducked her head under water, then came up again, blinking. 'Ugh. Very salty and stingy. So what are you going to do when we get back?'

Still on her back, Leanne kicked her legs, staring up at the sky. 'I'm planning to do something new and exciting. A whole new career. It's all going so well right now. The blogging, I mean. Why not build on that instead of letting it die?'

'You should. I bet you'd make a real go of it.' Maddy swam a few strokes. 'But what about teaching? You signed a contract for another school year. And Carlo? Where does he fit into all of this?'

Leanne sighed and turned, joining Maddy in a breast stroke. 'I can write in my spare time. And Carlo? Who knows? I haven't got that far in my plans for him.' She grinned at Maddy. 'But hey, whatever. Isn't life grand all the same?'

Maddy agreed that life was indeed, right there and then, perfectly grand. And in that mood, laughing and teasing, they returned to the yacht to live the good life.

Chapter Fourteen

Models and other wildlife

Poštovani dragi! (Croatian for 'hello darlings'). I hope life is as grand for you as it is for us, suffering in the hot sun of the Dalmatian islands. But as you will see, my new outfits are very comfortable, even if they're a little, ahem, unusual. But baggy clothing is the new trend these days, they say, whoever 'they' are, and this new fabric is surprisingly cool... Not that fashion is my hobby or anything. I'm more into writing silly blogposts about lovely holidays. If only one could do that for a living...

This morning, Maddy and I went snorkelling and we floated for hours in the balmy water studying the amazing marine life that we never knew existed. It was the most incredible experience! Like floating, weightless in space, in this blue, shimmering world full of fish of all the colours of the rainbow. They glimmered and glittered like jewels and it was hard to tear ourselves away from the gorgeous sights. Now lunch on the rear deck and then perhaps a snooze if I get sleepy. This caviar and champagne life is a tough job, but someone's got to do it.

Later, dragi! Sleepy hugs from moi and Maddy.

*

Lucilla sent the modelling photos to Leanne when they had finished lunch. 'I think they can be used for your Instagram posts. No big reveal, just a hashtag or two. Keep it low key, like you said. How did you feel wearing those clothes?' she asked, as they were relaxing on the rear deck with a cup of coffee after lunch.

Leanne avoided Lucilla's piercing eyes. 'Uh, hmm, I was surprised at how they felt. I think it's something to do with the fabric. All so natural and soft.'

Lucilla nodded. 'That's a good marketing point. We should make a slogan around that. What do you think?'

'Yes, sounds good,' Leanne replied. 'I have to look at all the photos first. But there doesn't seem to be a good signal here, so can we wait till we get to that little fishing village on Hvar?'

Lucilla nodded. 'Good idea.'

Maddy poured herself a cup of freshly brewed coffee. 'Hvar? Isn't that a town?'

'Yes,' Claudia volunteered. 'It's both. Hvar is a town on the island of Hvar, isn't that right, Nico?'

'Yes,' Nico called from the saloon, where he was studying the charts and checking the shipping forecast on the radar screen. 'We are going to dock in Jelsa, a nice fishing village with good restaurants.'

'Oh, phew,' Leanne sighed. 'Restaurants. Then I can invite you all to eat in one of them. It's my turn to cook, but believe me, you wouldn't want to eat whatever I managed not to burn.'

'So when are we setting off?' Claudia enquired. 'Is there time for a little siesta before we go?'

'Yep,' Nico called from the saloon. 'We'll go in half an hour. Not much wind, so you can stay asleep on the way.'

'Thank you, Nico.' Claudia got up and yawned. 'I'm exhausted after this morning.'

'What made you so tired?' Maddy asked. 'Power yoga?'

'No,' Claudia sighed. 'Making my bed. I'm beginning to regret not having staff on the yacht. All this housework is so dreary and tiring.'

'Says the woman who never made a bed before,' Leanne muttered to Maddy.

'I'll say ciao for now,' Claudia said and shuffled off to her cabin.

Lucilla followed in Claudia's wake, declaring the photo shoot had exhausted her, closely followed by a sleepy-eyed Maddy, with Bridget trotting behind her. But Leanne, still on a high after the morning, didn't feel like sleeping. She stayed on deck under the awning, and tried her phone again, but it was no use – still no signal. She'd have to wait until they got to Hvar. She could have looked at the footage from this morning, but she wanted to see it all when she was alone.

'Hi,' a voice said behind her, making her jump.

Leanne looked around to find Tony climbing aboard from the dinghy. 'Hi. I thought you'd already left.'

Tony jumped onto the deck. 'No, not yet. We're waiting for better wind. And Carlo wanted to take a nap. He was tired after the modelling session, he said.'

'Seems like everyone's tired,' Leanne remarked. 'I'm the only one still awake, apart from Nico.'

'You didn't feel like sleeping?'

'No. I feel wide awake for some reason. What about you?'

Tony sat down in one of the deep chairs by the railing and propped his feet on the lifebuoy. 'I'm not very good at sleeping either.'

'Oh. But you do look tired, if you don't mind me saying.'

Tony took off his glasses and pinched the bridge of his nose. 'I don't sleep well generally.'

'Insomnia, eh?' Leanne said, feeling suddenly sorry for him. 'Maybe you think too much.'

Tony put his glasses back on his head and leaned back, his hands behind his head. 'Yes, that's the problem. I'm supposed to have a break and rest, but it's easier said than done.'

'You want to talk about it?' Leanne asked gently. 'I mean, there seems to be something troubling you.'

Tony turned to look at Leanne. In the shade of the awning, his eyes were nearly black and his face so pale his freckles stood out like dark dots across the bridge of his nose. Lines of exhaustion were etched around his mouth. 'Yeah, maybe it would be good to talk.'

Leanne sat back against the cushions in her chair. 'I'd be happy to listen.'

'It's not very pretty.'

'I'm sure it isn't.'

Tony turned to look out across the still water. 'It's... well... I'm not sure where to start.'

'Is it your job?' Leanne asked. 'You were working as a doctor abroad, you said. In Africa?'

'That's right. With Doctors Without Borders. Five years of hell.'

'Five years? That's a long time to spend in hell,' Leanne remarked. 'Couldn't you get out sooner if it was so bad for you?'

'I could, but I didn't want to.' Tony twisted in the chair and looked at her. 'It wasn't all hell for me, you see, but for *them*. The children, the mothers, the pregnant women living in war zones, getting hit by bullets and shrapnel, having limbs blown off in mine fields, watching their children die of hunger or bullet wounds.'

'Holy shit,' Leanne whispered. 'How terrible. But it's amazing that you were there to make a difference. You must have saved many lives.'

'Yes. Sure I did. All of us. Nurses and doctors, even if there weren't enough of us. But you know what? If I had a shitty day and got no sleep, someone could die as a result. And of course that happened sometimes. A wrong diagnosis because I was too tired to think straight, or going to sleep and leaving the care of a patient in the hands of an inexperienced nurse. Stuff like that. Not often, but it did happen. And you never stop blaming yourself.' Tony looked at his hands. 'Five years of that, and I had to get out. I was burnt out and no good as a doctor to those people.'

'What are you going to do now? After this holiday?' Leanne asked. She wanted to take his hand, or stroke his cheek to comfort him somehow, but she didn't dare.

'Now?' he said. 'I'm going back to Ireland. I want to train as paediatrician. I love kids and I love making them better. The health service in Ireland is going through a crisis, as you know. Maybe I can do something to help improve it.'

'That's a very good idea,' Leanne said. 'We do need doctors in Ireland and especially young doctors like—' She stopped. 'How old are you?'

Tony laughed. 'Thirty-four. But I probably look ten years older to you.'

'No. You look young and worn out, that's all. I'm only two years younger.'

He looked surprised. 'Really? But you don't look much older than my little sister. She's twenty-five.'

'What does she do?'

'Kate?' Tony smiled. 'She's working in Dublin at one of those big IT companies. But I could be wrong. She's changed jobs so many times, I've lost track.' His eyes focused on Leanne. 'So, thirty-two and not married or in a relationship? How come?'

'I'm working on it,' Leanne said with a wry smile. 'But so far no luck. You have to kiss a lot of frogs before you find a real prince, or so they say.'

'So that's what you're doing? Kissing frogs and teaching?'

'Yeah. Takes up a lot of my time.'

'And then you're taking a break from all that and touring around Europe.'

'Thanks for telling me the story of my life,' Leanne teased, only pretending to be annoyed. The conversation had taken on a more playful tone, which seemed to calm Tony. His eyes were less troubled and his body more relaxed as they continued to banter.

'And now you're modelling the latest fashion on the Internet,' Tony continued, unabashed. 'I can see that finding the perfect husband would be hard for a high-flyer like you.'

'It is,' Leanne sighed, with a twinkle in her eyes. 'Who could live up to my standards, I wonder?'

'What about Carlo?' Tony asked, with a mischievous expression.

Leanne felt her face flush. 'Who knows?' she said, with pretend nonchalance. 'I haven't seen enough of him yet.'

'I'm sure that's only a matter of time.'

'Really?' Despite her resolve, Leanne felt a dart of embarrassment. 'You can read minds and see into the future, can you now?'

'You don't have to look into anything to know what's going on. Latin lover meets hot Irish chick with attitude. Would make a great rom-com.'

Leanne bristled, cheeks blushing. 'I'm not sure what you mean?'

Tony shot her a contrite look. 'I'm sorry. I was only joking.'

'How come nobody laughed?' Leanne snapped, feeling vulnerable all of a sudden.

Tony made a pleading gesture. 'Ah come on, let it go will you? I was being stupid. I like talking to you. I love teasing you too. But I didn't mean to—'

Her anger gone as soon as it had started, Leanne waved her hand in the air. 'Nah, it's okay. I shouldn't be so prickly. But it's a sore spot. My love life is a bit tricky to say the least. Too much baggage I suppose.'

'I know. And the older we get the more we have.' Tony got up as the awning flapped in a sudden gust. 'I see the wind's up. We'd better get going if we're to get any sailing this afternoon.' He hesitated at the railing. 'Thanks for listening. It felt good to share a little bit about – well, you know.'

'Any time,' Leanne replied. 'I'm here, if you—'

'Thanks. Much appreciated,' Tony said a little stiffly, as if he regretted baring his soul to her. 'See you later.' He leapt over the railing into the dinghy and rowed away.

Leanne watched him head back to the sailing boat, her mind on what he had told her. He was obviously suffering from a trauma that affected him daily. There had to be something he could do to make it better and help him at least get a night's sleep. Therapy was probably the best option. But he probably wouldn't want to look for that kind of help, being a doctor himself.

Leanne turned her mind to the present as the anchor chain rattled and Nico started the engine. The boat began to move in the choppy water. They'd be in Jelsa in a little over an hour.

She checked her bag to see if she had her phone, cash and credit cards, sunglasses and sunscreen all there. Then she found the little bottle with the perfume her dad had made up for her and sprayed some of it on her wrists. The scent brought back the memory of their reunion and how hard it had been to hear his side of the story. *Oh, Mam,* she thought, *how could you have been so cruel, only thinking of yourself? I was only twelve and it broke my heart when he left. And then he never called or even wrote me one single word. Or so I thought…*

Leanne sat back in the deck chair and stared out across the sea, thinking about it all. So much pain that could have been prevented. But now, because of her lottery win, she had been given more than money – a reunion with her father who loved her. A gift, but also a burden in the form of his expectations. Leanne sighed and decided to park it all at the back of her mind. 'I'll think about it later,' she said out loud and smiled at the bright blue sky, dotted with soaring seagulls and fluffy white clouds. The sun and the soft breeze caressed her skin and the smell of her perfume evaporated along with her worries. Life was too good right now to be sad and lonely. Who knew what the future would bring?

Chapter Fifteen

Maddy woke up when the boat started to move. She looked around the plush cabin and noticed her laptop, still open, on the little table beside the porthole. She had intended to write an email to Erik, but then felt too sleepy. In any case, there had been no signal, so she had left it and stretched out on the soft bed, her eyes closing, drifting off to sleep. The intense heat and the morning of swimming had exhausted her.

Bridget, who had curled up at the foot of the bed, stirred, yawned and went back to sleep. 'Good idea, girl,' Maddy said and patted her. 'I'll take you for a good long walk when we dock.' She got up and decided to continue writing as they would soon be within range of the masts on the island of Hvar.

> Dear Erik, Maddy wrote, here we are on the high seas. Well, not quite, as we spent the night and morning in a lovely bay and are now on our way to the island of Hvar, where we will stay in the harbour of a cute little fishing village for the night. Leanne is treating us all to dinner. It's her turn to cook, but as she is no Nigella, she's cheating. So far the cruise is hugely enjoyable despite us no longer being two

*girls on a trip. We've ended up with some rather unusual
people, most of them part of Lucilla's extended family. And
the glorious hunk Carlo, of course, on whom Leanne seems
to have a huge crush. He seems quite interested, but please
don't worry. She could end up with someone far worse, as
I'm sure you know...*

Maddy paused, thinking about Carlo, wondering if what you saw
was what you got, or if there was something else brewing behind
his smooth good looks. He was nice, courteous and easy-going with
eyes that could be flirtatious and mischievous. Then he also seemed
to have a cool head for business and a drive to make his ideas work.
Ambitious and hard-working. Nice and polite. What could possibly
be wrong with that? Nothing, of course, but Maddy had a niggling
worry that he was not the right man for Leanne. But was that really
any of her business? Leanne was an adult and Maddy had no right to
interfere. Yet the twelve years of life experience that separated them
had led her to her distrust people that seemed too perfect. And there
was something about Carlo she couldn't put a finger on that rang
false. Was it his way of beaming that film star smile at everyone, or
the way Lucilla watched him when she thought nobody was looking?

Maddy sighed. Watching what could end up a train crash was
not exactly good for one's peace of mind. But maybe she was being
too protective. She shrugged and continued writing. Que sera, sera
and all that.

*The other people in the party consist of Lucilla, who you
know from the marketing firm, and her cousin Tony, who*

happens to be half Irish. Nice man, who looks as if he's been
through something difficult. But haven't we all? Then Lucilla
and Tony's aunt Claudia, a former New York socialite who
seems to be on the run from something or someone – pos-
sibly the gutter press, since she left her husband, famous
horror writer Oliver Wilde. I nearly said Oscar Wilde, but
this guy's oeuvre would be far removed from such heights
of literature. Anyhow, despite a little tension here and there
and Claudia playing the lady of the manor, it's going well
and we're all enjoying this stunning part of the Adriatic.

Maddy stopped and read through what she'd written. All very
nice and breezy but without any personal note. Should she write
something more intimate, telling him how much she missed him and
that their short time together was constantly in her mind and her
dreams? No. Better keep a little distance for now. Sweet and cheery.

Your perfume is lovely and reminds me of you, she contin-
ued. Especially when I dab it on certain parts of my body…
Claudia wants to know where she can buy it but I told her
it was bespoke and made especially for me, so now she
wants you to create one for her. Be prepared to meet a
real-live diva!

We seem to be docking, so I'll sign off now. I'm sure
you're following the blog, anyway, so you'll get the updates
on this wonderful get-away. Can't tell you how much I'm
loving this trip! And I'm spending money like there's no
tomorrow, which is totally irresponsible but all in a good

cause. I don't want you-know-who to get his greedy paws on
my cash when we start dividing assets, even if he assured
me he won't claim any of it. But there'll be very little left by
the time it comes to the crunch.

All the best for now, dear pen pal. Please write and tell
me how your plans are coming along.

Maddy xx

She quickly read through what she had written and pressed
send. Not quite as bland as she had planned, but she didn't want
to appear too cool and distant. She missed Erik and looked forward
to seeing him again, but this trip was just what she needed after the
intense few days with a man she had felt immediately drawn to. He
had wanted too much too soon, not just a brief fling. He'd made
his intentions clear – he was after a steady relationship, something
to build on for a future together. That was something she couldn't
deliver right now. The complications of her life made things difficult,
and it would take time to sort all that out. But Maddy couldn't help
feeling a pang of regret at the thought that she could have stayed
and got to know him better. But the distance between them would
make him miss her too, which was part of her plan, if she was honest
with herself. This interlude in her life, with a looming divorce from
a marriage that had begun to feel like a prison, was something she
found hard to deal with. Tom had quickly found a new woman
and that stung even though she no longer loved him. But meeting
Erik, with whom she could imagine living high in the hills above
the blue Mediterranean, had been just what she needed in order
to find herself again. She dug out the little bottle of perfume from

her handbag and sprayed some on her neck, breathing in the lovely floral scent. It reminded her of Erik and their night together, but also of her new life and what lay ahead. She was free, and at forty-four still relatively young. A good place to be. If only she didn't care so much about Leanne and her happiness…

Jelsa was a gorgeous fishing village, home to a sheltered harbour lined with little shops and cute fish restaurants tucked away in old stone-faced buildings. Steeped in history, the houses and streets harked back to Grecian times and beyond. The cobblestones, laid by the Romans, were polished by many feet through the centuries and the higgledy-piggledy houses that lined the streets and narrow lanes had an irresistible charm to them. Maddy and Leanne had decided to tour the town together, taking Bridget with them on her lead.

'I could live here forever,' Leanne sighed, looking up at the old façades where roses rambled all the way up to the red tiles of the roofs. She breathed in the warm air, laden with the fragrance of flowers, spices and a whiff of the sea breeze. 'It makes me feel so relaxed,' she continued, happy to have Maddy on her own. The others were fun but she was craving some quality time with her friend.

'Me too,' Maddy agreed. 'But I bet these houses are cold in the winter.'

'I'd say they're freezing,' Leanne agreed. 'But maybe a summer house would be an idea?'

'The property prices all over these islands have shot up in the past few years,' Maddy remarked. 'I looked it all up when we were in Trogir. It struck me that a little house here would be so fabulous. But not very practical, I suppose.'

Leanne put her arm through Maddy's. 'There you go being all sensible again.'

'Boring, huh?'

'No. Comforting. You're so grounded. I'm more like a hot air balloon at the moment.'

Maddy squeezed Leanne's arm. 'I noticed. Let me know if you want me to pull you down to earth.'

Leanne smiled. 'At the moment it's good to float.' She looked up at the blue sky above, not a cloud in sight. 'The view is pretty good from here.'

'Have you looked at the photos from the morning's shoot?'

Leanne stopped walking. 'Yes. The photos are great. Everything worked really well and the light was perfect. Carlo and I suit each other in an odd way and the clothes aren't as bad as they seemed. But...' She stepped back and ran her hand through her hair. 'If this low-key approach doesn't work, Lucilla and Carlo won't be very pleased.'

'I'm sure it'll be okay,' Maddy soothed. 'Hey, let's go and have ice cream in that little square down below. Tony told me the ice cream here is nearly better than in Florence. I feel like one of those sinful sundae things topped with whipped cream, nuts and hot chocolate sauce. Don't you?'

'Now you're talking.' Leanne took Bridget's lead and pulled Maddy along to the beautiful main square with its white flagstones, old buildings and bars and restaurants festooned with colourful umbrellas. The square opened onto the harbour and had breath-taking views straight out to sea, sparkling under the bright sun.

Maddy looked around. 'What a stunning place.'

'Gorgeous. Let's find the ice cream parlour and get stuck in.'

Twenty minutes later, they were sitting at a table outside the ice cream parlour looking at each other across two tall glasses stuffed full of ice cream sundae, topped with a huge mound of whipped cream and a bright red cherry perched on top. They dug in, laughing, and didn't speak until the last blob of chocolate sauce had been scraped from the glass.

'Oh my God,' Maddy sighed, wiping her mouth. 'That was delicious.'

'Are you kidding? It was pure heaven,' Leanne said, licking her spoon. 'I don't think we'll have room for dinner.'

'I'm sure we'll make space,' Maddy replied.

'I felt like a kid eating that.' Leanne looked around the square and the other tables, where couples and families were enjoying an assortment of desserts. 'Seems like a popular spot.' Glancing around, she noticed a lone figure behind them. It was odd to see someone on their own in this family kind of place. But why wouldn't anyone want an ice cream on a hot day? She felt a little sorry for the man and wondered if he had a family or a wife with him.

Maddy looked around. 'Yes. Everyone's getting into the ice creams. Except...' She leant towards Leanne. 'That guy over there, at the table behind us... He's not eating anything. And I think he took a photo of us with his phone.'

'What?' Leanne followed Maddy's gaze and saw that the man was still sitting there. He had a blond beard and wore a white sunhat and sunglasses. He looked in her direction but his eyes were hidden. She couldn't tell if he was looking at her or at the view of the town and the little church behind her. 'I noticed him a moment ago. Thought he looked lonely. But I'm sure he didn't take a photo us, just of the town and the harbour. Lovely view from here.'

'Yeah. Probably.' Maddy paid the bill and got up. 'Ready to go? I want to look into those little shops. They sell hand-printed silk scarves and sarongs for the beach that would make nice gifts to bring home.'

'Okay.' Leanne gathered her things. 'I want to write a blog post and then upload the first photo of the marketing campaign on my Insta page. We need to book a table for dinner too, don't we?' She put her hand on her stomach and groaned. 'A very late dinner.'

'And light,' Maddy filled in. 'If we keep eating like this we'll turn into blobs. Let's get going, then.'

'Don't forget Bridget,' Leanne said and peered under the table. But the spot where Bridget had been sitting was empty. Leanne looked at Maddy, panic rising in her chest. 'She's not there.'

Chapter Sixteen

'What?!' Maddy exclaimed and bent down to look. 'She's gone.' She looked wildly around the square, but there was no sign of the little poodle. 'Where could she be?'

'I don't know,' Leanne moaned, panic rising in her chest. 'Please tell me she wasn't stolen.'

'Maybe she just wandered off?' Maddy looked around the tables again. 'We have to ask around. Let's start with that guy who took the photo. He might have seen—'

'He's gone too,' Leanne said, looking at the empty table. Now seriously worried, she grabbed a passing waiter by the arm, nearly knocking the tray crammed with ice cream sundaes out of his hands. 'Please, our dog is lost, have you seen her? A little black poodle with a red collar.' The words rushed out of her in a panic.

'Yes.' The waiter nodded and steadied the tray. 'I saw her.'

'Thank God,' Leanne breathed. 'Where is she?'

'I saw her when you sat down. She was under the table. Then I didn't see her any more.'

Leanne squeezed his arm. 'Is that all? You didn't see her get away – or someone taking her? You must have!'

'No.' The waiter raised his eyebrows, looking at Leanne as if she might be dangerous and pulled away. 'Sorry, but I have to serve the ice creams.' He walked off towards another table where a family was eagerly waiting for their treat.

'Shit,' Leanne exclaimed, cold sweat breaking out in her armpits. 'Where the bloody hell is she? We have to find her, Maddy, we have to!'

'Calm down. I'm sure someone has seen her. We just have to keep looking.' Maddy started to move around the tables, asking people about Bridget, showing them photos on her phone. Everyone shook their heads and shrugged. No, they hadn't seen the little dog.

Leanne walked up to a family digging into huge banana splits. Mother, father, two small boys, and a girl of about twelve, her hair in pigtails and huge round glasses perched on her nose. Maybe... She walked up to the table. 'Do you speak English?'

'Yes,' the father said. 'Sure we're Irish.'

'Thank God,' Leanne sighed. 'I mean not thank God you're Irish, aren't there enough of us already? I meant thank God you speak English. We've lost our dog, you see, and we were wondering if you've seen her? A little black poodle. Her name's Bridget and she wears a red collar...'

They all shook their heads, except the girl, who pointed at Leanne. 'It's her. The one from the blog.'

'Stop pointing, Sinead,' the mother corrected. 'It's rude. What blog?'

'*Women Now*,' Sinead said, looking important. 'I follow it.'

'What?' her mother snapped. 'You follow a... blog? Have I not told you to stay off the Internet when we're not around ?'

Sinead rolled her eyes. 'Jesus, Ma, you're so old-fashioned. Everyone in my class goes on the Internet on their own.'

'But you're not allowed to have a Facebook account until you're thirteen,' the father protested.

Sinead sighed. 'Oh, please, Dad. Facebook is so yesterday. I'm on Snapchat and Instagram. And the Wordpress blogs.' She looked at Leanne and smiled, her braces glinting in the sun. 'Your blog is *awesome*. Most of my friends follow it.'

'Oh, thank you.' Leanne smiled at the girl. 'Glad you like it. We didn't know we had so many young fans, did we, Maddy?'

'Not at all,' Maddy said, walking closer.

'What's the blog about?' the father asked, eyeing them suspiciously.

'It's about how they won some money on the Lotto,' Sinead said. 'Then they bought a sports car and took off on a trip across Europe with their little dog. Leanne had a date with a hot Italian the other day and then they set off on this trip on a yacht. And now they're here and—' Sinead's face fell. 'You lost Bridget?!'

'Yes,' Leanne said, 'But I'm sure we'll find her. She might even have gone back to the boat all by herself.'

Sinead shot up. 'But we have to find her,' she exclaimed. 'Ma, Dad, please help them find Bridget.' She pulled at her brother beside her. 'Sean, get up, we have to help Leanne and Maddy find Bridget.'

'But I want to finish my ice cream,' Sean protested.

'Who's Bridget?' The father asked. 'Your daughter?'

'Gee, Dad, you haven't been listening,' Sinead groaned. 'Bridget's their *dog*. A small black poodle. So cute and cuddly. And we have to help look for her. If we all split up, we might have a better chance.'

The father got up. 'Of course, we'll help. Why didn't you ask in the first place?'

'They did,' Sinead groaned. 'You weren't paying attention.' She hauled a phone out of the pocket of her jeans. 'I just had an idea. I'm going to ask that girl I met at the marina. She might have seen something.' Sinead punched in a number, while Leanne and Maddy waited, holding onto each other. 'Hi, Fidelma, Sinead here. Guess who I just met? Only Leanne and Maddy from the blog!' She paused while listening to the voice at the other end. 'Yes, it's them. I swear. Right here, beside me. Okay, we'll do a selfie later. The thing is they've lost Bridget. She seems to have wandered off while they were eating ice cream. Have you seen her?' Sinead listened for a moment and then gave a shout so loud they all jumped. 'What!!?? She just passed you?' Sinead yelled, her eyes on stalks. 'Where are you? Tell us quick!'

'Where?' Leanne shouted, grabbing Sinead by the shoulder.

'The harbour,' Sinead said, pointing just past the house on the corner. 'Fidelma said a man is walking towards her with a poodle on a red lead. Let's go!' Sinead took off at a run, Maddy and Leanne behind her, followed by Sinead's dad.

They rounded the corner and raced down the quay at breakneck speed. 'I can see her!' Sinead shouted and started to sprint ahead.

'Where?' Leanne panted, her heart beating, her breathing ragged.

'There,' Sinead shouted, pointing ahead. 'That man, there. He's pulling her along.'

Leanne spotted the man who had been at the table behind them, walking swiftly towards a small motorboat, pulling a yelping Bridget with him. He stopped and scooped the dog up in his arms and continued half-running, looking over his shoulder.

'Stop!' Leanne shouted. 'Give us our dog back!'

The man hurried away, but Sinead had nearly caught up with him. Then she lunged for his legs and the man toppled over, crashing to the ground, losing his grip on the dog. 'Fuck!' he shouted and scrambled to his feet, pulling away from Sinead who was still hanging onto his legs.

'Bridget!' Leanne called and held out her arms. The black furry bundle ran like the wind away from the man and jumped into Leanne's arms, whining, barking and furiously licking Leanne's face. 'Oh, my baby, what happened to you?' she breathed into the soft fur.

Sinead got to her feet. 'He's getting away,' she shouted and pointed at the strange man jumping aboard a small motorboat with a red stripe painted on the side. Then the boat pulled out into the bay, the dog thief at the wheel. He revved the engine and took off, soon disappearing around the headland.

Maddy and Sinead's dad caught up with them, breathing hard and sweating profusely.

Sinead's father wiped his face a handkerchief. 'That was some race.'

'You're my hero, Sinead,' Leanne said, still hugging Bridget. 'You saved Bridget. I don't know how to thank you.'

'Ah sure, it was Fidelma,' Sinead said with false modesty. 'But of course I had the brains to call her, so yeah, I'm quite proud of myself.' She stroked Bridget's head. 'I'm so glad she's back with you. I bet that man thought he could kidnap her and ask for ransom money or something.'

'Could be,' Maddy agreed. 'Or maybe he was hoping to sell her?'

'He looked kind of familiar,' Leanne said, casting her mind back to when they had seen him sitting behind them at café. 'I can't quite put my finger on it, but I could swear I've seen him somewhere.'

Maddy took Bridget from Leanne. 'How could you see that? He wore a hat and sunglasses and had a beard covering most of his face. Not much to recognise there.'

Leanne shook her head. 'Nah, you're right. I'm probably barking up the wrong lamp post.'

'Hey, could we do a selfie now?' Sinead cut in.

The father stepped away. 'Not with me in it, please. I have to think of my business and my reputation.'

Sinead giggled. 'I don't think your clients would even blink.'

'What's your business?' Leanne asked, intrigued.

'I'm an undertaker,' the father replied.

'Oh.' Leanne exchanged a glance with Maddy, willing her not to laugh.

The dad smiled. 'Sinead's right. My clients wouldn't kick up a fuss.' He tapped his daughter on the nose. 'Cheeky girl. But I still don't want to be in that selfie.'

Sinead sighed. 'Why on earth would we want you in it? But you can take the photo.' She picked up her phone. 'I'll get Fidelma to join us. She's earned this.'

'She certainly has,' Leanne said with feeling.

It didn't take long before they were joined by Fidelma, a tall girl with black hair and a dimply smile. Sinead made them all stand together while her father took several shots with Sinead, Leanne and Fidelma's phones, before they all hugged and said goodbye.

'See you on the blog!' Sinead called as she and her dad walked away.

'That was lucky,' Maddy sighed as she buried her face in Bridget's fur. 'You bad girl, how could you get away from us?'

'Maybe that guy lured her with something?' Leanne suggested. 'Some treats? You know she can't resist them.'

Maddy placed Bridget on the ground and grabbed her lead. 'Could be. And we were too busy stuffing our faces to notice. Thank God for Sinead. Who knows what would have happened if she hadn't been there?'

Leanne shuddered. 'Horrible.' She suddenly stopped and looked out at sea. 'Horrible…' she muttered. 'Or… horror?'

Maddy blinked. 'What?'

Leanne felt her heart race. Could it be? 'Oliver Wilde,' she said out loud. 'That's who he looked like, that man who stole Bridget.'

Chapter Seventeen

When they returned to the yacht, Tony and Carlo had arrived after a long sailing trip around the islands. The wind was so good and they had wanted to try the big red balloon sail known as a spinnaker. They were both in high spirits, drinking ice cold beer on the rear deck. Claudia was sipping ice tea and Lucilla had gone for a walk.

Leanne glanced at Maddy as they walked up the gangplank, Bridget in Maddy's arms. 'Will we tell Claudia? I mean if it is him, shouldn't she know he's around?'

'No,' Maddy whispered. 'It's such a long shot. You're probably wrong.'

'Yeah, maybe,' Leanne muttered. 'But we still have to be careful. I have an idea about tonight anyway, which will throw him off our scent, if I should be right and he's stalking us or something.'

'Stalking us? Come on. That's totally off the wall.' Maddy let Bridget down on the deck. 'Can we forget about it and move on, please?'

'Alright then,' Leanne agreed. 'But I have to write a short blog post to thank Sinead. She was a true star.'

'You should. But don't broadcast your suspicions about that man.'

'I doubt Claudia will read it. But I won't mention him.'

'Good. Anyway, let's go and have tea and a chat with the lads. They look like they've had a great afternoon. I'll be with you in a sec. I just want to settle Bridget after her adventure and check my emails.'

'And I'll go and write that post. Sinead will be looking out for it and I don't want to disappoint her. See you in a little while.' Leanne kissed Bridget on the top of her silky head and went to write up the post.

Kidnap drama!

Hello! I thought I'd report a huge scare we had today when we visited Jelsa, a little fishing village on the island of Hvar. Maddy, Bridget and I were enjoying a mountain of an ice cream at a lovely café in the main square, and as we were leaving we noticed our darling pooch was missing. You can imagine the panic and near-heart attacks! We ran around the square like mad things asking everyone if they'd seen her and would have given up if an Irish girl called Sinead hadn't stepped in and used her network of teenage girls all around the marina. One of them, a super girl called Fidelma, spotted Bridget as she was whisked away by a stranger, who was trying to get her onto his boat. We ran like the wind to catch up but he was too fast. Then Sinead raced ahead and bravely threw herself forward and grabbed the legs of the dog-napper in a rugby tackle worthy of the Irish world cup team and brought the man down, freeing Bridget, who raced into my arms, crying like a baby. Oh the poor little thing! So scared she was shivering like a leaf. But

hip-hip hooray for Sinead, who, I suspect, is an undercover
agent for MI5 – or at least Interpol. As you can see in the
photo taken by her lovely dad, she's also very cute and will,
when the braces come off, be quite dangerous! Fidelma is
also an excellent example of young, strong womanhood
and looks like a real trooper. Many, many thanks Sinead!
Bridget has now calmed down and is snoozing on Maddy's
bed, exhausted by her HUGE fright. Big phews all around!

Leanne posted the piece, smiling and shaking her head. Those
girls. So brave and independent. They should go into politics when
they grew up. The world would be a better place with such brave
women in charge.

When she had finished the post and freshened up, Leanne walked
through the saloon to the rear deck. This was the first time she had
seen Carlo since their photo shoot. 'Hi,' she said. 'You look cool
and comfortable.'

Tony waved his bottle of beer towards her. 'Yeah, a cool beer
is just the thing after the sailing we did. You want some Ožujsko?
It's a Croatian beer. Very nice. I bought a few bottles and put them
in the fridge.'

'No thanks,' Leanne said, staring at Carlo's back. 'I'll just have
some ice tea.'

'Coming right up,' Tony said and went to fetch it for her.

Claudia got up. 'I'm going to freshen up in my cabin, as we're
going out later.'

Leanne nodded. 'Good idea.' She could hear Tony and Nico talking in the saloon, something about the weather and the direction of the wind the following day.

Carlo turned and smiled at her. 'Hey there, *bella*. Did you see the photos?'

'I did.' Leanne sat down beside him. 'How about you?'

Carlo put his arm along the back of her chair. 'Oh, yes. Loved them.' He leaned so close she could feel his warm breath tickle her neck and smell that spicy aftershave he used – it made her tingle. 'I felt that we were doing something very… intimate while we posed. And when I saw it on the screen, it was even better.'

'Oh,' Leanne mumbled, shivers going up her spine. Her voice trailed away, while Carlo lightly kissed her bare shoulder.

Suddenly Tony appeared behind them. He slid a tall glass towards Leanne with a wink. 'I think you need this. It'll help cool you off.'

'Thank you.' Leanne avoided his probing eyes and sipped the cool drink. She held the cold glass to her hot cheek for a moment. It wasn't the heat that made her cheeks flush, but Carlo's eyes on her and his arm resting lightly on the back of her chair, his fingers touching her bare skin. He smelled so good too. It was irresistible.

Tony sat down and finished his bottle of beer. 'So, you're treating us to dinner tonight, I hear?'

Leanne nodded. 'Yes. But not here in Jelsa. I found this cute little village about twenty minutes from here by motor. It's around the headline to the north. A village called Vrboska. So I thought we could all go on the yacht and leave your sailing boat here until we get back tonight.'

'Or we could all pack up, leave here and moor our boats over there for the night?' Tony suggested. 'I'll ask Nico if there are any free spots in the marina there. He can contact the harbour master.'

'That's a great idea,' Leanne exclaimed. 'Why didn't I think of that?' She sat back, relieved. This way, they'd be gone and that man – if he *was* spying on Claudia – wouldn't be able to find them. Leanne decided to change tack with her blogposts as well, only mentioning places after they had left, just in case. Even if the man was just some weirdo, meeting Sinead had made her realise how very public their posts were. They had around a hundred thousand followers and more to come, she thought with a shiver. It suddenly dawned on her how huge the blog had become and how recognisable she and Maddy were. They'd better sharpen up and be more vigilant in future.

'Why so serious all of a sudden?' Tony asked. 'You looked all soft and dreamy there and now you're frowning. What's up?'

Carlo pulled her close. 'Something wrong, *cara*?'

Leanne briefly brushed Carlo's shoulder with her cheek. 'Nothing wrong. I was just thinking about the blog and how popular it's become. I think we need to be more careful in future and not announce where we're going and when, that's all. You can never be too safe, can you?'

Carlo nodded. 'I know what you mean. I think this is important. And we are in a very popular area with a lot of people passing through.'

'Is that why you picked Vrboska for our dinner?' Tony asked.

'Yes,' Leanne replied. 'But I also found this little fish restaurant. It's near the harbour where everything they serve is homemade.

Even the wine is homegrown. And we don't have to dress up, it'll be nice and casual.'

Tony laughed. 'Who's going to break that to Claudia? She's doing a major overhaul in her cabin, she told me. Face mask, make-up, hair – the lot. And she's picking out an outfit right now.'

Carlo looked highly amused. 'Don't tell her. Just say we're going to a fashionable spot up the coast.'

Leanne grinned and slapped his arm. 'You cruel man.' She reluctantly pulled out of Carlo's embrace and got up. 'I'm going to do that Instagram post now, while we have a signal. That first photo we took. I'll put in a few hashtags and then we'll see.'

Carlo smiled at Leanne. 'I'm sure it'll be picked up. If only because you looked so good in those things.'

'The fabrics do feel amazing,' Leanne agreed. 'And they look heaps better on than just hanging up. Okay, that gives me lot of ideas, thanks. See you later, lads.'

'Maybe we could agree to meet up at the restaurant?' Tony suggested. 'Carlo and I will set off right away and sail up towards Vrboska. We'll book a table for—' He checked his watch. 'Eight o'clock? Then you might have time for a swim beforehand.'

'I never say no to a swim,' Leanne replied. 'Sounds heavenly.'

'I looked it up on my phone,' Carlo said. 'There's no beach but across the bay from their harbour, there is a place with flat rocks where you can dive in.'

'Great.' Tony picked up the empty beer bottles from the table. 'I'll take these for recycling. See you later, girl.'

Behind Tony's back, Carlo pulled her close. 'Swimming is good, but later, we could find a spot for just you and me,' he whispered, his hot breath tickling her cheek. I want us to be on our own… you know? But only if you do, too.'

Leanne sighed and pressed her chest to his. 'Do I want *you*, you mean?'

'Yes.' Carlo put his hand on the small of her back and let it slide further down. 'That's exactly what I mean.'

'You must know I do. But…'

'But?'

'Where can we be alone?'

He stroked her cheek. 'Do not worry, *cara*. I will take care of it. After dinner. Okay?'

'Absolutely wonderful,' Leanne breathed, her heart hammering.

'Ciao, darling.' He kissed her lightly on the lips and walked away with the grace and suppleness of a cat.

Lightheaded, Leanne held on to the railing and stared out across the harbour. How incredible. This beautiful man wanted her as much as she wanted him,. She had seen it in his eyes and felt it in his kiss. She sighed. Could life be any more perfect?

Chapter Eighteen

The restaurant in the harbour of Vrboska proved to be an excellent choice for dinner. There was a great buzz under the stripy awning, where tables were crammed close together, all packed with groups of people eating, laughing and drinking. They had to weave around the busy tables as a cheery waiter showed them the only free one, set for six, right at the edge of the water.

'Fantastic choice, Leanne.' Lucilla beamed her a surprisingly warm smile as she sat down.

'Yes,' Claudia agreed. 'Such a quaint place. And the town is so picturesque. I saw people actually living in those little houses. I waved at them and they waved back. So very charming.'

'Jesus,' Leanne whispered to Maddy. 'What does she think this is, a Disney theme park?'

Maddy giggled. 'I know. She does the lady of the manor so well.'

'Fantastic place,' Carlo said behind them. 'Much nicer than Jelsa. And just look at that view.'

Leanne turned and saw what he meant. The little town was enchanting with ancient stone houses, cobbled streets and a tiny, steepled church. A humpback bridge straddled the canal that ran into the sea at the end of the harbour, where the water lay like a huge blue mirror, its surface only broken by two swans swimming leisurely around. As the sun cast its final golden rays on the scene before it disappeared behind the mountains, the sky slowly turned a deeper blue. 'It's stunning here, I have to say.'

Carlo pulled out a chair for her. 'Sit here, beside me, so you can show me the Instagram post and we can check the comments and likes.'

'Thank you.' Leanne sank down on the chair, wondering how she would manage to eat. Butterflies churned in her stomach as he sat beside her, lightly brushing her thigh with his leg.

He touched the sleeve of her white top. 'I see you're wearing part of the collection. Looks nice on you.'

'Yes,' Claudia agreed from her place across the table. 'That top is wonderful on you. Looks soft and comfortable too. I would never pick something like that, it's so daring, but on you it works.'

'Thank you,' Leanne replied. 'And I'm sorry that you had to go back and change. That Vera Wang black shift with the pearls was lovely. But not right for this place, I suppose.'

'Not really, no.' Claudia adjusted her sleeveless cream silk blouse and smoothed her hair. 'But you have to go with the flow, as the saying goes.'

Claudia looked relaxed and happy, Leanne reflected, all the tension gone from her face. She didn't even complain when the home-grown wine arrived, served in two big flagons.

Maddy studied the menu. 'Looks like everything comes from either the sea or the garden behind the restaurant. How wonderful.'

'That's right,' the waiter replied, his pen and pad ready to take their orders. 'I can recommend the deep-fried calamari with aioli, or the grilled sardines for a starter. And maybe, if you don't want to eat more fish, there's pork with crispy crackling.'

'I'll have the calamari followed by the seafood pasta.' Leanne looked up at the waiter. 'Is there garlic in that?'

'Oh, yes. The pasta comes with a lovely garlic sauce.'

'Oh.' Leanne glanced at Carlo sheepishly.

'I'll have that, too,' he announced. 'Then we'll both smell just as bad as each other,' he whispered in Leanne's ear while the others ordered.

The waiter poured them all some white wine and then went to place the orders. Claudia took a careful sip, and then another, smiling happily. 'Not bad really, this wine,' she announced.

'Delicious,' Maddy agreed when she had tasted it. 'What do you think, Leanne?'

She smiled and lifted her glass to her nose. 'Pears,' she said and sniffed again. 'And a touch of lemon with a hint of—' she winked at Tony '— snips, snails and puppy dogs' tails.'

Tony smiled back. 'No sugar and spice?'

'Not tonight,' she laughed and knocked back the wine in one go.

'Be careful, though,' Tony warned. 'It's very strong, like all wines in this area.'

Leanne coughed. 'I can take it, don't worry.'

'It says fourteen per cent on the bottle,' Maddy remarked.

Claudia shrugged. 'So what? I'm not planning to drive or operate machinery. Remember, I'm Italian. We can hold our wine better than anyone.'

'She's already tipsy,' Maddy whispered in Leanne's ear. 'She downed two glasses as if it was water.'

'The food will help,' Leanne mumbled back. 'But what does it matter if she gets drunk? She's having a good time.'

Maddy laughed and grabbed her wine. 'So am I. Cheers, pet. Great choice of restaurant.'

'Accidentally, yes,' Leanne laughed. 'Cheers, Mads.' She sighed as the starter arrived, crisp golden rings of calamari on a bed of fresh lettuce topped with creamy aioli. 'This smells divine. What did you order?'

'Grilled sardines, followed by seafood risotto.' Maddy licked her lips as her starter was served. 'Smells fantastic. I didn't think I'd be able to eat anything after our ice cream pig-out, but here I am, starving.'

'I know.' Leanne dug into her starter. 'Me too. I'm so glad Nico offered to stay in the boat to mind Bridget. Not that I'm worried,' she added, 'but you never know.'

'I think we can forget that weirdo,' Maddy said. 'It was probably just a fit of madness. Or he was just playing a prank on us. For fun.'

'Something like that,' Leanne said, deciding to let her suspicions go. Maddy was probably right. 'Already forgotten,' she said, her mouth full of calamari.

The food was delicious, even to foodie snobs like Claudia and Lucilla, who both had something called *brudet*, a local fish stew, for their main course, which they declared was excellent. Leanne closed her eyes and groaned as she tasted the seafood pasta, filled with juicy prawns, sweet clams and mussels, with a buttery, flavourful sauce, silky and smooth in her mouth.

'Good, no?' Carlo said beside her.

'Heaven on a stick,' Leanne sighed. 'I'll stink of garlic for days but I don't care.'

'We all will,' Tony said. 'Everything is laced with garlic here.'

'And it's delicious,' Maddy declared. 'Don't know when I've ever eaten better food.'

'Yeah, but…' Tony started. 'You'd miss the auld spud, though.'

Leanne burst out laughing. 'Ye're a bit of a lad, aren't you?'

'More than a bit,' Tony replied. 'But I won't deny that garlic is very good for you.'

'And so is wine,' Claudia said, into her fifth glass. 'Cheers, everyone!'

'Cheers!' they all shouted and raised their glasses, clinking them in celebration.

The sky darkened as they ate and a huge full moon rose over the harbour, its reflection shimmering in the dark water. Maddy looked at the sky and declared she wanted to go for a stroll in the moonlight after dinner. Everyone agreed it would be the perfect end to the evening.

'Look,' Claudia exclaimed, scanning the dessert menu. 'Croatian coffee with brandy from here. Like Irish coffee but…'

'Sounds dangerous,' Lucilla remarked. 'But why not? A little nightcap with coffee to sober us up.'

'More likely to make us even drunker,' Tony said. 'But hey, what the hell. Might as well be hanged for a sheep as a lamb, as we say in good auld County Cork.'

Maddy laughed. 'Geez, you're more oirish than the oirish themselves.'

'Spend a little time in west Cork and it rubs off on you in no time,' Tony replied with a wink. 'Makes a man out of you, even if you're a woman.'

Maddy laughed. 'Must go there and see if it works.'

They ordered Croatian coffee for everyone and it proved to be very good, even if it didn't quite taste like the Irish variety.

Having finished their drinks, Carlo touched Leanne's arm. 'When can we get away?' he mumbled in her ear.

Leanne looked around the table. Maddy was talking to Claudia, and Tony and Lucilla seemed to be having a heated discussion in Italian. Everyone had laid into the wine big time and had finished their Croatian coffees, looking more than relaxed.

'They're all a little sloshed,' Leanne whispered. 'Don't think they'll notice if we slip away.'

She was right. None of them glanced in their direction as, in the cover of the dim light, Carlo and Leanne sneakily made their way around the tables. Leanne quickly paid the bill and followed Carlo out onto the cobblestones of the street.

He turned to Leanne when they were out of sight of the restaurant. 'We got away,' he whispered, pulling her close and kissing her hard on the lips. 'I have waited for this all evening,' he breathed against her cheek.

Leanne wrapped her arms around his neck. 'Me too.' His touch, his lips, the heat of his body and the scent of aftershave mingled with a whiff of garlic, made her giddy with lust. 'Where can we go?'

He kissed her again, his tongue doing things to the inside of her mouth that almost made her knees buckle. She pulled away. 'Stop it, or you'll have to carry me.'

He laughed and touched her cheek. 'You're as hot as I am. Come on, *cara*, I'll take you to the perfect place.'

'Where?' Leanne asked, breathless, pulling at him. 'Take me there.'

Carlo took her hand and broke into a run. 'It's across the bridge and around the headland. A small boating club with a clubhouse.'

Leanne stopped. 'Too far. What about the boat?'

'Nico's there with your dog.'

'No. I meant the sailing boat. They'll be nobody there for hours. They're all going for a walk through town in the moonlight.'

'Okay. A little risky, but I don't think we'll be long.'

'The risk is part of the excitement,' Leanne whispered, light-headed with anticipation. She felt like a teenager.

'Why are we waiting?' He pulled her along the quay until they reached the sailing boat, moored a short distance away from the yacht.

Carlo pulled the boat in and, with their shoes off, they jumped on board and scrambled across the deck down to the saloon, tearing off their clothes and throwing them aside as they went. By the time they reached the saloon, Carlo was naked and Leanne left standing in her tiny knickers.

'Where's your cabin?' Leanne asked, looking wildly around.

'I'll show you later.' Carlo pulled her close as they sank down onto the couch, the moonlight streaming in through the portholes.

Leanne's skin was on fire as he touched her. A wave of joy coursed through her. This was it. She was finally doing what she had longed for ever since she first saw him – their chemistry undeniable from the off. She matched his caresses with some of her own that made him groan with pleasure and she arched her hips, ready for him. 'I can't wait,' she whispered.

He lay down on top of her, ready to finish what they'd started. 'You're amazing,' he breathed into her ear.

'So are you. Oh, Carlo, I think I'm falling in love with you,' she whispered, overcome by emotion.

He suddenly froze.

'I can't wait any longer.' She closed her eyes and waited for him to respond.

But he suddenly pulled away and collapsed in a heap on top of her, his body slick with sweat.

'What's the matter?' she asked, confused.

'I'm sorry,' he mumbled into her chest. 'It's not working. Too much wine.'

'What? But we're just going to…' Leanne looked at him, shocked. He couldn't do it after a few glasses of wine? She sat up and stared at him. This was not what she had expected. He strutted around like some sex god and now this?

He grunted something into the cushions.

Leanne realised he was very upset and felt a surge of pity. She stroked his hair. 'It's all right. Perfectly understandable.'

'Sorry if you're disappointed.'

'Not at all. Happens after a lot of booze,' she soothed. 'Not your fault.'

'No, it was both of us.' He rolled onto his back, looking at the ceiling.

'What?' Leanne stared at him. 'Both of us? What did I do to put you off?'

'You were, you were too… demanding.'

Leanne glared at him. 'What do you mean? Too demanding? Cast your mind back to a few minutes ago. We were both so into it we couldn't wait. I wanted you, you wanted me, and then…'

'Please,' he mumbled. 'Don't rub it in. You expected too much. That put me off.'

'Put you off?' Leanne scrambled off the couch and groped around for her clothes. 'Gee, I'm sorry. I didn't expect that much, really. I thought… maybe we'd make love and then we'd…' Her voice trailed off. It started to dawn on her what had happened. He had wanted a quickie, and she had expected romance. She had mentioned the word 'love' and that had scared him. That was the true reason he hadn't been able to finish what they'd started. So he was right, she thought bitterly. It had been her fault. Why oh why had she let herself fall this hard for a man again? Why hadn't she listened to the warnings of her mother?

'You won't tell anyone about this?' he mumbled.

'Why would I? I'm going now,' she said, when she had pulled her shorts and top back on, shame coursing through her. 'Can't find my knickers, but you're probably lying on them.'

He didn't reply. She stood there for a while wondering what to say, but then she heard it. Loud snoring. He had fallen asleep. That's how much he cared. Her legs like jelly, Leanne climbed the steps onto the deck, found her shoes and jumped ashore. Not wanting to return to the motorboat, she sat on the edge of the quay, her feet dangling over the still water, staring at the dark sky studded with glimmering stars. *It was the wine,* she thought. *I shouldn't have agreed to have sex just like that. And I shouldn't have said anything about falling in love. That was so stupid.* Next time they'd skip the booze.

If there was a next time.

The walk through town in the moonlight was enchanting, Maddy thought as they walked up the narrow streets, where they could see lights in some of the houses, and people sitting outside drinking wine. They crossed the bridge to the other side and paused for a moment to admire the view to the sea and the moon hanging above the islands. The water lay like a sheet of glass reflecting the heavens above them. Maddy looked up at a myriad of stars and sighed happily. 'How beautiful,' she said to Tony, who was standing beside her.

'Lovely.' He leant on the parapet and looked into the dark water. 'The air is so still, not a breath of wind.'

'I hope it'll start blowing tomorrow. I know how much you love sailing.'

'Yes. It's my favourite thing.'

Maddy looked down the bridge. 'Where are Lucilla and Claudia?'

'They said they'd head back to the boat.'

She nodded. 'Good idea. It's late and that wine was strong. We should go back too.'

They started to walk back. 'I hope Leanne and—' He stopped.

'What? That Carlo and Leanne are all right?' Maddy laughed. 'I'm sure they're absolutely fine. It's such a romantic evening.'

'So it is,' he said flatly, walking a little faster.

Maddy fell into step with him. 'Are you worried about something?'

'Not really. They're grown-ups.'

'So they are.' Maddy looked at him but it was too dark to make out his expression. What was that all about? Was he worried about Leanne? Or did he have feelings for her? *Oh come on*, she told herself. *Don't turn this into a love triangle drama.* Tony was far too sensible to let Leanne break his heart.

But she knew from experience that love had absolutely nothing to do with good sense.

Chapter Nineteen

The Instagram photo had the desired effect. Leanne had nearly a thousand more followers the next day and hundreds of likes and comments, all positive, most of them asking about the clothes.

'This is excellent,' Lucilla said as she checked it all on her phone at breakfast on the rear deck. 'And we've had an offer of a feature from two major newspapers. Carlo will be pleased. And so will our client.'

'Where is Carlo?' Maddy asked. 'I thought he'd call in before they set off.'

'They left very early,' Claudia said. 'The wind was up and they didn't want to miss out on it.'

Lucilla nodded. 'Okay. We'll see them at lunch when we anchor outside Zlatni Rat.'

'What's that?' Leanne asked, idly stirring her coffee, her mind on the night before.

'It a very famous beach on the island of Brač,' Nico replied from the saloon, where he was mapping out the day's journey on the charts.

'That's right,' Maddy said. 'I looked it up in the guidebook. Great place for a long swim.'

'Good,' Leanne said, not really listening. She was relieved Carlo had not appeared this morning and wondered how she should handle the situation with him. The thought of facing him made her sick with nerves.

'You okay?' Maddy asked, studying her. 'You look pale.'

Leanne forced a smile. 'Too much wine, I think. And very little sleep.'

'Yes, that wine was a little strong,' Claudia remarked, pouring herself coffee from the pot. 'I have a bit of a headache myself.' She glanced at Leanne. 'But you were already in bed when we came back. I thought you were asleep.'

'Not really,' Leanne murmured into her coffee. 'I heard you come back. I was awake quite a long time after that – thinking.'

Lucilla shot her a probing look. 'Too much thinking, perhaps?'

Leanne shrugged. 'Yeah. Maybe.' She got up. 'I'm going to do a little work on the blog. Give me a shout when we arrive at – whatever that beach is called.'

'Zlatni Rat,' Nico repeated. 'Then we'll head off towards Korcula, with a stop for the night on the way.'

'Fabulous,' Leanne said, feeling anything but, and went into her cabin, banging the door shut. She sank down on her bed and buried her face in her hands. She needed to cry, but the tears would not come. Instead, she kept playing what had happened the night before over and over again, chiding herself for having got it so wrong. 'Stupid, stupid, stupid,' she railed and lay face down on the bed. Then the tears started to fall and she cried silently into the pillow until she was too tired to do anything except lie there, exhausted.

There was a knock on the door. Before she had a chance to answer, Maddy slid inside, closing the door silently behind her. Leanne was about to tell her to leave, but Maddy held up a hand.

'I'm not going until I see you're all right.'

'I'm fine.' Leanne turned onto her back and stared out the porthole. She could hear the engine and feel the boat moving out of the harbour. 'We're on our way,' she mumbled.

Maddy sat down on the bed. 'Yes. We'll be at that beach by lunchtime.' She touched Leanne's shoulder. 'Was Carlo horrible to you last night?'

Leanne cringed just thinking about it. 'No. It was me. I made a huge mistake.'

'Oh. You mean…' She paused. 'Do you want to tell me about it? Maybe I can help?'

'Help with what?' Leanne demanded. 'You can't turn the clock back and undo my stupidity.' She flung an arm across her eyes. 'You see, it was all so romantic last night. The wine, moonlight, the harbour, him kissing me like I was the most gorgeous woman on earth. Jesus, that guy can kiss.'

'Why am I not surprised?' Maddy said, with a glimmer of a smile. 'I'm sure he's good at everything else too.'

'Oh, yes, that's what I thought.' Leanne sat up and stared at Maddy. 'We were so hot for each other, he made me feel like I was on fire. We ran to the sailing boat and tore all our clothes off. We were on the couch in the saloon because we just couldn't wait. He was so amazing, so *sexy*. We were about to – you know. But then…' She stopped.

'Then what?'

'I had to go and say something that totally put him off.'

'Like what? Like… you know, it wasn't big enough?'

'Jesus, no. Why would I say something like that? It was much worse.'

Maddy looked confused. 'What on earth was it? Come on, spit it out. You'll feel better when you've told me.'

Leanne pressed her face against Maddy's shoulder. 'I said I was falling in love with him,' she whispered.

'I see. Well, maybe that was a mistake...'

'The biggest ever,' Leanne sobbed. 'And I said those stupid words just as we were about to – you know. And that made him freeze and then he just collapsed saying he couldn't do it. And then he fell asleep and started snoring. Great end to a romance, don't you think?'

Maddy made a strange sound. 'Oh. Okay. I see.'

Leanne stared wildly at Maddy. 'See what?'

'You scared him. I'd say all he wanted was your body, but then you held out your heart to him. To a man like that, it would have been frightening.'

'A man like what?' Leanne looked suspiciously at Maddy. 'Do you know something about Carlo I don't?'

'No. I don't. But I know the type. Good-looking and confident on the surface, scared shitless of commitment inside. Sex is fine but don't ask him for anything more. Shallow as anything.'

Leanne nodded. 'Yeah, that was my thought too. I tried to make him feel better by saying it was okay and that it happens after a lot of booze. Not that I meant it, but I thought it'd help. Then he said it was my fault because I expected too much from him. I mentioned love and he just crumbled.'

Maddy smoothed Leanne's hair from her face. 'Saying he was falling in love, or giving you more than just sex was what he must have meant by "too much".'

'Yeah, I suppose that's it,' Leanne said miserably.

Maddy took a deep breath. 'You know what? In a way that makes him a better man. I mean, how many times have men said "I'm in love with you" and not meant it, just to get what they want? To Carlo, it would have been a lie and it sounds like he couldn't say it and not mean it.'

'Full marks to him, then. Nul points to me.' Leanne collapsed against the pillows. 'I shouldn't have opened my stupid mouth. But at that moment I felt so full of love for him I thought I was going to burst. What was that, then?'

'Infatuation.'

Leanne thought for a moment, reality sinking in. 'Yes. That's probably what it was. Real love doesn't happen so soon, does it? What did I think this was, the movies?'

'How do you feel about him now?'

'I don't know. The way he behaved afterwards wasn't very nice. Not coping with what I said made him look like a bit of a wimp, to be honest. But I'm supposed to work with him and do a few more shoots. I can't even bear to face him right now.'

'Just pretend nothing happened,' Maddy suggested. 'If anyone can style it out, you can.'

'But I can't.' Leanne's eyes filled with tears again. 'I got carried away and came on to him last night, Maddy. I can't get that out of my head. The shame of it.'

Maddy took Leanne's hand and looked into her eyes, willing her to listen. 'Don't feel ashamed. Who hasn't had too much to drink and fallen into bed with some sexy guy? Don't you think a lot of women – and men – wake up after a night out and wonder what they were thinking? Wine and the moonlight and a guy like Carlo kissing you… how could you resist?'

'Well…' Leanne started. 'That makes it sound a lot better.' She looked at her hands, then at Maddy. 'You're not going to tell Dad about this, are you?'

'Of course not,' Maddy exclaimed. 'It's your private business. All of this stays between you and me, I swear.'

Leanne nodded. 'Okay. It's just that it hits me sometimes that you're my best friend and you're dating my dad. It feels very strange.'

'It feels strange to me too,' Maddy confessed. 'But I would never discuss the things you tell me in private with Erik. That's up to you.'

'God, no!' Leanne exclaimed, jumping up from the bed. 'I'll never tell him or anyone else. I couldn't bear it.'

'Good. Then try to get over it and act like you don't care. Can you do that?'

'I'll try.'

'Good. It'll be okay. I'd say he'll be perfectly polite and then he'll say something to you in private and you can both move on. Carlo is a nice guy behind it all, Leanne. He's probably as confused as you are right now.'

'I bet he's wondering how he's going to get me to back off. And he had the nerve to ask me not to tell anyone.'

'And then you told me.'

'You're not just anyone though. You're Maddy.'

Maddy's eyes softened. She got up and put her arms around Leanne and hugged her tight. 'Don't be sad. You're my best friend too and I love you.'

Leanne hugged her back, feeling better with her friend's arms around her. 'Love you too, Mads,' she said into Maddy's shoulder.

'Your dad loves you very much too. And Bridget.'

'Bridget? Where is she?'

'Lucilla took her for a walk before we left. I think she's asleep in one of the chairs on the rear deck.'

'Oh. Good.' Exhausted after all the emotion, Leanne pulled out of Maddy's arms and lay down again. 'Thank you for the TLC. I feel better now.'

'Good.' Maddy patted Leanne's leg. 'You have a snooze and I'll wake you up in an hour.'

Leanne smiled weakly. 'Okay. Go and finish your breakfast with Lucilla and Claudia – sorry to tear you away. I really like both of them, you know. They're great fun.'

'And Lucilla likes you too, even though I know you were worried, and Claudia thinks you're fabulous. Tony's very fond of you too.'

'Tony's great,' Leanne mumbled, her eyes heavy. 'He's like a big rock you can lean on.' Her eyes closed and she fell asleep before Maddy had closed the door.

Maddy returned to her breakfast, deep in thought. What a mess Leanne had got herself into. But maybe the turn of events was a good thing? Her blurting out that she was falling in love with Carlo, in the heat of the moment, had frightened him away, but his reaction might also have shown that he wasn't right for Leanne. That all he was after was sex and nothing more, and Leanne deserved better than that. But would it turn her off him, or make her even more determined to get him?

Maddy sighed and took a big bite of the flaky croissant Claudia had bought at the bakery this morning. It was still warm and deliciously buttery. Why was life so complicated? Why couldn't they have a normal holiday without all this tension? The situation with Leanne was not the only trouble brewing under the glitzy surface. There was also Lucilla hovering in the background, her eyes on Carlo. Then Claudia, who seemed on edge most of the time, constantly checking her emails and watching everyone around her when they were in public places. And Tony, who looked like he'd been in some kind of hell. Carlo was the only one who didn't seem too concerned about anything, except now he probably was. And Maddy herself, with her soon-to-be ex-husband and looming divorce, and this budding romance with a handsome Norwegian, who just happened to be Leanne's dad. So much drama. You couldn't make it up.

Maddy gazed out over the blue water and the white sails on the horizon, the islands dotted in the distance and motorboats going to and fro. It was a lovely, breezy day with just a few clouds, birds soaring in the air, and she enjoyed the cool wind on her face and the cries of the seagulls. They were keeping a fast pace, passing smaller crafts on the way. Maddy waved at a group of people in a speedboat and they waved back, revving their engine to whizz past them.

'Lovely day,' Claudia said, sitting down beside her.

'It's a grand day, all right,' Maddy agreed. 'So fresh here out at sea.'

'We should really clean up after breakfast, but I think we'll wait until we stop or we'll break everything,' Claudia said with a laugh.

'You're right,' Maddy said. 'And the coffee's still warm if you want another cup. But I ate the last croissant. Sorry.'

'I'm glad you did.' Claudia poured herself some coffee. 'I shouldn't really eat all that gluten. But the food here is too good to be true. I'll have to go on a diet when I get back home.'

'Where's home?' Maddy asked. 'New York?'

Claudia made a face. 'No. I left New York for good. I'm moving back to Florence. My family owns the palazzo with Lucilla's family. We all have apartments there. Mine's in need of extensive repairs but I can stay with Lucilla until it's ready.'

'Must be expensive. The repairs, I mean.'

'Oh, yes. I'm going to make it ultra-modern and rip out the old kitchen and bathrooms. I want to be comfortable and I don't intend to move ever again.' She sipped her coffee, watching the boats speeding ahead of them. 'Everyone's in such a hurry. What's the point?'

'Maybe they're hooked on speed?' Maddy said with a laugh. 'You must be happy to move back home?'

'Happy and sad,' Claudia said. 'And very stressed, to be honest. My husband's being difficult.'

'I thought the divorce was all done?'

Claudia looked into her cup. 'No, not quite. We're separated and I have a lawyer, but he's dragging his heels. We signed a prenup before we got married, but he's so clever, I wouldn't be surprised if he managed to figure out a way to get his hands on my assets. So in the meantime, I'm making sure it's all secured. I'm selling the Park Avenue condo and moving everything to Florence. The properties here are owned by my family, so that's safe, and I'm pouring money into the repairs, so that's not something he can claim. Except if he comes and rips out the bathrooms, of course,' she added with a wry smile. 'But he'd be too lazy.'

'What was the problem between you?' Maddy asked without thinking. She put her hand to her mouth. 'Sorry, that just came out. Didn't mean to be nosey.'

'It's okay,' Claudia said and smiled. 'In America everyone spills their heart and soul out all the time. I've learned to talk about personal things, and in a way, it helps. To put it in a nutshell, I married a man with irresistible charm who turned out to be a bad sort. He was controlling and possessive and it took me quite a while to realise what was going on. But one day I suddenly woke up and then I packed my bags and ran out.'

'But isn't he staying in the apartment?'

'No. He didn't want to live on Park Avenue. He already had an apartment in the West Village, so we lived there during our marriage. I let the condo to a French diplomat, and when he was posted back to Europe, I decided to sell it. Thank God I kept it in my own name, otherwise he would have been able to claim half the money I'll get for it.' Claudia sighed and looked out over the sea. 'Enough of that. I don't have very pleasant memories of my marriage.'

'Of course you don't,' Maddy soothed, shocked by Claudia's revelations.

Maddy picked up a pair of binoculars from the side table and started to watch the marine life and the boats. 'These are great binoculars,' she said, scanning the shoreline of the nearest island. 'I can see every detail.' She moved her gaze over the water and saw something move. 'Oh my God, a dolphin!' she exclaimed, fascinated. 'It's following that little boat just behind us.'

'How lovely,' Claudia squealed. 'Can I see?'

Maddy handed her the binoculars. 'It's there, just beside that small white motorboat with the red stripe across the stern. Keep the binoculars trained on the hull and you'll see the dolphin jump.'

'Oh, yes!' Claudia shrieked. 'It's jumping as if it's playing with the boat. I hope the person driving is careful.'

'I'm sure he is.' Maddy saw the driver, a man in a blue baseball cap, looking down into the water. But… She stared at him. He looked familiar, even from this distance. And the boat… It suddenly struck her. It looked like the same boat as the one they had seen speeding away from the harbour in Jelsa. And that man looked exactly like the person who had tried to steal Bridget. Even from far away, his strong features were recognisable. Had Claudia seen him? She turned as Claudia gulped and dropped the binoculars.

'It's him,' she croaked, pointing a finger at the boat. 'My husband.'

Chapter Twenty

Maddy stared at Claudia. 'Are you sure?'

'Oh yes, I'm certain,' Claudia said in a shaky voice. 'He's following me.' Her face was pale and her chin wobbled. 'I knew he'd find me somehow, the bastard.'

'But how did he know where you were?'

'He could have hacked into my email. He's done it before.' Claudia sat rigid in the chair. 'He even hacked into my bank account once and siphoned off a huge amount of money to feed his gambling addiction. I didn't notice it until they called me from the bank.' She shuddered. 'That's part of the reason I left him. And now he's after me to get me back. Or to get money from me.'

Maddy's heart broke for Claudia. 'That's terrible. What are you going to do?' She looked at the boat again. It was still the same distance away. She picked up the binoculars and inspected him more closely. 'He has a beard, but I recognise him from photos I've seen in the media. No mistaking that broken nose and square jaw.'

'He couldn't disguise those away.' Claudia got up and went into the saloon. 'Can we go faster, Nico?' she called to the bridge. 'We think someone's following us.'

'Of course,' Nico shouted back. 'We're going quite fast already, but do you want to speed it up even more?'

'Yes please,' Claudia shouted. 'We want to get away from that motorboat behind us. The one with the red stripe across the side.'

'Who's following you?' Nico asked.

'My husband,' Claudia replied. 'It's a long story. Can we go at top speed?'

'No problem,' Nico replied, pushing the accelerator.

They could hear the engines roar and the boat surged forward, throwing up sprays of water in their wake. It didn't take long to lose the little motorboat. They turned sharply around the next island, in through a narrow sound, and then a slight gap between two rocks, the sides of the yacht barely scraping past. Another sharp turn and they were in a small bay, where Nico expertly steered the yacht to an outcrop, behind which they were hidden from view. He killed the engine and they stopped, rocking gently on the waves.

In the ensuing silence, only broken by the cry from a lone seagull and the loud chirping of the cicadas from the nearby shore, Maddy and Claudia looked at each other and exhaled.

'Is this okay?' Nico shouted. 'Will I drop the anchor?'

'Yes please,' Maddy called back. 'This looks perfect, Nico. Thank you.'

Leanne peered out of her cabin. 'What's happening? Have we stopped?'

'Yes,' Maddy replied. 'Nice little bay. I think we can stay here for a while if you want a swim.'

The chain of the anchor rattled at the same time as the door to Lucilla's cabin burst open and she came charging out. 'What's going on?'

'We were being followed by a speedboat,' Claudia said. 'And we think it's my husband.'

'What?' Lucilla stared wildly at Claudia. 'Your husband? That's crazy. How could he find you?'

'I don't know,' Claudia replied, sinking down on a chair, her hands covering her face.

'Is this true?' Lucilla asked Maddy. 'Did you see this man?'

'Yes.' Maddy showed her the binoculars. 'We were looking at a dolphin and then we saw the boat that it was following and the person driving it. Definitely Oliver Wilde.'

'But how is that possible?' Lucilla looked at Claudia. 'I thought you had made sure you couldn't be found.'

'I did. I even changed my phone and number. I set up a new email address and told nobody where I was.'

Maddy looked at Claudia's troubled face and realised that this must be why she had been looking over her shoulder and hiding behind her sunglasses all the time.

'This is very strange,' Lucilla said, sitting down. She patted Claudia's shoulder. 'Don't worry. I'm sure we managed to lose him during this mad race. I practically fell off my bed!'

'I hope we lost him,' Claudia sighed.

Lucilla picked up her phone. 'But just to be sure, I'm going to call Carlo. This might be a problem that can be solved by *la famiglia*.'

'Whose family?' Maddy asked. 'Yours?'

'No, Carlo's,' Lucilla said. She paused while she punched in a number. 'He's from Naples. Huge family and they all help each other.'

'You mean like some kind of mafia?' Leanne asked, returning from her cabin wearing her bikini.

'No,' Lucilla said, laughing. 'Just a family network. Some of the cousins are on holiday in Dubrovnik.' She waited for a while and then hung up. 'No signal. Tony and Carlo must be on their way.'

Leanne looked over the railing. 'Very quiet here. Nobody around except seagulls. I'm going to jump in for a swim. Anyone want to join me?'

'In a minute,' Maddy replied. 'But you go ahead, I'll catch up with you.'

'Okay.' Leanne threw her leg across the railing and jumped into the crystal-clear water, swimming away to the shore just as the sailing boat glided around the outcrop and settled beside the motorboat with a splash of the anchor. Tony threw a fender over the side to stop the boats knocking against each other and waved.

'Hi there! Got Nico's message so we changed our course. Nice little bay. We're in time for lunch, I hope?'

'Lunch?' Claudia exclaimed. 'How can you think of lunch at a time like this?'

Tony looked surprised. 'A time like what?'

'Did you see a motorboat with a red stripe across the hull when you came through the sound?' Maddy asked.

'Yes, we did,' Tony replied. 'Going hell for leather towards Dubrovnik.'

Claudia let out a long sigh. 'Oh, that's good.'

'What's this all about?' Tony asked.

'Nothing. Just someone we wanted to lose,' Maddy said, seeing how uncomfortable Claudia looked. 'Lunch isn't ready yet, but we'll rustle something up.' She went into the galley. 'Hard boiled eggs, salad, cheese and bread okay?' she called out.

'Sounds good,' Tony replied. 'We'll bring beer. If there's any ham, I'd be more than happy. How about you, Carlo?'

Carlo didn't reply. Already in a pair of red Speedos, he dived from the deck of the sailing boat and followed Leanne with an easy crawl.

Maddy watched him swim away, praying that whatever happened next, it wouldn't be worse than last night.

Leanne lay on a rock on the shore of the little island, her eyes closed to the sun. The water had been cold and she was enjoying the sun warming her. The hot rock beneath her, the sound of the cicadas chirping and the waves lapping the shore were soothing her worries away. After her long siesta on the yacht, she felt rested and much calmer than before. Whatever happened, she'd cope with it, even if the thought of facing Carlo made her cringe with embarrassment.

She heard feet crunching the pebbles and opened her eyes. Carlo, dripping wet in a pair of tiny red Speedos, made his way to the rock. *God, what a beautiful body*, she thought, before the anger hit her.

'What are you doing here?' she snapped, her voice hoarse. So much for playing it cool.

'I want to talk to you.'

She closed her eyes again. 'I'm not ready to speak to you yet.'

'Then just listen.' Carlo sat down on the rock beside her, his leg barely touching hers.

'How can I avoid it?'

'Please. I need to explain. First of all, I want you to know two things. The first is how sorry I am about what happened. I shouldn't have flirted with you like that, and I shouldn't have tried to make love with you like that. It was all wrong.'

'Wrong?' Leanne sat up and glared at him, her hand shading her eyes against the sun. 'Yeah, it was,' she said bitterly. 'And I was wrong to believe you were falling for me the way I was for you. I didn't mean to say what I said, actually, only that I felt so—' She stopped and looked at his face. 'You have no right to be angry with me.'

'I'm not angry. I'm sad about what happened – or didn't. It was a mistake and I'm sorry. I thought you were... that we were just...' He stopped and rubbed his eyes. 'This is difficult.'

'What is? That you don't fancy me and that you were just looking for a quick screw?'

'No... yes, I mean...' He looked away. 'I do like you, Leanne. But there's something about me you need to know.'

Leanne gasped. She couldn't believe it. He couldn't be...? 'Are you trying to tell me you're... gay?'

Carlo snorted a laugh. 'No, of course not. But there's something else.' He looked at his hands. 'I can't get involved with anyone.'

'Why not?' Her heart was beating so fast she thought it was going to burst out of her chest.

'Because of Lucilla.'

Leanne sighed. 'Okay. I knew it. She owns you or something. Or you love her and she doesn't want you.'

'Stop making things up,' Carlo ordered. 'The thing is... Lucilla and I are engaged.'

Leanne gasped. 'To be married, you mean?'

Carlo got up. 'Yes. To be married. What other kind of engaged is there?'

'But you broke up,' Leanne said, confused. 'That's what you told me.'

'No, not really. We're taking a little break from each other. We're going to be married next year. But we have decided to split up for a while and see other people. She felt I needed to… get around. She knows I like to play the field. But that will end when we're married, so…'

Leanne suddenly understood what was going on. 'You needed to sow some wild oats before you go into that to-death-do-us-part life sentence, you mean?' she started. 'Lucilla wants you to fool around for a bit so that when you're finally Mr and Mrs, you won't stray again? Sleep with a few floozies and have a ball before the wedding bells ring? Am I right?' She got more and more worked up as she talked.

'Yes,' Carlo replied, looking shamefaced.

'And then when you met me, you thought I'd be one of those fun girls who sleeps around with no hard feelings afterwards?'

'Something like that,' Carlo said.

'Exactly like that, I bet.' Leanne hugged her knees to her chest. 'And then all was well until I had to go and say the magic words which scared you shitless. I see it all now.'

'You've explained it better than I could.'

'Yeah, but I have to say, it's weird. She lets you fool around, in fact she's there to see it happen, like last night. She must have known what we were up to.'

Carlo shrugged. 'I don't know.'

'And she loved the photos we took. She must have felt the vibes between us. But as it was good for business, so she didn't protest. Is that right?'

He shrugged again. 'She doesn't involve her feelings when she is working. Business is business for her. If the campaign is a success, we're made.'

'Of course.' With a feeling of distaste, Leanne climbed off the rock. This was too much. She didn't want to hear any more. 'Well, whatever,' she drawled. 'I'm going back to the boat.'

Carlo grabbed her arm. 'Don't go yet. I want you to hear the rest.'

'You mean there's more?' Leanne peeled his hand off her arm. 'I'd appreciate it if you didn't touch me.'

'Sorry.' Carlo sat down on the rock and folded his arms. 'But I want you to hear this. I come from a big, very poor family in Naples. Five brothers. Four sisters. I'm the youngest. I've worked hard all my life to help the family. I worked as a model in New York so I could send money to them and to my mother, who is old and unwell.'

'What about your dad?'

'He's dead.'

'Oh, God. I'm sorry. But go on.'

'Then I went to Nice and studied marketing. That's where I met Lucilla. We started dating, and then when the course was finished we began working for your father. After that, we set up our own business, hoping to make something of ourselves. During this time, we fell in love, but her family didn't approve. It wasn't until last year, when the business started doing well, that they've welcomed me into the family. They're noble and rich, you see, and I come from nowhere.'

She could see it all now. Lucilla, the classy aristocrat with connections and money, and Carlo, the handsome poor boy with a great head for business. Together they would be hard to beat. And they both knew it.

'I have worked so, so hard to be where I am today,' Carlo continued. 'I'm the head of my own company, and I'm engaged to marry this powerful woman with enormous standing in society. Together we will found a dynasty.'

'And she gives you a little time off beforehand to fool around,' Leanne remarked, a sharp edge to her voice. 'Seems a little heartless to me, but hey, I'm not a businesswoman.'

'No. I don't think you really understand the whole thing.'

'That's putting it mildly.' She looked at him, and all the anger and embarrassment faded away. She wasn't really in love with him, she realised. She was attracted to him, that was for sure. And she had wanted him to want her. Body and soul. But he was only after one thing and just for a night. A bit of fun before the real deal. She thought about Carlo and Lucilla – their relationship didn't sound like the kind of true love she dreamed of. 'Do you love Lucilla?' she had to ask. 'I mean really, really love her? Like you'd die for her?'

'Yes. She's perfect for me. Beautiful, smart, classy. And we have the same outlook on life. She can be a little cold and calculating at times. But that's her sharp mind. I wouldn't be where I am now if I hadn't met her.'

'I see.' This made her feel sad, not only for herself, but also for him. But she had to cut her losses and appear cool and in control. Leanne swallowed and held out her hand. 'Let's shake hands and agree to be friends. No more fooling around. We'll work as before but no more flirting, is that clear?'

Carlo took her hand and kissed it. 'Very clear.'

Leanne snatched her hand away. 'No kissing hands, either.'

'It's the Italian way.'

'I don't care.' Leanne started to wobble over the sharp rocks to the water. 'I'm going back. I think lunch would be good – I'm suddenly starving.' She stopped and thought for a moment, then she looked at Carlo. 'Take some advice from an auld woman like me. Stop all this "taking a break" crap. It'll only make you and everyone else miserable. You'll hurt a lot of people along the way, just like you've hurt me. Go back to Lucilla and say you've finished playing and now you want to be a grown-up.'

He nodded, looking contrite. 'You might be right.'

'You bet I am. See you around, pet.' Leanne turned, threw herself in the water and started to swim away, shedding the pain and embarrassment with every stroke. So Carlo and Lucilla were getting married? Good luck to them. She was better off out of it.

As she swam, she tried to put the whole sorry affair behind her. *Nobody died,* she thought. *I got carried away with the romance of it, thinking I could choose who to fall in love with. Carlo was there, right under my nose, so handsome, sexy and flirty. What an eejit I was to fall into that way of thinking.* She slowed down and switched to breast stroke, looking up at the blue sky, enjoying the feel of the cool water on her skin, telling herself it was going to be okay. It was a sin not to enjoy this dreamy part of the world, the yacht, the food, the wine and the fun. It was the trip of a lifetime, not to be spoiled by a silly infatuation for a man who didn't deserve it – no matter how gorgeous he was. *End of story*, she thought, mentally closing the door on the whole affair. Life was good. It was time to wake up and enjoy it.

She reached the boat and climbed the ladder to the rear deck, dripping with water. 'How about some lunch, then?' she said and shook her wet hands at Tony. 'How about a sandwich and a beer, and make it snappy! I'm ravenous.'

'And happy,' Tony remarked, smiling at her. 'You're suddenly sparkling.'

'I know.' Leanne grabbed a towel from the railing and wrapped herself in it. 'I seem to have gotten rid of something heavy back there.'

'Oh?' He looked intrigued. 'Sounds good.'

She nodded, pressing the towel to her face, taking a deep breath. 'More than good. A lesson learned and a new direction.' She turned and looked at the island and Carlo slowly swimming back. 'I was blinded by the stars for a moment. But now I can see everything clearly.'

Chapter Twenty-One

Leanne's good mood rubbed off on everyone else except Claudia, who had withdrawn into her cabin, not wanting lunch. When Maddy sat down, she looked at Leanne, who made a thumbs-up sign. Maddy smiled, looking relieved. When Carlo came on board, having changed into shorts and a polo shirt, Leanne was able to greet him with a casual 'hi' and continue eating as if nothing at all had happened, even though she was still a little shaken. Lucilla glanced at them both but then, sensing the lack of tension, shot Leanne a friendly smile. They all feasted on the salad of fresh tomatoes, crisp cucumbers, avocados and salty cheese, followed by fruit Lucilla had prepared from her finds at the little market in in Vrboska that morning.

'Wonderful fruit,' Maddy remarked, biting into a plump apricot. 'So fresh.'

'All from the local farms in the area,' Lucilla said. 'These islands have an ideal climate to grow fruit and vegetables and the quality is fantastic.'

'That wine last night was really good too,' Maddy said. 'Except you had to be careful or it would go straight to your head.'

'Not to mention that Croatian coffee,' Tony said. 'There was more brandy than coffee in it. I think we were all a little sloshed.'

'Please,' Leanne muttered into her salad, 'let's not go there.'

'No,' Lucilla said, with a glance in Carlo's direction. 'We have other problems today.'

'What problems?' Tony asked.

'Claudia's husband.'

'I thought he was an ex by now,' Carlo said.

'No. Still married, apparently.' Maddy popped a piece of the apricot into her mouth.

'So why is he a problem?' Leanne asked.

'He's following us,' Lucilla replied.

'What?' Leanne stared at her. 'So I was right then?'

'Yes,' Maddy said. 'That guy who tried to steal Bridget is Oliver Wilde.'

'I knew it!' Leanne exclaimed.

Tony swallowed his beer noisily. 'What? Oliver Wilde? He tried to steal your dog?'

'Yes,' Leanne replied. 'When we were in Jelsa at the ice cream place. He ran off with her when we weren't looking. But we managed to get her back. Didn't want to say anything in case it wasn't him and it upset Claudia.' She frowned. 'But why on earth did he do it? What was the idea?'

'How weird,' Tony said. 'And now he's following us? How do you know it's him?'

'We saw him,' Maddy replied. 'But then we lost him thanks to Nico. He knows these waters like the back of his hand.'

'Oh.' Tony looked thoughtful. 'Is that why Claudia's locked herself in her cabin?'

'I suppose so,' Maddy replied. 'She's very upset.'

Tony took another sip of his beer. 'So what do we do now?'

'I think we should stay here tonight,' Lucilla suggested. 'And then head for Dubrovnik tomorrow as planned. We had agreed to stay at this nice hotel for three days, but we might have to change our plans if we can't get rid of Oliver Wilde in the meantime.'

Leanne gasped. 'Get rid of him?' she whispered. She knew Lucilla was ruthless, but that was pushing it.

Lucilla laughed and shook her head. 'I didn't mean it the way it sounded. I meant we should see if we can get him to leave Claudia alone. She has filed for divorce and they've been separated for nearly six months. She has no idea why he's doing this.'

'Maybe it would be an idea to ask him what he wants,' Tony suggested.

'Claudia says he wants her money,' Maddy explained. 'But she has it all locked up in property and trusts funds for her son. And anyway, there's a prenup.'

'Why can't she just ask him what he's doing here?' Leanne wondered.

'Because he can't be trusted,' Maddy replied. 'She has changed her phone number and email address, and refuses to contact him. She's trying to get in touch with her lawyer in New York right now, but the signal's bad here.'

Tony got up. 'Maybe if someone else talked to him, he might be more truthful. I'll go and ask Claudia if she'll give me his contact details. Maybe I can help out.'

'She won't want that,' Lucilla argued.

'Do you have a better idea?' Tony asked coolly.

Lucilla shrugged. 'No.'

'Let me know if you get one.' Tony went into the saloon and knocked on Claudia's door. There was no reply, but after a few minutes, Claudia, her face white, opened the door and peered out. 'Yes?'

'It's only me,' Tony said. 'I had an idea that might help.'

Claudia sighed. 'What idea? Nothing will help. We have to call the FBI. Or Carlo's family network or something.'

'I don't think we have to go that far,' Tony said. He smiled and put his hand on Claudia's shoulder. 'You're stressed. Come out to the deck and have a glass of wine and we'll see if we can sort this out.'

'Okay, if you insist.' Claudia sighed again and shuffled through the saloon to the deck where she sank down on the chair Tony pulled out for her. Maddy got her a glass of white wine and Lucilla offered her a plate with salad, cheese and fresh bread.

With Tony's arm around her, Claudia sipped some wine and picked at the food, looking a little calmer. 'Thanks, Tony. You're so kind.'

'Feeling better?' he asked.

'A little.' She looked at him. 'So what was it you were saying?'

Tony quickly explained his plan. Claudia reluctantly agreed and gave Tony all the details he needed. After several attempts, Tony finally managed to send a text message to Oliver's phone. 'There,' he said. 'I sent it. The signal comes and goes, so it might be a while before he gets it.'

But it didn't take longer than five minutes before Tony's phone pinged. He opened the message, his eyes widening. 'Weird,' he muttered. 'Is this guy deranged?'

'What did he say?' Claudia demanded, her eyes like saucers.

Tony held out his phone to her. 'Read this.'

'"I am being followed by the IRA and need Claudia's help to get them off my back,"' Claudia read. 'The IRA? As in the Irish terrorist group? He's finally flipped.'

'What an earth?!' exclaimed Leanne.

Claudia nodded. 'Nothing about this man would surprise me,' she said, looking grim-faced.

'So,' Leanne said. 'We're hiding from the author of horror stories who's being pursued by the IRA. This trip gets weirder and weirder.'

'But why does he think Claudia can get the IRA off his back?' Maddy wondered.

Claudia shrugged. 'No idea. As I said, he's crazy.'

Tony typed on his phone. 'I'm asking him to explain.'

The reply came only a minute later. Tony read it and burst out laughing.

'What?' Claudia exclaimed. 'Just don't sit there laughing.'

'"Correction,"' Tony read out loud. '"I meant the IRS. This phone has a crazy keyboard."'

'He never knew how to type on a phone,' Claudia said with a derisory snort. 'So it was the IRS? Doesn't surprise me.'

'What's the IRS?' Leanne asked.

'The Internal Revenue Service. Otherwise known as the US tax office,' Tony replied. 'He must be in debt to them.'

'I bet he's been cheating on his tax returns,' Claudia said. 'And now they're after him. No wonder he's panicking. Those guys take no prisoners. He probably wants me to help him out.'

'Would you?' Maddy asked.

'You must be joking,' Claudia drawled. 'Tony, tell him to get lost. I'm not going to give him a cent of my money. If he's been cheating on his taxes, let him rot in jail.'

Tony picked up his phone. 'I'll just tell him you're sorry but can't help him right now.'

Claudia waved her hand. 'Okay, whatever.'

Tony sent the message, but it wouldn't go off. 'The signal's gone again,' he said, getting up. 'We just have to wait and see what he says. Maybe he'll give up. But there's a nice wind out there and I'd like to do a little sailing. Wilde is not after the sailing boat, so I think it'd be safe to go out for an hour or two. And he's left the area anyway. Who wants to come?'

Carlo shook his head. 'Not me. I'll stay here.' He exchanged a look with Lucilla. 'Maybe we could have a meeting about the business? I need to straighten a few things out with you.'

Lucilla nodded. 'Okay.'

'I'll come,' Leanne suddenly shouted, jumping up. 'I haven't sailed for ages but I'd love to have a go.'

Tony grinned and gave her a thumbs-up. 'Brilliant. Anyone else? There's a strong north easterly, so it should be quite fun.'

'Count me out,' Maddy said, yawning. 'I don't want to get seasick. I'm taking my siesta and then I'll take Bridget in the dinghy to the shore for a walk.'

'How about you, Claudia?' Tony asked. 'It might be good for you get your mind off things by coming with us.'

'No thanks. I'm a bad sailor.' Claudia rose and started to gather plates and glasses. 'I'll get Nico some lunch and make some coffee.'

'It's just you and me, then,' Tony said to Leanne. 'I'll go and get her ready. Bring a jacket or a shirt. It can get a little chilly with the strong wind.'

'Aye, aye, captain.' Leanne saluted, happy to get away from everyone for a while. The winds, the sea and the sailing would blow away the lingering sadness. And this time she had a feeling she'd be with a kindred spirit.

Chapter Twenty-Two

They left the little bay with slack winds but as soon as they rounded the island, the strong north eastern caught the sails. The boat leaned over so much they had to sit on the hull to stop the water gushing into the cockpit. Tony steered the boat into the wind and told Leanne to reduce the mainsail.

'Here,' he shouted, handing her a life vest. 'Put this on first.'

'Okay,' Leanne called back, shrugging on the vest. She found the winch for winding the line and quickly reduced the mainsail, which had the desired effect. The boat straightened up somewhat and she jumped into the cockpit to help out with the jib, the small front sail, when they tacked.

'Great to be in such a modern boat,' she said to Tony. 'The sail is tucked into the boom when it comes down and the winches are automatic, so you don't tear the skin off your hands.'

Tony, his hands on the wheel, took his eyes off the course and smiled at her. 'Yes, that takes the pain out of it. It's a great boat to sail in strong winds. Carlo loves it too. We've had a lot of fun sailing in these waters.'

'I can imagine.' Leanne scanned the waves and saw other boats in the distance, all leaning over, some of them with crews sitting on the side as counterweights. 'I love this,' she exclaimed, overcome with the exhilaration of the wind and the waves slapping the hull, the salty tang of the sea and the excitement of battling the elements. 'Haven't done it since I was a kid. My dad used to take me to Kerry where we hired a boat. He taught me to sail.' She looked at Tony standing by the wheel, solid and strong, and felt happy to be in his calm, comforting presence. She felt like nothing bad could happen when she was with him. He had a quiet maturity that soothed her. 'I'd forgotten how wonderful it is,' she said.

Tony smiled. 'I can see you know your way around a boat. Hey, you want to have a go at steering?'

'I'd love to.' Leanne jumped up and joined him. Tony stepped aside and she put her hands on the wheel, trying her best to hold the same course.

'Aim for the little island over there and hold that course,' Tony said and went behind her, putting his arms around her for a moment, steadying the boat. 'Okay. I think you've got it.'

'Yup,' Leanne said as he stepped away, wishing he'd stay with his arms around her for a bit longer. It felt so comforting, reminding her of when her dad had taught her and held her the same way. But Tony wasn't her father, she realised, and when their eyes met she felt a sudden spark of something. He was a good-looking man, with strong, clean-cut features, only he wasn't quite her type. But what was her type? she wondered as Tony came back to take the wheel and they touched again, setting off another little spark. With Carlo, she had felt something different, something intimate and exciting – and she had been proved totally wrong. With Tony, she felt calm and protected. And safe. Was that so bad?

The wind dropped as they came closer to the big island across the straights. Tony told Leanne to let out the sail and the speed increased, the boat leaning a little more, but without the dramatic surge they had experienced earlier. Tony relaxed and they chatted idly while they looked at the shore of the island as they approached. It looked inviting with waves lapping onto a curve of golden sand and tall pine trees that cast deep shadows on the far end of the beach.

'We'll have to tack here,' Tony called. 'Ready with the jib?'

'Yes,' Leanne replied, her hand on the winch.

'Watch out for the boom,' he shouted as the boat turned and they both ducked to avoid being hit. The boom swung across to the other side and the boat took off again, faster and faster as they left the shelter of the island.

'You want me to reduce the sail again?' Leanne asked.

'No. It's okay. We'll be going back soon, and then we'll have the wind behind us. We could put up the spinnaker then and we'll be back a lot quicker.'

'I don't want to go back,' Leanne blurted out, unable to hold it in. 'I want to sail with you like this forever.'

'Oh?' He looked at her, surprised. 'Whatever made you say that?'

'I don't know,' Leanne replied, feeling sheepish. 'It's just the way I feel right now.'

He looked out at sea again. 'Because of whatever happened between you and Carlo?'

'No. Yes. I don't know.' Confusion overcome her. The memory of the night before made tears well up in her eyes and Leanne blinked furiously to stop them spilling down her cheeks. 'Forget it.'

'If you don't want to talk about it, I understand. He didn't say anything to me, in case you were wondering.'

'Nice of Carlo not to mention it,' Leanne said, a bitter edge to her voice. 'But if anyone knew, it wouldn't be good for his image.'

'Or yours?'

'My image?' Leanne shrugged. 'I don't have one. Didn't you know? I'm the tart of the century. I do anything for—'

'Money?'

'No. Love. A much harder currency.'

Tony didn't reply for a moment, while he busied himself with steering the boat and watching the sails. 'I see. No need to tell me more if you don't want to.'

'Nothing happened, you know. Not that I didn't want it to, of course. So it was just a technicality really. But it's okay. I've moved on.'

He nodded. 'I know what you mean. A moment's madness brought on by wine and the full moon and a handsome Italian man paying you attention.'

'Not hard to figure me out, is it?'

His hazel eyes softened behind the glasses. 'That's not the way I see it. Don't be so hard on yourself, Leanne. You're worth more than Carlo. A lot more.'

Startled by the sudden passion in his voice, Leanne stared at him. 'Oh,' was all she managed. 'Thank you.'

'For what?'

'For making me feel better about myself.'

With his eyes once again on the course, Tony nodded. 'You have to learn to like yourself before you can truly love someone. A very wise woman said that to me before I left Africa. And it took me a while to realise that it's true.'

'You didn't like yourself?' Leanne asked.

'Not much, no.'

'Because you blamed yourself for making mistakes? And for leaving when you were still needed?'

'Something like that. I still haven't totally cracked it but I'm beginning to heal. This trip has been very good for me. And meeting you.'

'Me? I haven't done much.'

'You've listened without judging. That helped me a lot.' Tony looked up at the sail. 'The wind is changing a bit. But we have to get back, I'm afraid, my sweet friend. So we'll turn and sail slowly without a spinnaker. How's that?'

'Perfect,' Leanne laughed and put her hand on the winch. 'Ready to take the jib, captain.'

'You're a great crew.' Tony turned the wheel and the wind filled the sails from the stern, carrying the boat forward on the waves.

Leanne looked up at him. What a great photo it would make with him standing there, the wind in his hair, his eyes on the horizon and the white sail billowing behind him. She picked up her phone and took a shot.

Tony glanced at her and grinned, his teeth white in his freckly face. 'Hey, I'm no model.'

'But you look so fabulous there at the wheel. Like the master of the sea and of your destiny.'

'I wish,' he said with a laugh. 'But get back to the job, darlin', or we'll sink.'

'Aye, aye, captain.'

Leanne felt a surge of happiness as the boat steadied and they set the course on the little island in the far distance. 'Thank you for taking me sailing. I feel better about everything. Even Carlo. I'm just going to ghost him from now on, except for when we're doing the shoots.'

'Ghost him?'

Leanne laughed and pushed him. 'Get with the programme, Tony, and join the twenty-first century! Ghosting someone is the same as ignoring them. It usually means not answering their texts or emails. Get it?'

Tony laughed. 'Yes, sure. Except in this case, you have to see him in person every day. So not quite possible, is it?'

'Nope. But I'll do my best.'

'Good.' He grinned and then leant over and kissed her lightly on the lips, pulling back just as suddenly with a contrite look. 'Sorry. Didn't mean to do that. It was just that you looked so cute just now.'

The kiss startled her, not because it had shocked her but because of how it made her feel. How soft his lips were and how good he smelled. She hadn't expected that at all. 'I forgive you,' she said, placing her hands on his cheeks and pulling his face close, pressing her lips to his in a long, sweet kiss. 'You look cute too,' she whispered when they pulled back. 'And you've made me feel so good today. Thank you for that.'

'You did the same for me.' They stared at each other for a moment full of unspoken words, until Tony tore his eyes away and checked their course. 'We're nearly there,' he announced, his voice hoarse.

'Already?' Leanne squealed and looked ahead. 'That was quick.'

'Time flies when you're having fun,' Tony quipped. 'And we did. Didn't we?'

Leanne looked at his mouth, wishing she could kiss him again. 'Oh yes,' she sighed. 'We did.'

Chapter Twenty-Three

As the sun dipped on the horizon, Maddy watched Leanne and Tony steer the sailing boat into the little inlet. As they tidied away the sails and ropes, putting out fenders and dropping the anchor, she was struck by the calm complicity between them. When they had left earlier, Leanne's eyes had revealed a lingering pain, despite her best effort at putting on a brave face. Even though she had been perfectly friendly with Carlo, there had been an undeniable tension between them, she thought with a pang of pity for Leanne. Her pale smile earlier hadn't fooled Maddy. She knew Leanne was both hurt and ashamed about what had happened. But then Tony had asked her to go sailing with him and it looked like he might have been able to cheer her up. She couldn't help thinking there was something sweet between them. Tony could be good for Leanne, like the big brother she never had. Maddy smiled at them as they jumped onto the deck of the yacht.

'Hi, there,' she said. 'You look as if you've had a good afternoon.'

Leanne beamed. 'Yes, it was amazing. Despite the very strict captain barking orders at me the whole time.'

Tony sighed in mock despair. 'What could I do with a crew like that? I had to make sure we didn't sink.'

Leanne stuck her tongue out at him. 'Yeah, right. I did a brilliant job. You just can't bear to admit it.'

Tony laughed and ruffled her hair. 'You were great, girl. Good job, considering you haven't been on a boat for a long time. Is there any beer?'

His phone pinged before Maddy had a chance to reply. 'Maybe a message from Claudia's man?' she suggested.

Tony looked at his phone. 'Yes. It's from him. It says he needs Claudia's signature on some papers, that's all, and can we meet up in Dubrovnik tomorrow. He promises not to make trouble. And that we're not to tell anyone where he is.'

'What was that?' Claudia asked, coming out of her cabin. 'You heard from Oliver?'

'Yes. He wants to meet you in Dubrovnik to sign some papers.'

'What papers? It's a trick,' Claudia muttered. 'He's trying to get me back.'

'I think you should talk to him,' Tony said. 'I'll come with you. We can meet him in a bar or café. Somewhere public where he can't do anything.'

Claudia shrugged. 'Okay. I suppose I'd better find out what he's up to. I've finally managed to contact my lawyer. He says Ollie has started proceedings and will be hiring a lawyer. So that's something, I suppose.'

'That sounds like he's going to cooperate,' Leanne said.

'Yes, but it might also be a trick.' Claudia turned and went into the galley and tied an apron around her waist. 'I'm cooking tonight. Pasta followed by grilled fish that we got from the market in the harbour. Then the rest of the fruit. Not much else, but we have plenty of wine.'

'I think I'll skip the wine tonight,' Leanne said, turning red.

'I think we should do the grilling on the island,' Tony suggested. 'Otherwise the whole boat will stink of fish. In fact, why don't we have a picnic and get a barbeque going? Forget the pasta, Claudia – we'll do grilled zucchini and those little potatoes we bought the other day. Then some salad and what's left of our bread. How's that?'

'Fun!' Leanne shouted. 'Like scout camp.'

'More like boot camp,' Claudia muttered. 'But fine, if that's what you want.'

They did. When Lucilla and Carlo emerged from her cabin, Leanne was so busy helping Tony put everything together that she didn't have time to pay them much attention. Maddy looked at her with a huge sigh of relief. It'd be okay. Leanne would move on and the holiday could continue in relative peace. Dubrovnik, the pearl of the Adriatic, beckoned. *The highlight of the trip*, Maddy thought with a tingle of excitement. She had always wanted to visit this ancient city and now she'd be able to explore it. Things were settling down and all was well. For the moment.

The improvised barbeque turned out to be as much fun as Leanne had hoped. Even Claudia joined in, dressed in a pair of white shorts and a denim shirt she had borrowed from Lucilla. 'I didn't bring an outfit for this kind of thing, but it'll do, I suppose,' she declared.

Leanne looked at her pristine hair and make-up, gleaming white shorts and Gucci sandals and laughed. 'Yeah, you look a total wreck. Mind if I take a shot?' She aimed her phone at Claudia. 'You might as well come out of hiding now that your hubby has spotted you.'

'Yes, but… the IRS,' Claudia started.

'They're not interested in you,' Leanne argued. 'In any case, I managed to upload the photos of Carlo and me to my Instagram page, so that should stir things up a bit. Most likely no one will pay you much attention.'

Maddy picked up her phone. 'I got a bit of a signal. Here are the photos.' Her eyes widened as she watched the screen. 'Oh my God, they're amazing,' she exclaimed. She stared at Leanne and Carlo in turn. 'You two… You made those rags look fabulous. Everyone will want them now.'

'Incredible.' Claudia looked at the photos over Maddy's shoulder. 'This should cause a sensation.'

'Already doing well on Twitter,' Carlo announced. 'Hashtag #sexyrisorcenaturali. And the company have set up their own Instagram account. They'll take over the campaign as soon as the buzz gets started.'

Lucilla grinned and high-fived Carlo. 'We did it!'

'Yes, great,' Leanne interrupted, annoyed at their assumption it was all their doing. She'd played a part, hadn't she? 'All done now. How about putting some food and drink together for the barbecue?'

'I'm on it,' Tony declared. 'If you get the food together here, I'll go and get beer, crisps and sausages from our boat. Then we'll meet on the island. Carlo, come on. Let's get this party started!'

Tony's good mood was contagious and suddenly everyone was busy packing food and putting chilled wine into the hamper Lucilla had prepared. 'Lamb chops, zucchini, aubergine and potatoes can all be grilled together,' she said. 'And the sausages too. We have more than enough.'

'I'll put in some fruit and bread,' Maddy offered. 'And there are paper plates and plastic glasses for the wine in that cupboard. Could you take care of that, Claudia?'

'And I'll take care of Bridget,' Leanne volunteered.

They all packed into the rubber dinghy, which Nico steered carefully to avoid underwater rocks. Tony and Carlo were already gathering firewood and lighting the fire on the island and once they had carried everything ashore, the smell of delicious grilled meat soon filled the air.

Leanne sat back on her beach blanket when she had finished eating and sighed with pleasure. What could be better than this? Food and wine and good company in such a beautiful place, the dark sky dotted with glimmering stars and the full moon slowly rising over the treetops. It was perfect. Only one thing was missing. She sat up. 'Music,' she called out. 'We need music. Can we sing a song or something?'

'I have a terrible voice,' Claudia declared. 'But maybe Carlo could sing an Italian song?'

Carlo laughed and got up from his place beside Lucilla. 'I'm no Pavarotti, but I can give you "O Sole Mio". Please tell me to stop if it hurts your ears,' he said with a laugh. He took a big breath and started singing. He had a nice, deep voice with a slightly hoarse timbre, but he missed a note here and there, making Leanne wince. When he finished, they all applauded, and he bowed and sat down. 'Not very good, but I haven't sung in a long time, forgive me. He looked at Tony. 'How about some Irish music on the thing you play sometimes?'

'What thing?' Leanne asked. 'Don't tell me you have a guitar or a fiddle?'

'No fiddle, I'm afraid, but…' Tony groped into his breast pocket and pulled out a small metal flute.

'A tin whistle!' Leanne exclaimed. 'How perfect. Please play us a tune.'

'Oh yes,' Maddy sighed. 'Something Irish, please.'

Tony started to play a lilting, haunting melody that echoed across the still, black water, bringing tears to Leanne's eyes. 'Oh,' she whispered when he stopped playing. 'How beautiful. What was that tune?'

'Seán Ó Riada. "Mnà na hEireann" – "Women of Ireland",' Tony replied. 'I'll play another one of his, if you like.'

'Yes, please,' Claudia said, looking dreamily out over the bay. 'That music is heavenly –there's something otherworldly about it.'

Leanne took out her phone. 'Hang on. I want this on video. What are you going to play?'

'This one is simply called "Tin Whistles".' Tony put the instrument to his mouth and yet again, the sweet sound filled the air while they all listened with bated breath, letting out a collective 'oooh' when the music ended.

'*Mille grazie*,' Lucilla said. 'That was incredible. Irish music is so lovely.'

'Especially Seán Ó Riada,' Maddy sighed.

'Can you sing something, Maddy?' Lucilla asked.

Maddy shook her head and laughed. 'I'm not very musical but I know Leanne has a nice voice. Why don't you sing something, Leanne?'

'Feck off,' Leanne protested. 'I'm in no mood for singing.'

'Why not?' Tony asked. He played a few notes on his tin whistle. 'You know this one?'

Leanne nodded. '"Danny Boy".'

'Come on,' he urged. 'I'll play it if you sing.'

'Do I have to?'

'I won't take no for an answer.'

'Okay, then.' Persuaded, Leanne closed her eyes and cleared her throat. She took a deep breath and started to sing, shakily at first, but with growing confidence as Tony accompanied her on the tin whistle. The beautiful words and music carried her away to another place, another time, singing Irish songs in her granny's kitchen when she was a child. She wiped away a tear when she had finished, noticing in the dying glow of the fire and the beam of the moonlight, that everyone else was doing the same.

'That was beautiful,' Claudia said, dabbing her eyes with the edge of her shirt. 'But sad. Can we have something cheery now, please?'

Then Tony played a lively jig and they all started to chat and laugh as the mood lifted. After they gathered up the remains of the meal, they all piled into the dinghies, but before Leanne clambered aboard, Tony gently pulled her aside. 'You have a beautiful voice.'

'And you play that thing to perfection,' Leanne replied. 'Want to start a band?'

Tony laughed. 'Not at the moment, but you never know. You should post a video with your singing on your blog, too.'

'Only if you play.'

'Why not? We were good together, weren't we?'

Leanne looked at him, unable to make out his expression in the dark. 'We were,' she said.

His glasses glinted as he leant closer. 'Good night, my sweet Irish colleen,' he whispered, kissing her cheek before he left to board the other dinghy.

As Leanne watched them leave, the splash of the oars was the only sound in the quiet, still night. She hugged Bridget to her chest and placed her cheek against the dog's soft head as Nico started the engine and the rubber dinghy slowly made its way back to the yacht. It had been a lovely evening, a sharp contrast to the night before. Funny how feelings can change so quickly. Last night she had thought Carlo was the man for her, and that making love would be the beginning of a relationship with him. How wrong she had been. He had revealed himself to be the exact opposite to the man of her dreams.

And then Tony... She smiled as she thought of him. He was serious, a bit of a nerd really, but with hidden depths and a sweet, caring side she found so touching. He looked at her as if he thought the world of her... Not to mention how he made her feel when they touched, and his talent for music, and that kiss... It was all so unexpected. Leanne smiled to herself as the engine stopped and they glided in beside the yacht. She didn't notice Bridget stiffen until she was growling and then barking furiously. They all looked up at the deck and froze.

'It's him,' Claudia whimpered.

Chapter Twenty-Four

'Him?' Lucilla mumbled, looking at the dark shape on deck. 'You mean…'

'Yes,' Claudia whispered back.

'Good evening, ladies,' a gravelly voice said in a Yorkshire accent mixed with a touch of New York. 'Please come aboard slowly without making too much noise.'

Dumbstruck, they silently started to climb the ladder.

'What shall I do?' Nico muttered in Leanne's ear as he helped her onto the deck. 'I can try to alert the coastguard on the satellite radio inside when I get a chance?'

'Yes,' Leanne whispered. 'Please do.'

They said nothing else, all huddling together on the rear deck, while Bridget, barking and whining, struggled to get out of Leanne's grip. The man switched on the light above the entrance to the saloon, springing into view. He was taller than his photos had indicated, with square shoulders and an equally square jaw. It was as if he were hewn out of a block of granite. Then he smiled and his features softened, the crinkles around his eyes making him look suddenly charming. But then something glinted in his hand and Leanne gasped.

'A gun!' she shouted. 'He has a gun!'

They all backed away. Leanne held the wriggling, barking Bridget in a tight grip, her eyes on the man. She was very sure she didn't want to die. Not right here, right now at the hands of this stranger. 'Please. I beg you. Don't shoot us,' she pleaded.

'Don't do anything stupid and I won't,' he growled.

'Won't what?' Claudia asked, stepping forward. 'Don't be ridiculous. That's not a gun, it's a phone. Not the least bit dangerous unless you're planning to text us to death.'

Feeling relieved, Leanne giggled. 'Judging by his typing skills, that'd take him a while.'

'Oh, okay,' Oliver Wilde said. 'Relax, everyone. I'm not armed. Who do you think am I?'

'What do you want from us, Oliver?' Lucilla asked.

'I want you to help me,' he replied. 'My boat broke down just outside the bay. So I managed to row to your yacht and now I need help to get out of here. And I want to talk to my wife about something else, but that can wait.'

'But why are you here?' Maddy asked, trying to sound confident.

'What's going on?' Tony asked, climbing up the ladder at the back. He stopped dead when he spotted Oliver. 'Holy shit,' he gasped. 'It's Oliver Wilde.'

'It's me all right,' Oliver said. 'If you could all stop blathering, I'll tell you the whole story.'

'Okay.' Tony nodded. 'Let's go and sit down,'

'Great,' Oliver said, pushing past Nico into the saloon, where he sat down heavily on the couch. 'I wouldn't say no to a beer.'

'You never did,' Claudia remarked, sitting opposite him. 'There's no beer. But if you're nice, maybe we can get you a cup of tea.'

Oliver nodded. 'Okay, that's fine.'

'I'll make it,' Maddy offered. 'Put Bridget in your cabin, Leanne. She's still upset.'

Leanne settled the shivering little dog on her bed and then joined the others in the saloon, all seated around the table while Nico went to contact the coastguard. Maddy put a tray with mugs of tea on the table and they all helped themselves.

Tony pushed a steaming mug at Oliver. 'Herbal tea. Very soothing. Let's hear your story then.'

'No need for stories,' Claudia interrupted. 'I think I know the scenario. You cheated on your taxes and now the IRS are after you and you want me to help out, right?'

'Not quite,' Oliver grunted. He sipped some tea, made a face and pushed the mug away. He looked at Claudia. 'Yes, it's true that I have quite a big tax debt and those guys are after me, but that's not all. I need your help for something else.' He paused. 'The thing is, you see, that I'm going into politics.'

'Politics?' Claudia gasped. 'You mean… in America?'

Oliver nodded. 'Yes. I'm an American citizen, so I can, you know.'

Lucilla laughed. 'You're running for president?'

'No,' Oliver replied. 'If you all shut up for a moment I'll tell you. I'm going to be the next governor of California.'

'Oh, wow. Like… your man,' Leanne cut in. 'Whatshisname, Schwarzerknickers?'

'Schwarzenegger,' Oliver corrected. 'And yes, just like him.'

'Santa Maria!' Claudia exclaimed with a derisory laugh. 'That's ridiculous. Who on earth is going to vote for you?'

'Lots of people,' Oliver said. 'I have a campaign manager and quite a lot of money has been collected already. I'll have to try to pay back the tax debt before the elections and I was hoping you could help me. But this is not just about money, it's about…' He paused and looked pleadingly at Claudia. 'I need you beside me during the campaign. Your style and beauty – your charm and elegance are the best weapons I would have against the other candidates. With you at my side, I'd have a very good chance.'

Claudia stared at him. 'I can't believe I'm hearing this. After all I've put up with, you expect me not only to help you financially, but also to be some kind of trophy wife for these elections that you couldn't possibly win? Why should I?'

Oliver looked into Claudia's eyes. 'Because of what we had once, you and I,' he said, his voice suddenly gentle. 'Have you forgotten?'

Claudia looked away. 'No. Yes… I mean… It was nice in the beginning,' she whispered. 'But then…'

'Never mind all that,' Oliver cut in and took her hands. 'We were in love once. Let's not forget that. Let's not ruin the lovely memories.'

'You already did,' Claudia snapped and pulled her hands away. 'And to think I was actually frightened of you. But now, looking at you talking about this ridiculous political career, I feel like laughing. Can't believe I put up with all the mental abuse without complaint for so long.'

Oliver looked contrite for a moment. 'I'm sorry about all that. But I will change, I swear. I'll be the kind of husband you wanted me to be, if only—'

Claudia got up. 'Not even if you beg. Forget it, Ollie. I'm not going around shaking hands and kissing babies. We're finished. The divorce is going through. Please try to accept that.'

Oliver didn't reply. He sat with his head bowed while they all stared, waiting for him to speak. Then he looked up and sighed deeply. 'All right. I give up. I thought you might see my side of things, but I realise it was too much to ask.'

'You bet,' Claudia muttered. 'Way too much.'

Oliver sighed. 'I had a suspicion that would be the case. But you can't blame a guy for trying.' He paused. 'But… maybe… for old times' sake… you could give me a farewell gift? That most precious thing you won't share with anyone… You know what I mean.'

Claudia gasped. 'What? You think I'm going to give *that* away? Never!'

'Ah, please,' Oliver begged. 'That was what made me fall in love with you in the first place.'

'What are you going on about?' Leanne asked, bursting with curiosity.

Claudia stared at her. 'He wants me to give him my grandmother's secret pasta sauce recipe.'

Lucilla gasped. 'What?! Nonna Angela's pasta sauce? It belongs to our family. You can't give that away, Claudia!'

'Of course not,' Claudia agreed. 'I never would.' She glared at Oliver. 'You should know that.'

He nodded, looking deflated. 'Okay. I understand. But could you at least get someone to help me with the boat?'

'We will,' Tony said. 'Did you manage to get through, Nico?'

'Yes,' Nico called from the desk. 'I've talked to them. They said they'd be here in the morning. '

'He's not going to sleep here, is he?' Leanne asked.

'I'll take him back to the sailing boat,' Tony offered. 'He can sleep in my cabin and I'll take the couch in the saloon.'

'Perfect,' Claudia said. 'But tell me, how on earth did you manage to find me?'

Oliver smirked. 'You leave huge footprints all over the place, sweetheart. And that concierge at the crumbling heap you call a palazzo doesn't mind spilling the beans if you press a few euros into her greedy paw. Then I just read all the blogposts on that website and followed the trail you left behind, including the name of the restaurant on the awning in that tiny village you thought nobody would see.'

'Shit,' Leanne moaned. 'I forgot about that. Should have been more careful.'

'That's for sure,' Oliver said. 'But what can you expect from a bunch of women?'

'That's enough,' Tony snapped and tugged at Oliver's shirt. 'Come on, mate. Let's go.'

'Okay,' Oliver grunted and struggled to get to his feet. 'No need to get rough.'

'Just one thing before you go,' Maddy interrupted. 'Why did you try to steal our dog?'

'I was going to use her to get Claudia to give me that recipe. The mutt for the sauce,' Oliver replied. 'A bit of bartering, really.'

'Or blackmail. That kind of fell on its face,' Leanne remarked. 'But hey, just one little tip; if you're going into politics you might consider cleaning up your act. Start by being polite to women. That'll get you more votes. And you could try to look less scruffy while you're at it.' She wrinkled her nose. 'And maybe take a shower?'

'Thanks for the advice, m'dear,' Oliver grunted. 'But now I've had enough of this. Lead me to my bunk. Bye, darling wife. I'm sorry you didn't want to join me in my new adventure. Could have been fun, but no hard feelings. Sad to say farewell but maybe our paths will cross again one day.'

Claudia shrugged. 'Never would be too soon. Goodbye, Ollie.'

Leanne watched them go across the rear deck, Oliver first, Tony behind him. But where was Carlo? She noticed him then, at the back of the deck, leaving in the wake of the other men. So he'd been hiding behind the women, not daring to open his mouth. What a wimp. Still handsome, still a nice guy, still dashing in that gorgeous Italian way, but some of his masculinity, that she had been so attracted to, had disappeared and Leanne realised how superficial her feelings for him had been. But Tony...

She smiled at Maddy. 'Did you see that?' she breathed.

'What?' Maddy asked, laughing.

'Tony. Isn't he incredible?'

'Tony? I thought Claudia was amazing, standing up to Oliver like that.'

'I think she finally had enough. Very brave, I must say.'

'But Carlo just...' Leanne glanced around for Lucilla but she and Claudia had already gone into their cabins. 'He was such a chicken shit. Not Tony, though. He has probably been in some tough spots during his time abroad and has had to take charge. Seems to have been pretty scary most of the time.'

'That explains it.' Maddy yawned. 'Well, what a night. I'm going to bed.'

'Me too. Hope the coastguard will be here in the morning.' Leanne suddenly laughed. 'That guy is going into politics? How mad is that?'

Maddy joined in her laughter. 'Well if Schwazerknickers can get elected, so can he. Politics has turned really weird lately. Just look at some of the world leaders today.'

'You're right,' Leanne said with a yawn. 'I'm knackered. Must sleep or I'll pass out.'

'Me too.' Maddy kissed her cheek. 'Good night, pet. No need to wish you sweet dreams. I can tell by the stars in your eyes you'll have some lovely ones.'

Leanne laughed and felt herself blush. 'Yes,' she whispered to Bridget when they were tucked up in bed. 'I'll dream of music and singing and the stars in the sky. And that light kiss I can still feel on my cheek. And in my heart.'

Chapter Twenty-Five

The coastguard arrived the next morning, and after some conferring with Tony and Nico they took Oliver with them, towing his boat behind theirs. They all heaved a sigh of relief, especially Claudia. 'So glad to have that man out of my hair,' she sighed over the meagre breakfast that they had scraped together, as most of their supplies had been depleted during the barbeque.

'There's not much food left,' Leanne remarked.

'We'll be in Dubrovnik this afternoon,' Maddy said, as Nico started the engine and they made their way across the calm water of the bay. 'So we can stock up there. In any case, we have reservations at the Dubrovnik Palace Hotel. Looked amazing on their website. It's right on the water and a spit from the best beach in town.'

'Does it have a spa?' Claudia asked.

'Oh yes, spa, jacuzzi the works,' Maddy replied.

'Heaven,' Claudia sighed. 'Back to civilisation. It's been fun, but I think I might fly back to Florence from Dubrovnik in a couple of days.'

'We'll miss you,' Leanne said, realising it was true. Claudia had been great company, better than Lucilla, who despite her generosity and charm was a little too into herself. All she ever talked about was business. But Claudia had grown on her, revealing a fun, kind personality behind all the bluster.

'Have you checked Instagram?' Lucilla suddenly asked, as if she was reading Leanne's thoughts. 'I'd love to see the reactions to the new photos.'

'Not much of a signal,' Maddy said, checking her phone. 'But once we get nearer to the mainland, it should be better.'

'Okay.' Lucilla went back to her laptop. 'We'll have a look when we can connect.'

'Great.'

When they reached the choppy waters of the straights, Leanne looked to the far distance where she could see the sailing boat ahead of them, leaning over in the brisk wind, Tony at the helm. Carlo was on deck checking sails, wearing nothing but his tiny red Speedos. Probably topping up his tan before their photo shoot later that day. They had decided to do a few final shots on the beach below the hotel. She wasn't looking forward to it and she wondered how she'd be able to fake being attracted to Carlo, when all she could think of was Tony. It had seemed like such a good idea at the beginning. Who would have thought it would have gone tits up?

Her phone pinged. She glanced at it and saw it was a text from an unknown number. She opened the message and smiled as she saw who it was from. *Got your number from Carlo. How about a date tonight? You, me, pizza, wine and nobody else... So much to talk about, don't you think? T x*

Leanne chuckled to herself as she replied. *Pizza, wine –and thee how can I resist? Just checked my busy calendar and see I have a window, so I can fit you in. Please don't tell Carlo or anyone, and I won't either. L x*

She didn't know why she wanted their date to be a secret. It was as if it was something precious and special and somehow fragile at this early stage. She didn't want to share it with anyone yet, not even Maddy. Her feelings for Tony were all jumbled up in her head and her growing attraction to him confused her. She was normally drawn to traditionally attractive, glamorous men; Tony was the direct opposite. He was tall and gangly and seemed oblivious to the way he dressed, usually in a pair of rugby shorts from his college days, a faded green polo shirt and battered trainers. His curly red hair needed a trim but that was a detail that Leanne found cute. She wanted to run her fingers through those curls and smooth the lines around his mouth. His attraction lay in his kind eyes, his warm smile, and his sharp intelligence. And he oozed warmth and compassion. But there was something more that she couldn't put her finger on and she didn't want to jinx anything. She jumped as her phone pinged again.

A secret date? Yes! My lips are sealed. I will msg you later with time and place. Over and out. T x

'What are you giggling about?' Maddy asked.

Leanne blushed and switched off her phone. 'Nothing. Just a funny thing on Facebook.'

'Oh? Is the signal better now?' Maddy looked at her phone. 'No. Seems to be down.'

'It comes and goes,' Leanne replied. 'Must have been a glimmer of a signal just then.'

'I suppose,' Maddy said, looking suspicious. 'Are you up to something?'

'Me?' Leanne replied, her eyes wide. 'Up to what exactly?'

'Not much chance of being up to anything out at sea,' Claudia remarked. 'Even for Leanne. But I need to get online too, so I can book a spa treatment. A complete overhaul is long overdue.'

'Yeah, you need serious attention,' Leanne teased, looking at Claudia's nearly flawless complexion.

'Do I look a mess?' Claudia asked anxiously, fishing a mirror out of her handbag, studying her face.

'No, you look perfect,' Leanne replied. 'What's your secret? Botox? Fillers? Surgery? Whatever it is, it looks completely natural.'

'Botox?' Claudia scoffed. 'That's so yesterday. No, just a few non-invasive treatments like dermabrasion and microblading. Expensive and time-consuming, but worth it. And I stay out of the sun, eat healthy food, I don't smoke and try to keep alcohol to a minimum. Plus yoga, Pilates and regular workouts with a personal trainer.'

'A full-time job,' Maddy remarked. 'I'd never have time for all of that.'

'You have to make time,' Claudia declared.

'Sounds like a very boring existence,' Leanne said. 'I mean, no sunshine or wine? And no junk food like pizza, a big cheeseburger or beer?'

'Pizza is not junk food. Besides, you wear what you eat,' Claudia said, looking at Leanne's slim figure. 'You're still young, so you can afford to abuse your body. For now.' Her laser eyes moved to Maddy. 'But after forty, you have to start thinking about making changes. And rethink your underwear. Especially if you hope to find a new man.'

Maddy laughed. 'Rethink my underwear? You mean as in push-up bras and spandex?'

'Not quite,' Claudia replied. 'But some kind of support can't hurt.'

'But Maddy's already found a new man. A golden oldie,' Leanne quipped.

'Not that old,' Maddy protested. 'But quite perfect for me. He doesn't seem to notice the ravages of time or childbirth on a woman's body. He's amazing in bed, too.'

Leanne squirmed. 'Ugh. It's my dad you're talking about, you know. I really don't need details of your, ahem, relations with him.'

Maddy laughed. 'Okay, I get it. The idea of your parents having—'

Leanne got up. 'Please. Don't say the words "parents" and "sex" in the same sentence. So gross.' She picked up her phone. 'I'm going to see if the signal is better now that we're closer to the mainland.'

'It is,' Lucilla said from the saloon. 'And your Instagram account is hopping. I also just got a message from the client. They have a huge number of orders.' She beamed at Leanne. 'Well done. You and Carlo must do some more modelling for them.'

'I don't think so,' Leanne replied, making a face. 'I just did it for the craic. I'm not going to start a new career in fashion.'

'You never know,' Lucilla said, closing her laptop. 'Have look at the comments on Instagram. I think you'll be amazed.'

'Okay. I will.' Feeling the need to be away from the prying eyes of Lucilla, Leanne went into her cabin and closed the door. She sat on the bed and opened Instagram, looking at the photos. She stared at the images of the two of them, playing and flirting in the sun. Was that woman her? It seemed like a lifetime ago. What an unreal moment it had been. She shivered as she thought about her brief fling with Carlo and how it had ended so spectacularly. Not one of the best moments in her life to say the least, but it was a relief it hadn't gone any further. She realised now that even when her hormones had been in overdrive she had known, deep down, that it was all wrong, somehow. She hadn't told Maddy about her subsequent chat with Carlo, when he had revealed the truth about his relationship with Lucilla, nor did she want to. Better to leave all that in the past. She turned her attention back to Instagram.

There were over a thousand comments with everything from 'cool!' to 'sizzling hot couple', and 'fun in the sun'. When she switched to Twitter she saw the photos had an amazing number of retweets and comments. But instead of feeling thrilled, she was embarrassed and wished she could erase the whole thing. But it was there, all over the Internet, forever. Hopefully it would soon be forgotten.

Leanne looked up her recent photos on her phone and found the one she had taken of Tony at the wheel of the sailing boat. A gorgeous shot with his head and shoulders outlined against the blue sky and white sail. She'd match it with a fun little post.

While she was browsing, the phone pinged. A message from Tony with a time and place for their date. She replied with a thumbs-up emoji and he sent a kissing emoji back. Leanne smiled and lay back on the bed, looking dreamily out of the porthole at the bright blue sky overhead and the sea sending sprays of water against the glass. They'd be docking in Dubrovnik soon. She'd be able to freshen up in the luxury of the plush hotel room – and get ready for her secret date. She felt excitement buzz inside her, like champagne bubbles, as she thought of the evening ahead. She sat up again, too excited to rest, and opened her laptop.

Gone with the wind.

Hi from the ocean blue! We have nearly arrived at the pearl of the Adriatic, aka Dubrovnik. Can't wait to discover the delights of this city I've heard so much about. But I'm also still glowing from a wild sailing trip I took yesterday with the cute doctor. As you can see from the photo, he's one of the best sailors around, steering the boat through choppy waters and high winds without a flicker of an eyebrow. I crewed (as in helping with ropes and sails, don't you dare put an 's' in front!) as best I could but with all the modern equipment on this boat it was a breeze (in more ways than one). I haven't sailed since I was twelve but it all came back to me in a flash as the winds took us across the straits in super-quick time. It was exhilarating! The boat leaned over so much we had to sit on the side to weigh it down but then when we reduced the sail she (as in the boat) calmed down and we managed to get back without sinking. Must do this again very soon. Especially with the cute doctor ;)

Dubrovnik beckons. Watch this space for my review of this ancient city!

Chapter Twenty-Six

In the meantime, Maddy was making plans for the evening. She booked a table for six at the best restaurant in Dubrovnik on Claudia's recommendation, and after a little hesitation also booked a massage and facial at the hotel spa. It wouldn't do any harm to get an overhaul after the swimming and sunbathing that might have damaged her aging skin, according to Claudia. It was urgent, if she was to believe Claudia, who declared that even the nicest men were big liars who noticed dry skin, wrinkles, cellulite and stretch marks despite pretending not to. 'Men are very visual,' she declared. 'They get turned on by what they see. Women are sensual, where feel and touch are more important to us. That's why seemingly unattractive men appeal to women if they know how to touch them in the right way.'

'Oh,' was all Maddy managed before she hurried away to her cabin to send a message to Erik.

He had beaten her to it and she found a long email in her inbox when she logged in.

Dear, sweet Maddy,

I'm sitting at my desk wondering how you are. I've followed the blog and seen you're both hugely enjoying the trip. But when it comes to an end, I hope you will come back here for an extended visit and we can sort out what we want to do next. I know we only knew each for a short week, but I still feel we belong together. I understand and respect your wish to go back to Dublin for that last school year, and it will be a good way to test our relationship. During that year, I will visit you often, and I'd love you to come here for the longer holidays. After that I hope you will be ready to move in with me and share my dream that is now looking very real. I also hope you have had a talk with Leanne and managed to persuade her to accept my offer for her to take over my business once we've settled at the farm. I was pleased to hear about her romance with Carlo, which fits into my plans, as Carlo is based in Nice. They would make a fantastic corporate couple.

Maddy gulped and stopped reading. She had completely forgotten to speak to Leanne about Erik's plans for his firm, as she had promised him before she left Nice. And now with Leanne's supposed romance with Carlo dead in the water, the whole thing was doomed to fail. How was she going to break this to Erik? He was the kind of person who believed he could draw up a plan and then everything would fall into place, even other people's lives. His dream of building a new life on a little farm high in the hills above Nice depended on Leanne, and to a certain extent, Maddy, with whom he hoped to share it. She hated to shatter his dream, but he had to be told that some of the jigsaw pieces didn't fit and probably never would. It wouldn't be easy for him to accept it, she thought with a gulp. She continued reading the message.

> *So with these plans growing in my head, I will leave you for tonight, my dear pen pal and, hopefully, future partner. Will speak to you soon when your adventure comes to an end and the new one is beginning.*
>
> *Much love, min kjære. From your mad Norwegian*

She smiled. He was so sweet and loving. Except for a tiny spark of irritation at his absolute belief that everything would work out the way he wanted, she felt her feelings for him growing and she longed to see him again. But he had to be taught that other people might have other plans and other dreams, especially his daughter. Barging into her life like this after all those years apart would be wrong.

Maddy sighed and decided to talk to Leanne later that evening, just so she could tell Erik she had tried. Then he would have to work it out with Leanne and leave her out if it completely. Otherwise his dream would turn to ashes and he'd end up alone in that beautiful but remote farm. She had spent a lifetime living according to other people's wishes. She wasn't going to get into that trap again.

'Maddy!' Leanne called from outside. 'We can see Dubrovnik. Come and look. It's fabulous.'

Maddy turned off her laptop and hurried to the sundeck, where Lucilla, Claudia and Leanne were watching the ruggedly beautiful coastline and Dubrovnik in the distance. Maddy stared at the town shimmering in the bright sunshine, its red roofs and cupolas rising above the walls of the Old Town. The entire city seemed to be turned towards the sun and the sea, blazing with rich colours of the blossoming gardens and terracotta roofs, as if it were floating on the deep blue water, surrounded by green islands.

'Beautiful,' she sighed.

Claudia picked up the binoculars. 'Even better up close. Look at the Venetian architecture. Fascinating.'

'We'll be docking at the marina soon,' Nico announced from the bridge. 'Are you all ready to go ashore?'

'All ready,' Claudia replied. 'I've ordered a taxi to take us to the hotel.'

'I'm packed.' Leanne went to her cabin to get her bag and Bridget. 'But could you take Bridget, Mads? I have to go straight to the beach for the photo shoot, or we'll have nothing to post on Instagram later.'

'Of course.' Maddy took Bridget's lead. 'Come here, sweetheart. I just have to throw a few things in and I'll be with you.'

'Carlo and I are in the same hotel as you,' Lucilla announced. 'I'll look after her if you want.'

'She'll be fine with me,' Maddy said, picking up the dog. 'But I'll let you know if I have to go anywhere. I've checked with the hotel and they allow pets, so that's all sorted.'

They docked only minutes later and Nico laid out the gangplank. 'See you in a few days,' he said. 'I have to fill in the logs and report to the harbour master. Then I'll have dinner with some of the other skippers. Let me know your plans for the return trip when you know what you want to do.'

'We will,' Maddy said. 'Thanks for everything, Nico.'

Claudia handed him an envelope. 'We did a collection last night. A small token of appreciation for being such a terrific skipper.'

'That's very kind. Thank you. Enjoy Dubrovnik, ladies.' He took the envelope, smiled broadly and saluted as they left.

'What collection?' Lucilla asked in the taxi.

Claudia shrugged. 'I just thought of it before we left. But I believe it's customary to leave a tip to the staff even on a yacht.'

Lucilla looked glum. 'Of course. I should have thought of that. Thank you, Claudia.'

'Yes,' Leanne agreed. 'That was very thoughtful of you.'

'Let us know how much and we'll pay you back,' Maddy said.

'Fifty each,' Claudia said. 'We can settle during dinner tonight. Maddy booked a table at a nice restaurant for us all.'

'Oh. Sorry, but Carlo and I made other plans,' Lucilla said.

'And, uh, I…' Leanne stopped. 'I'm not up to going out tonight. Thought I'd get room service and watch some TV. I need to write a blogpost too and… stuff.'

'Don't forget the photo shoot in about an hour,' Lucilla reminded her. 'Just a few casual shots to finish off.'

Leanne nodded, glancing at Maddy. 'That's fine. I'll be there. But after that I'm just going to chill for a bit. Sorry to miss dinner, Mads.'

'That's fine. I understand.' Maddy looked at Leanne, wondering what was going on with her. She wouldn't normally pass up a meal at a top-notch restaurant. But maybe she was tired after all the upset with Carlo and the ensuing talk they'd had, which Leanne hadn't filled her in on yet. Hopefully they had made up and decided to go their separate ways.

'It's just you and me, then,' Claudia said. 'But that'll be nice too, won't it?'

'Of course,' Maddy replied. 'Looking forward to it. But I think I'll cancel the reservation at the restaurant and book a table for two at the hotel. What do you think?'

'Good idea,' Claudia said.

Leanne looked out the window of the taxi. 'Wow, this town is gorgeous. Look at those old walls and the amazing architecture. Can't wait to explore the Old Town tomorrow.'

They all looked out the windows and admired the ancient city, the curve of the harbour and the mellow stones of the city walls. The Old Town, which flew past them in the taxi, was steeped in history and oozed a mediaeval atmosphere. Throngs of people wandered around, peeking into quaint shops, drinking coffee outside picturesque cafés and taking photographs of the stunning views of the deep-blue sea.

Twenty minutes later, the taxi drew up outside the hotel and they stepped out into the brilliant sunshine. Leanne sniffed the air. 'I love the smell here. Such a gorgeous mix of rosemary, lemons, pine and good food.'

Claudia inhaled noisily through her nose. 'Can't smell a thing.'

Leanne laughed. 'That's because you don't have "the nose".'

'I suppose.' Claudia paid the driver and handed her bag to the uniformed porter who had just appeared. 'Let's check in.'

The hotel was a modern building backed by the pine-wooded slopes of Petka Hill, on the shore of the Lapad peninsula. It looked onto the open sea, the tiny rocky Grebeni islets, capped by a lighthouse, and the island of Koločep. Set in grounds planted with rosemary, oleander, olive trees and pines, it included a stunning beachfront and rooftop spa. The rooms were large and luxurious, each with spectacular views of the Adriatic.

Maddy could see straight down into the crystal-clear waters from her balcony. She stood there for a moment, looking out at the dramatic coastline with its rugged cliffs and inlets. This was truly paradise. How lovely it would be if Erik was here to share this experience. Then she remembered she hadn't replied to his latest email and felt a pang of guilt. She hadn't kept her promise to speak to Leanne and couldn't reply until she had.

She sighed as she leant on the railing and spotted Carlo and Leanne on the little beach far below. What was going on between them? And why hadn't Leanne told her what had happened during their discussion? She realised, with a dart of sadness, that she and Leanne were not as close as they had been during their drive through France. Something had shifted between them. Relationships, she thought, between friends or lovers, never stayed the same.

The phone on the bedside table rang. It was the hotel spa reminding her she had an appointment for a massage and facial in ten minutes. Maddy settled Bridget on a cushion, looking forward to an hour of pampering. It seemed selfish but it would be good to take a break from other people for a while – Erik and his plans, Leanne and her problems and even Tom and the divorce. She wished she could be more like Claudia, who thought of herself first, everything happening on her terms. Maybe that was the secret to survival? She'd soon find out.

Chapter Twenty-Seven

While Maddy continued her soul-searching during a massage at the spa, Leanne was striking a pose on the beach, dressed in a white strapless sundress. Carlo wore a pair of black shorts, his torso gleaming. Awkward and stiff at first, they tried to follow Lucilla's directions until she told them to stop. 'It's not working,' she said. 'You've lost that – thing you had before.'

Carlo glanced at Leanne and then looked down at the sand. 'We never had anything,' he muttered.

Lucilla waved away his explanations. 'All right, whatever. Just see if you can look a little less hostile, Leanne. And Carlo, you could maybe – I don't know – pretend to have a fight with Leanne?'

'Fight?' Leanne said and straightened up. 'Great idea.' She put up her fists. 'Come on, big boy, try to punch me.'

Carlo laughed and relaxed. His fist shot out and hit Leanne playfully on the jaw. 'There. Take that, *ragazza*!'

Just as he lunged forward, Leanne put out her foot and tripped him while Lucilla snapped away with her camera. 'Excellent!' she shouted. 'Now change into the tunic and shorts, Leanne, and we'll do a few with you on your own, standing in the water with your hair wet.'

Leanne quickly changed and waded into the sea until she was knee-deep, scooping some water onto her hair. 'Like this?'

'Perfect!' Lucilla shouted, taking several shots before she took the camera off the tripod. 'That's enough for today, Great finish, I think. Right, Carlo?'

'Yes,' Carlo replied from the water's edge where he'd been watching them.

'Great.' Leanne felt him looking at her, wearing a worried expression. Their eyes met for a split second. She waded back to the beach, touching Carlo's shoulder as she passed him. 'It's okay,' she whispered. 'I'm not mad at you or anything.'

'Oh. Good.' He relaxed and smiled, not the usual practised white grin, but a sweet little smile.

'I'm too tired and hot anyway,' she said to Lucilla. 'I just want to have swim and relax. We're on holiday after all!'

'That's okay,' Lucilla said. 'I want to swim too and then go and look at the photos.' She snapped her fingers. 'Come here, Carlo, and help me put everything away.'

'Yes, Lucilla,' Carlo mumbled and did as he was told.

Leanne walked to the sun lounger where she had left her towel. She stripped down to her bikini and was about to run into the sea when someone stopped her.

'Excuse me, but…'

Leanne turned and squinted at the tall, blonde woman. 'Yes?'

'Sorry to barge in on your photo shoot,' the woman said in a posh British accent, 'but I was wondering if I could have a word with you.'

'About what?' Leanne asked.

'The clothes you were modelling just now. I've never seen anything like them.'

'Why?' Leanne stared at the woman. 'I… Well, I'm not a model. And that little photo session was just for a new brand that I'm promoting for a friend.'

'Looks amazing.' The woman touched the tunic Leanne had thrown on the lounger. 'This fabric – it feels incredibly soft. Like… like the belly of a new-born puppy. What is it?'

'It's a new fabric. A linen and paper mix that's completely biodegradable. You just throw it into the compost bin when you don't want it any more and it melts away.'

'Fabulous,' the woman said, looking impressed. 'Love the concept of throwing last year's wardrobe away without guilt. Who was the genius who came up with that?'

'A company called Risorse Naturali. Actually, all the details are on my Instagram.'

The woman nodded. 'I see.' The woman took her phone out of her beach bag. 'So… Risorse Naturali… And your Instagram account?'

Leanne gave the woman the details before they said goodbye.

'Who was that?' Lucilla asked beside her, shaking water out of her hair.

Leanne handed her a towel. 'An English woman asking about the clothes. She was very interested. Sounded fierce posh too. I gave her all the details. You should tell your client to work harder on their Insta account, now that they've got a bit of notice from me,' Leanne suggested. 'Then you'll go seriously upmarket. That woman is one of the people you need to appeal to, not my friends and followers.' She glanced at Lucilla's voluptuous body in a black swimsuit. 'And you should start wearing those clothes yourself. They'd look fab on a body like yours.'

Lucilla looked at Leanne with a sour expression. 'That woman could be a fashion spy. She might steal the whole concept. I don't think it was a good idea for you to tell her everything.'

Leanne rolled her eyes. 'Jaysus, I'm not thick. All the details are already out there. I didn't tell her anything she couldn't look up herself.' She threw her towel on the lounger and picked up her bag. 'I'm off now. And off the whole marketing word-of-mouth thing. You're on your own. I think I've done my bit.'

Lucilla looked annoyed. 'So you have. Not that it was a huge effort to fool around with Carlo while I worked hard behind the camera, was it?'

Leanne stared back at Lucilla. 'Nah, that was easy.' She paused while their eyes locked. 'But what was going on behind the camera was a pain in the neck.' Without waiting to see if Lucilla got the full meaning of what she had said, Leanne walked off . *The nail in the coffin of a friendship that never was*, she thought. *Good riddance to her and her lapdog.* Leanne walked up the steps to the hotel with a heady feeling that the next chapter in her life was about to start. And a very important chapter too. Bring it on.

'You look so fresh and glowing,' Claudia said when Maddy joined her in the hotel restaurant.

Maddy smiled. 'Oh yes. I feel wonderful. That was a great overhaul.'

'What did you have done?'

'Everything. I must have shed a kilo of dry skin. And then the massage and the Thalgo body wrap and the facial... I fell asleep halfway through it.'

'I had a wonderful time too.'

'I can see that,' Maddy said, admiring Claudia's radiant face and flawless make-up. 'But then you looked great before, too.'

'Thank you.'

Maddy picked up the menu but Claudia stopped her with an imperious gesture. 'I already ordered. Grilled fish and salad, then a little cheese and a light lemon sorbet. A bottle of Pinot Grigio and a carafe of water. Is that okay? You can change it if you like.'

'No, that sounds perfect,' Maddy said, letting out a giggle. Claudia was an unstoppable force but you had to let her run with it or you'd be risking a heated argument or some scathing remark. How did she do it?

'What are you laughing at?' Claudia asked suspiciously.

'Nothing. I just feel very good right now.'

'That's not true. You find me amusing, so let me hear it.'

Maddy sighed. 'Okay. I was just thinking how you always get your way. It made me laugh but it also makes me envy you. If I had had just a fraction of your – self-confidence, I might have managed my life better.'

Claudia snorted. 'Self-confidence? I think you meant selfishness but were too polite to say it. Some call me a bitch but that's going too far. Not that I think this aspect of my personality has made my life a breeze, but it has certainly helped me survive. The women in my family are strong and independent. We're matriarchs more than wives and mothers. I'm sure you've seen that streak in

Lucilla too. She manages both her career and her personal life with an iron fist.'

'Yes,' Maddy had to admit. 'Lucilla is definitely one of those strong women. Poor Carlo –I mean…'

Claudia sighed and waved at a waiter. 'Bring us the wine, please.' She turned to Maddy. 'Yes, Carlo. Hmm. Their relationship is strange, to say the least. Lucilla keeps him on a long leash and he seems to like it. But that's their business. I'm glad Leanne didn't get too involved. That could have been a mess. But then again, she looks like the strong type too.'

'Well, yes, but she is also vulnerable. I wouldn't like to see her hurt.'

'She'll be fine.' Claudia nodded at the waiter who had just arrived with their wine in a cooler. Once they had been poured a glass each, she turned back to Maddy and lifted her glass. 'Chin chin, Maddy. I'm glad we have this evening to ourselves.' She drank deeply and put the glass on the table. 'So, what about you and that handsome Scandinavian, then? Are you getting serious?'

Maddy gulped down some of the crisp white wine. 'Uh, yes, we are. I mean it was quite hot when I left and now we're writing to each other and trying to work out what we're going to do. He wants to move to this little farm in the mountains in Provence. Gorgeous place. He has plans which sound—'

Claudia put up a hand. 'Hold it right there. He has plans? What are they? And do you agree to them?'

'Most of them, I think.' Maddy fiddled with her cutlery. 'And I'm sure I'll get used to the new life he's building. He's bought this old farm in the mountains above Nice, where he wants to start a new life. I love the place and I feel we could be happy there. It'll mean I'll have to give up some things and leave my life in Ireland, but that might be a good thing.'

Claudia stared at her incredulously. 'You've only known him a couple of weeks and he is already telling you how to organise the rest of your life?'

'Seems crazy, I know. But that's the way he is.' Maddy looked at Claudia, willing her to understand. 'I love him already, even though it hasn't been long. I know it sounds mad but I don't want to lose him.'

They were interrupted by the waiter placing a huge platter of grilled fish and a plate of salad on the table.

'Delicious,' Maddy said, savouring the salty, buttery flavour of the white fish and the crisp salad in an olive oil and lemon dressing. 'And with this wine, it's all heavenly.'

'Fabulous,' Claudia agreed. She paused, holding her fork up. 'So, you were saying?'

'Oh, nothing,' Maddy mumbled. 'My little problems aren't that important.'

'They are to you. I have a feeling you're the kind of woman who wants to please everyone even if it makes you miserable in the end. You have to stop that. You're too old to play the doormat.'

'I'm not old,' Maddy protested. 'I'm forty-four. He's ten years older.'

Claudia nodded. 'That's what I mean. You're at a very important crossroad. If you take the wrong path, you'll end up where you were before.'

Maddy looked at Claudia thoughtfully. 'You know what? You might be right.'

'I am,' she stated in a tone that didn't allow argument. 'Without knowing the details, I feel the only way forward is to give him your terms and stick to them. Make him fight for you. Don't just say yes to everything. If he's worth keeping, he'll respect you for it. Nobody likes a martyr, you know.'

'That's a good point.'

'Just one more thing before we get back to the delights of this meal: the mountains in Provence are freezing in the winter.' Claudia shivered. 'It can be like Siberia for over a month. Paradise in summer, yes. But a freezing hell in winter. Just give your Scandinavian hunk that thought, okay?'

Maddy frowned. 'Oh my God, I never thought of that. You're right. It was so warm and sunshiny when I was there. I forgot that there must be a winter. And a cold one so high up. Thank you, Claudia, for that piece of advice. And for the rest. You've given me a lot to think about.'

'Glad to help,' Claudia chortled. She raised her glass. 'To men. What would they do without us?'

Maddy laughed and clinked glasses with Claudia. What a hoot she was. And how wise. While they continued eating and chatting, Maddy started to compose a message to Erik in her head. Following Claudia's advice would really make him sit up. But how would he take it? And was she ready to risk this new chance of love?

Claudia looked at Maddy as if she could read her thoughts. 'Go for it,' she urged. 'Save the rest of your life.'

Chapter Twenty-Eight

The tiny restaurant, tucked into a wall in a narrow lane in the Old Town, had a rustic charm to it. Wooden tables covered in red and white checked tablecloths were crammed together in the vaulted room that Tony said had been a bakery centuries ago. Now it was a candle-lit Italian restaurant that smelled of garlic and oregano.

'Is this okay?' Tony said as he pulled out a chair for Leanne.

'It's lovely.' She sat down and placed the white napkin in her lap. 'So Italian. Even with the straw-covered Chianti bottle with a candle in it. Like in a nineteen fifties movie.'

'I know. A bit cheesy, but I'm told the food is really good. And really Italian, very authentic.'

'In Croatia,' Leanne remarked.

'I know. But I was feeling homesick.'

'*Buona sera,*' a waiter interrupted, lighting the candle and handing them menus. He then placed a carafe of water and a basket of fresh bread on the table, smiled, winked at Leanne and left.

Tony laughed. 'See? Very Italian, even a flirty waiter.' He looked at her with a glint in his eyes she hadn't seen before. 'You look gorgeous tonight. New dress?'

'Kind of.' Leanne blushed and smoothed the short skirt of her black dress. 'I bought it in Nice before we left.'

'Black suits you.'

'Thank you.' Leanne smiled and nibbled on a piece of bread. 'And thanks for asking me out tonight. I didn't feel like spending the evening with anyone else.'

'Especially Carlo?' Tony asked casually.

Leanne looked away. 'Yeah. Especially him.' She looked back at Tony. 'Oh, I know I was a compete eejit over him. But it was a flash in the pan really. A bit of madness in the moonlight. Nothing happened. Not that I didn't want it to at that moment, but it was just... I was... Oh, God.' She felt her eyes sting and before she could stop it a single tear escaped and rolled down her cheek. 'Shit.' She fanned her face. 'I'm sorry. I don't want it to ruin this thing between us.'

Tony smiled and brushed the tear away with his finger. 'Shh. Don't be sad. It's okay. You don't have to tell me anything. You drank too much wine and you got carried away and thought he felt something else for you.' He stopped. 'Is that what happened?'

Leanne nodded. 'Yes,' she whispered. 'We were on the boat and—'

'I know,' Tony interrupted. 'I found your knickers in the couch the next day. Do you want them back?'

'No. Throw them away,' Leanne replied, going bright red.

He nodded, looking pleased. 'So then we can forget it and move on?'

Leanne laughed, feeling better already. 'Oh, yes. Absolutely.' She picked up the menu. 'We'd better order. The waiter is hovering.'

'What do you want to eat?' Tony asked from behind the menu. 'Pizza? Or something else?'

'How about the aubergine and mozzarella bake? Never had that.'

'It's like a lasagne without the pasta or meat. Really nice.'

'Let's try that. And a salad?'

'Great choice. And a bottle of Chianti. Or –' Tony smirked '– maybe some of that Croatian wine? A guy could get lucky.'

Leanne stuck her tongue out at him. 'Ha ha, very funny.' Then she couldn't help laughing. 'Okay, that was funny.' She looked at Tony, and before she could stop herself, it all came out in a long stream. 'You know what? The whole thing was ridiculous. There we were, going at it like rabbits and then I said I was falling in love with him even though I didn't really mean it and he just collapsed like a pricked balloon.' She giggled and put her hand over her mouth. 'Shit, now you know the whole story. Sorry,' she said looking at his inscrutable face. 'A typical case of TMI. Feck it, me and my big mouth. Maybe I should just go?'

Tony's mouth quivered. 'And leave me here looking stupid? Come on, Leanne, don't feel bad. I'm glad you told me. And now, can we really, really forget it?'

'Oh yes, please,' Leanne sighed, feeling a flood of relief wash over her. She had told him everything and it didn't seem to matter.

'These things happen,' he soothed. 'Do you think my love life hasn't been full of mishaps?'

'Uh, I have no idea. I thought maybe you were this cool, intellectual who never put a foot wrong.'

'Ha, my foot has been in my mouth many a time. I can tell you worse things than your little fling. But let's not go there, okay? We're here now and the past is the past. Let's keep it that way.'

'Good idea,' Leanne said. 'And now I'm starving, so please feed me.'

The waiter approached and Tony placed their order. Then he turned back to Leanne and put his hand on hers. 'But enough about that. Here we are, in this romantic place… Let's talk about us.'

Leanne looked at their hands. Hers, small and brown, and his freckly, fair-skinned one. He had nice hands, with the long fingers of a pianist – or surgeon. Gentle, healing hands. She looked at his sweet face, the glasses slightly askew, his unruly red hair and his honest hazel eyes. 'Us,' she said. 'Yes, let's talk. Starting with you. What will you do now? I mean when this holiday is over?'

He didn't move his hand but gripped hers a little harder. 'I told you I want to go to Ireland and qualify to be a paediatrician. And now I've just got an email from the secretary of one of the top paediatricians in Dublin that he will have me on his team. It won't be easy, fitting in studying with hospital, but I'm looking forward to it. Then I want to work towards a better health care especially for children across the country. Maybe start a campaign to build paediatric emergency clinics in remote rural areas. But that's a long way off.'

Leanne couldn't help admiring him. 'Sounds amazing. Hard work, but I have a feeling you thrive on that.'

'I'm a bit of a workaholic all right.'

Their food arrived and they were momentarily distracted by the delicious aroma of tomatoes, herbs and garlic.

Tony picked up his fork, still holding Leanne's hand. 'Do you think we can eat like this? Holding hands and talking and eating at the same time?'

'Of course,' Leanne replied, not wanting to let go of the feel of his warm hand on hers.

Tony laughed. 'We're nuts. But I like being nuts with you.'

'Me too.' Leanne smiled and took a bite of the aubergine bake, with its rich tomato sauce where garlic and herbs mingled in a delicious mix of flavours.

'Your turn,' Tony said when he had taken a few bites and drunk a little more wine. 'What do you want to do next?'

Leanne put down her fork and thought for a moment. 'You know, I haven't thought much about that until now. It was all about planning for the holiday, leasing the car, driving through Europe, doing the blog, spending the money, getting away from my mam, finding my dad and, ahem, meeting sexy men.' She blushed. 'The last bit wasn't so clever, but I thought it might be fun. Until now.'

'When you're sitting here with a not-so-sexy man who wants to know your plans for the future?' Tony removed his hand.

'No!' Leanne grabbed his hand again. 'Now I'm with an interesting, attractive man I want to know better. And who I want to spend more time with. With whom, I mean.' She stopped and blushed. 'You know what I mean.'

He smiled and touched her cheek. 'Yes. I was only teasing you. But go on.'

Leanne took another bite of the aubergine bake. 'Okay. What I want to do next is… Go back to Ireland. Buy a flat and move out of my mam's house. Then go back to teach science at St Concepta's for the next year and then – who knows? I've actually been thinking about the blog and how much I love writing. I might see if I can keep doing that and turn it into something bigger. Just an idea, but…'

'A very good one. I like it. Especially the bit about being in Dublin. Then we can keep seeing each other.' He paused, cleaning his plate with a piece of bread. 'What about your dad and his company? Didn't I hear you say something about taking over from him eventually?'

Leanne shrugged. 'Oh, that. I haven't thought much about it until now. And I don't need to because I'm quite sure. I don't want to take over from him. Then I'd have him breathing down my neck even though he says he'll go native and live like a hippie with Maddy in the mountains. Because he won't want to let go completely. It's his business, and I feel like I need to do my own thing. In addition it would scare me rigid, to be honest. Especially as I'm lousy at maths and accounts and anything to do with big money.'

'And your mother? I know this is none of my business, but are you going to tell her about your reunion with your dad? And confront her about how she kept him from keeping in touch with you?'

She stared at him. 'How did you know about that?'

'Maddy told me a little bit about it.'

'Oh. I see.' Leanne nodded. 'Yes. I'm going to have a serious chat with her when I get back. We need to talk about it. Don't know how she'll react but I'm guessing she'll be upset. But we need closure on all of it.' She sighed. 'Anyway, I don't even want to think about that right now. I just want to enjoy the rest of the holiday.'

'Me too.' Tony hesitated. 'I have an idea for the trip back to Trogir.'

'Yes?' Leanne looked at him, noticing he looked a little nervous.

'I… well… this is just a suggestion, but I was wondering if you'd like to sail back with me rather than going back on the yacht? Carlo and Lucilla seem to be reconciling and will probably share her cabin on the yacht, which might make it awkward for you.'

'Sail back with you?' Leanne felt a dart of sheer joy at the thought. Sailing with Tony in that fabulous boat through that wonderful archipelago. Heaven. 'It would be lovely,' she said, trying not to sound too eager. 'But I'll have to clear that with Maddy. She and I are a team, so…'

'Yeah, but you're not like Siamese twins, are you?' Tony remarked.

'Of course not. I'm sure she'll say it's fine. But then there's Bridget. I feel she's very attached to me so…'

'Why can't she come with us? She's a lovely little thing.'

'Oh.' Leanne couldn't think of more obstacles. 'Then in that case…' She felt her face break into a happy grin. 'I'd love to come sailing with you, Dr O'Grady.'

Tony winked. 'Welcome aboard, Miss Sandvik.' He looked around for the waiter. 'Now I suggest we get out of here and get an ice cream from the stand nearby for dessert. Then I'll escort madam back to her quarters before I retire to my cabin on the boat.'

'The boat? I thought you were staying at the hotel?'

He sighed. 'Ah, no. My budget doesn't stretch to five-star accommodation, I'm afraid. I like sleeping on boats in any case. The gentle rocking and the clucking of the water against the hull is very soporific.'

Leanne nodded. 'Yeah. It makes you go to sleep as well.' She winked. 'Thought I didn't know big words, did you?'

Tony laughed. 'You're a scream, Miss Sandvik.'

'Ah sure, I try me best to entertain.'

After paying the bill and leaving the restaurant, they walked to the ice cream stand, where they bought two cones of coconut and chocolate ice cream topped with whipped cream. Licking the delicious concoction, they continued hand-in-hand down the street, looking into shop windows, peering at the beautiful old buildings and talking until they reached the bus stop.

Leanne chewed on the last of her cone. 'Lovely evening. Thank you, Tony. I can take the bus from here back to the hotel. No need to go out of your way.'

Tony pulled her close. 'Your way is my way. Oh, and you have ice cream on your nose.'

'Lick it off,' she ordered.

With a cheeky grin, he did as Leanne commanded. 'Nice flavour.' He held her tight. 'I don't want to let you go.'

Leanne put both her arms around him and hugged him tighter. 'I know. I want to stay like this.' She breathed in his clean scent and closed her eyes, enjoying the sense of security and peace she felt with him. 'Do you want to come with me to the hotel?' she whispered into his chest. 'I'll show you a five-star bedroom. It has amazing views of the sea.'

'I have a better idea.' Tony stepped away and looked into her eyes in the dim lamplight. 'How about coming with me to the boat?'

'Oh, I...'

'I have a couple of cans of Guinness and a bag of crisps. And –' he stepped closer '– I'll fry sausages for breakfast,' he whispered into her ear.

Leanne closed her eyes and smiled. 'Ohhh. Guinness, crisps and sausages. How can a girl resist?'

'Is that a yes?'

Leanne laughed. 'It's a what the hell are we waiting for?'

'Perfect. And there's a cab.' Tony raised his arm, yelling: 'Taxi!'

The car came to a screeching halt and they jumped in, laughing and holding hands until they arrived at the marina. Tony paid the taxi fare and they got out and wandered along the deserted jetty in the moonlight until they reached the boat. Leanne looked up at the glistening moon and breathed in the cool, clean air. 'It's so close you could nearly touch it.'

'Beautiful night,' Tony said grabbing the rope and pulling the boat in. He took off his shoes and jumped aboard. Leanne removed her sandals and followed him onto the cool deck.

He took her hand. 'Come on. It's late. We need to rest.'

Leanne hesitated. It was odd being with him in the same space where she and Carlo… She pushed the memory away. No. This was real. This was Tony. A true-blue, she felt. Someone who'd never let her down. Someone she might even be able to love at some stage and who would love her back. Except this love wouldn't have to be earned – it would just be there, waiting for her, like a big, warm beating heart. She followed him into the boat, nerves racing through her, into his cabin where they lay down together. They looked into each other's eyes and knew it was the start of something special.

Chapter Twenty-Nine

Later that night, Maddy arranged to have a Skype conversation with Erik. Having struggled with several drafts of a reply to his earlier email, she gave up, realising that she had to see him and talk to him directly. This was too important to cram into a written message. It would decide their future together – if they had one. What Claudia had said still echoed through her mind and she knew she had to make Erik see her point of view.

She logged into Skype and waited for Erik to come online, her heart racing. She clicked on his number and heard the ringtone, then he came into view.

'Hello, Maddy,' he said and smiled that broad smile she remembered so well. 'How wonderful to see you.' He peered at her. 'You look beautiful from here. Very tanned. Are you having fun?'

'Oh yes,' she replied and shot him a cheery smile. 'It's been an amazing trip. And now we're in Dubrovnik. Such a heavenly place. I'd love to come back here with you sometime. You'd love it.'

'Good idea. Maybe next year? When we're together for good.'

'That'd be fabulous. And how are you?'

'I've been working hard up at the farm. Things are falling into place. The planning permission has gone through and I've been looking into the olive production and planted some more trees. Can't wait to show you when you come back.' He paused. 'Oh, by the way, have you had that talk with Leanne?'

Maddy squirmed. 'Uh, no. I…' She hesitated, wondering how to put it. Then Claudia's words echoed through her head. *Save the rest of your life.* She took a deep breath. 'I haven't talked to her because I didn't feel it was my place. Your relationship with Leanne is your affair. If she says she doesn't want to take over your firm, then you should respect that. And I don't want you to use me to try to make her change her mind.'

Erik's face had taken on a stony expression. 'I see,' he said. 'Okay. Fair enough. I just thought you'd help me get the point across to Leanne. But if that isn't okay with you, I'll talk to her myself.'

'Good. Thank you. But that's not all I wanted to say to you.'

He nodded. 'I thought so. Please go on.' His blue-green eyes were suddenly serious and Maddy felt a wave of panic. Maybe she shouldn't say anything about her misgivings. Hadn't she annoyed him enough? But a little voice inside her told her she had to go on. She couldn't keep humouring him at the expense of her own future happiness.

'Okay.' She folded her hands in her lap. 'It's about your plans for the farm and your dream of moving to the mountains. The thing is, I'm not sure I can do that.'

'Do what?' he enquired politely.

'I can't shut myself away from everything for the rest of my life,' Maddy exclaimed, exasperated. 'You keep going on about what you want to do, how much you love that old place and how you can't wait to move there with me. It's all about *you*. Have you ever stopped to think how I'm going to fit into all of that?'

'I thought we'd discussed that,' Erik said with a hint of annoyance. 'You'll go back to Ireland for that final year with your students and to sort out your divorce and then you'll be free to join me. Wasn't that what we agreed?'

'No!' Maddy exclaimed. 'That's what *you* told me I should do. I never said it was set in stone.'

Erik blinked. 'Oh? Forgive me for misunderstanding when you said you couldn't wait to live in that gorgeous place and how you simply knew we were meant to be together.'

Maddy squirmed. 'Oh, eh… yeah, I might have said that when I was feeling romantic and I had been drinking wine and I missed you so much. But…' She wrung her hands. 'Oh, feck it, you make me feel so confused.'

Erik stared at her. 'I would truly appreciate it if you could get it all off your chest right now. You seem to find it difficult to be honest with me.'

Maddy looked at him, her heart drumming. 'Yes, you're right. I do find it difficult. I'm not sure I can shut myself away in the back of beyond. A lovely back of beyond in the summer but what about the rest of the year? I believe it gets very cold there in the winter months and that you can even get snowed in sometimes.' Once she had started, the words came tumbling out of her mouth in a torrent. 'You seem to forget that I'm a woman and that I like going out to dinner, and shopping and visiting museums. I also love to swim in the sea and sit in a café and watch the world go by. And I have two children I'd like to see sometimes, friends in Ireland I want to keep in touch with and also a lovely new friend I've just met who lives in Florence and…' She stopped. 'I'd like to have a bit of fun from time to time now that I'm free to make my own choices. After so many years, I want to… feel young again.' Maddy drew breath and suddenly burst into tears. 'And I want you too, so much, Erik,' she sobbed. 'But I can't give up my whole life for you.'

Erik looked at her coldly. 'Oh,' he said. 'I see. That puts a completely new complexion on everything.'

Maddy's shoulders slumped. 'I suppose it does.' They looked at each other through cyberspace, each struggling with their own emotions until Maddy couldn't bear it any more. 'I'm sorry if I upset you. Goodbye, Erik,' she sobbed, switching off her laptop.

Still drunk on wine, romance and sex, Leanne arrived back at the hotel in the early hours of the morning. The sun was rising over the mountains in the east when she tiptoed down the corridor. She was just about to slide into her room, when Maddy's door swung opened and she peered out, Bridget in her arms.

She did a double take when she saw Leanne. 'You've been out all night?'

Leanne smiled. 'Yes. Wonderful night. Can't tell you about it right now, but it was…' She yawned. 'God, I need to sleep. Sorry. Later…' She went into her room and closed the door on Maddy, who was standing there looking like she hadn't slept either. It suddenly hit Leanne how awful her friend looked and she opened the door a crack. 'Are you okay? You look a little pale around the gills. Tummy bug or something?'

'No. Something else.' Maddy let Bridget down. 'Long story. I'll tell you at breakfast. Must take Bridget out for a bit.' She walked down the corridor, pulling at an unwilling Bridget, who seemed to want to get back to Leanne.

Leanne watched her go, wondering what on earth had happened. Maddy's obvious distress removed some of the gloss of her own new-found happiness, but not for long. She took off her dress and slid between the cool sheets, unwrapping the chocolate the maid had put on her pillow the night before. Lying there, she went over the evening in her head again from when she and Tony had held hands and talked, followed by the walk through the Old Town and the ice cream and the taxi ride and the boat... Oh what a night it had been. And how right it had felt to make love with Tony and then lie there afterwards talking, before doing it again and then sleeping and waking up, eating sausages at sunrise and kissing, laughing, and not wanting to say goodbye. They had only known each other for a short time and they hadn't clicked immediately, but they had found each other during that sailing trip and now she felt such a strong connection to him she knew wouldn't be broken. *It's all about trust*, she thought, unable to ignore the feeling they were meant to be together. All this was so new and so precious she was afraid to share it with someone else, in case it shattered the dream. Of course she'd have to tell Maddy at least. Soon. But right now, it was her own lovely secret, hers and Tony's. She fell asleep with a silly smile on her face.

Chapter Thirty

When Maddy returned from her walk, she felt there was no point going to her room and trying to sleep. She knew she couldn't. She headed for the terrace and the breakfast buffet in order to drown her sorrows with coffee and pastries. She had lost Erik. She didn't have to worry about her weight any more. She loaded a plate with two mini croissants, a raisin bun and a big Danish and sat down at a table near the end of the terrace, as far away as possible from the other guests.

'Maddy!' Claudia called from across the terrace. 'May I join you?'

Maddy smiled and nodded. 'Please do. I'll order coffee and orange juice for two. Go get some yummy buns and sit down here.'

Claudia eyed the array on Maddy's plate. 'So it didn't go so well, did it?'

'How do you know?'

Claudia gestured at Maddy's plate. 'I can tell by the mountain of carbs. Comfort food?'

Maddy nodded. 'Something like that.'

'You want to tell me what happened?'

'Okay.' Maddy didn't really feel like company, but Claudia would provide a good shoulder to cry on. She'd understand like nobody else.

But Claudia offered no comfort. 'He couldn't accept your wish to be independent?' she snorted when Maddy had finished telling her. 'Then he's not worth it. Save your tears, honey. With your looks and charm, you'll meet someone a lot better in no time. Come with me to Florence and stay for a week or two, why don't you? You can help me do up my apartment. We can raid the lovely furniture and interior design stores in Florence. And we'll shop for clothes and shoes and go to glamorous parties. There are plenty of attractive men in my circle of friends. They'll love you.'

'Oh, I don't know,' Maddy sighed. 'I think I'll just go back with Leanne. She'd be upset if I said I wanted to do something without her.'

'You're not joined at the hip, are you? I'm sure she won't mind. In any case, I have a feeling she has plans to be with someone else...'

Maddy sat up. 'Who?'

Claudia winked. 'I'm not going to tell tales. I'm not even sure I'm right. But I have a feeling...'

Maddy frowned. 'Please don't tell me she's taken up with Carlo again? I think he's big trouble.'

'She's an adult,' Claudia remarked. 'Let her make her own mistakes. Otherwise she won't learn anything.'

'But what if she doesn't learn? What is she's a rigid as her father?'

'Then she's a lost cause. She'll end up like him. Alone.'

Maddy's eyes stung with tears. 'That's awful.'

Claudia's eyes softened. She put her hand on Maddy's arm. 'I know you're upset about breaking up with him. But believe me, he would have ended up making you miserable. Come with me to Florence. It'll cheer us both up. I like you a lot, you know. I think we could be very good friends.'

Maddy smiled. 'You're very kind, Claudia. I think I'll take you up on that. But I have to sort things out with Leanne first. We went on this adventure together and she might be upset if I just bail out on her like this.'

'Of course. I understand. You have to do what's right. And if you don't come with me to Florence now, you can visit me anytime.' Claudia turned her attention to her breakfast. 'So let's try to enjoy this marvellous place and the fabulous food. And then we'll go and explore the Old Town together. So much to see here, you know.'

Maddy sighed and nodded. 'I know. This town is packed with history. I'm going to take photos and get as many books and brochures as I can for my students. I teach history as well as French, you see.'

'Must be nice,' Claudia said politely.

'I love teaching young people. It's a challenge to make it interesting enough for them to want to learn. The class I'm teaching now is lovely. A small class of only twenty girls that are very keen—' Maddy stopped when her phoned pinged. A text from Leanne saying she had something to share and she would wait at the beach café below the hotel. *Please don't scream when I tell you*, the message ended.

Maddy stared at the message. Oh God, now she'd have to tell Leanne what she thought of her going back to Carlo. They had probably had a night of hot sex and Leanne would have stars in her eyes and say she'd been wrong about him. Maddy got up. 'I have to go. Leanne wants to see me.'

Claudia raised an eyebrow. 'Oh? Maybe she'll give you the details of her romance.'

'Maybe. I don't know what to say to her.' Maddy sighed. 'Could you keep an eye on Bridget for me while I go and sort this out? She's asleep under the table.'

Claudia glanced at the little furry bundle at her feet. 'Oh so that's what it is. Of course, darling. I'll look after her. You can come and collect her when you and Leanne have sorted it out. I hope you'll be telling me you'll fly to Florence with me in the morning.'

'We'll see,' Maddy said as she left the terrace, not looking forward to her confrontation with Leanne. But she had to speak her mind. Leanne needed to see that Carlo was very wrong for her. And the other thing, much worse, was to break the news that she and Erik had ended their brief romance. What a roller coaster her life had become.

Leanne sat at a table in the shade outside the beach café drinking iced coffee while she waited. She had slept for several hours and woken up feeling refreshed and happy. Then she'd had a swim and a long think. It was time to break the news about her and Tony, while the afterglow of their night together was still fresh in her mind.

What was it about Tony that was so different from other men she had dated? she wondered. His whole attitude to women for a start. When he looked at her it wasn't just flirtatious but with true interest in her and who she was and what was on her mind. But then, when they touched and kissed, it was a whole other matter. It made Leanne hot just thinking about it. When Maddy arrived she greeted her with a cheery, 'Hi! Lovely day isn't it?'

Maddy came to a stop in the sand, glaring at Leanne. 'Lovely? Well you certainly seem to think so, after a wild night with that gobshite. But I have to tell you before you go on that I think you're making a huge mistake. That guy is so wrong for you and he'll end up breaking your heart. I told you so before, so don't come crying to me when it all goes apeshit and he leaves you for some other—'

Leanne blinked. 'What are you going on about? How do you know what I was doing last night?'

'A little bird told me. I know you won't listen to me. You're just as rigid as your dad and you'll end up just like him; all alone and bitter.'

Leanne stared at Maddy as if she was deranged. 'Are you feeling all right? You seem to have lost your marbles completely.' Her eyes narrowed. 'Have you and dad had a fight?'

'We broke up, if you must know,' Maddy said, her voice hoarse. 'And it's probably my fault, but I had to tell him that I couldn't let him take over my life.'

'You told him all that? Wow.' Leanne was impressed. Maddy had finally flipped and told her father where to get off, something that nobody else had dared to do – not even her, his own daughter. 'How did he react?'

Maddy shrugged, her head bowed. 'He got all cold and silent on me. I hung up in the middle of our Skype call. He didn't call me back. It's over.'

'I'm so sorry,' Leanne said, getting up to give Maddy a hug. 'What a pity. I thought you were so good together.'

Maddy pulled back. 'Well, it's all over, so no use talking about it.'

Leanne sat down again. 'I suppose not.' She pulled out the chair beside her. 'Hey, sit down. Have a coffee.'

Maddy sat down on the edge of the chair. 'No thanks. I had breakfast with Claudia just now.'

'Oh. Okay.' Leanne paused. 'What you just said… That rant about me and some… gobshite, I mean. I think you got it all wrong.'

Maddy looked at her coldly. 'No, you did. How could you take up with him again after what happened that night?'

Leanne jumped up so fast her chair tipped over. 'Will you shut up for just a moment okay?' She lifted the chair back up. 'Please just listen if you can manage that.'

Maddy looked sullenly back at Leanne. 'Okay. This'd better be good.'

'It is.' Leanne stood over Maddy, her arms folded. 'I wasn't with Carlo. I was with Tony. We had a date for dinner, and then… things just kinda happened and—'

'What?' Maddy gasped, her eyes widening. 'You were with – TONY?'

'Yes. No need to shout. I thought, with your astute antennae, you might have picked up the vibes between us… They've been there for a while, you know, only I didn't see it. I think it was on the ferry when he was looking after everyone that I discovered what a kind heart he has. I was so blinded by my stupid infatuation with Carlo but it slowly dawned on me. And when we went out sailing just the two of us, we connected in a way I can't describe. It just happened.' Leanne couldn't help letting out the buzz of happiness and her face broke into a wide smile. 'I think I'm in love. Really, truly, madly. I don't care how little time we've known each other for or how long this will last but I just adore him. I've never felt like this in my whole life, not even when the captain of the rugby team at Trinity asked me for a date.'

'Or when Carlo was all over you that night before—'

Leanne snorted. 'You had to bring that up, didn't you? No, Carlo never made me feel like this. With Tony, it's deep down in my *soul*. Sounds mad, I know, but…'

'No,' Maddy mumbled, looking down at her feet. 'I know what you mean. That's how I felt about Erik.'

Leanne sank down beside Maddy. 'Oh, Mads, I'm so sorry. Maybe you'll get back together again?'

'No. Don't think so. Not after what I said. His silence said it all.'

Leanne sighed. 'That's sad. For both of you. But most of all for him.'

Maddy patted Leanne's arm. 'Thank you. But now about you and Tony. I would never in my wildest dreams have imagined you with him.'

'Why? Oh, I know, he does look a little nerdy at first. And forbidding, the way he studies people and seems to be able to see into their minds. He's serious but he has a great sense of humour too. And he's so romantic. He got up early this morning and cooked sausages for me and then he played a beautiful Irish love song on the tin whistle. You have no idea how amazing it was to sit there on the deck and look over the still water and the boats and the islands while he played that gentle, lilting music.' Leanne sighed deeply. 'He has such depth and soul.'

'I can see that.' Maddy smiled. 'You look so happy. As if you've landed somewhere nice and safe. That cheers me up.'

'Oh, that's good.' Leanne got up. 'But there's something else. We have another day here and then…' She paused. 'I hope you won't take this wrong, but Tony wants me to sail back with him to Trogir tomorrow. Is that okay with you?'

'Oh. Of course. But what about Carlo?'

'He and Lucilla will be on the yacht. They've decided to get back together. Again.'

'I see.'

Maddy's sad face made Leanne feel guilty. 'Please don't be upset. I know we should be doing this trip together to the end, but now…'

Maddy nodded. 'It's okay. I had made other plans in any case. Claudia has asked me to fly back to Florence with her and stay for a week or two. I thought it sounded fun and just what I need after…'

Leanne laughed. 'Brilliant! And here I was agonising about how to break it to you.'

Maddy smiled. 'And I was worried you'd be upset.'

'But there's one person we haven't considered – Bridget.'

Maddy sighed. 'I know. I'd take her, but it'd be a little complicated to get her on a plane.'

'Well, we want her!' Leanne exclaimed. 'I was going to ask if you'd be able to bear parting with her. Tony adores her and she's so used to boats now. She'll love being with us.'

Maddy let out a sigh. 'Oh, that's wonderful.'

'And I'll continue the blog and wind it up during the sailing trip back. Everything's solved, then,' Leanne said happily.

'Except my love life,' Maddy said glumly. 'I don't think I'll get over that. Ever.'

Leanne put her arm around her friend. 'I know. But if he let you go that easily, he doesn't deserve you. I know he's my dad, but I'm disappointed in him.'

'So am I,' Maddy whispered, wiping away a tear. 'But life goes on. I'll just have to try to get over it.'

'With Claudia in charge, I think you'll soon be thinking of other things,' Leanne remarked. 'Talk about a party princess. She won't give you a chance to mope.'

Maddy got up. 'You're right. Come on, let's get this new chapter started.'

'That's the spirit,' Leanne laughed. 'Don't let men crush you.'

'Never,' Maddy declared with fire in her eyes.

Chapter Thirty-One

After a day's sightseeing with Claudia, Maddy returned to her room to put up her aching feet and rest her stiff back. Hours of walking on the cobblestones in the ancient city, visiting churches and museums had helped her turn her mind away from her sorrow. And how could this city not blow her mind, with its stunning architecture and history oozing out of every stone? She found Dubrovnik to be a friendly, open-hearted town, where every narrow street opened up to the glittering sea and the horizon beyond. It had been fun to browse in the little shops full of quaint crafts and cute trinkets. But now, exhausted, as she lay on her bed with the French windows open to let in the cool evening breeze, she felt the pain in her heart return with full force. She tried to think about all the interesting sites, the history, the artefacts that she would share with her students when the new school year started in September. She'd put the photos and brochures together into a slideshow. That'd be a good start to the term. Hopefully, by then, she'd have put the hurt of the break-up behind her and started to move on, building a new life for herself.

She felt her eyes close and drifted off for a moment, the knock on her door not quite registering until it rose to an insistent crescendo.

She sat up. 'Leanne, please go away. I want to rest for a while,' she called. But the knocking continued.

Maddy slowly got up. 'Okay, I'm coming,' she grumbled. 'Stop that racket.' Irritated and sleepy, she pulled the door open. 'What do you want?' she snapped at the tall figure. It took her a second before she registered who it was. She gasped and felt her knees wobble. 'Erik?' she whispered.

'Yes.' He looked at her for an instant before he came inside, letting the door slam behind him. 'It's me.'

She stepped back, staring at him. 'What... I mean how...?'

'By plane. Two planes, actually,' he said. 'I had to fly to Rome and change planes there.'

She suddenly noticed his pale face and the bags under his eyes. 'You look wrecked.'

He pinched the bridge of his nose. 'I haven't slept since... well, since you hung up on me yesterday. And then I had to get here as fast as I could. I didn't even bring as much as a toothbrush.'

'Oh.' She didn't know what to say. He looked worn out. His crumpled white shirt and creased jeans were far from his usual cool elegance. 'But... why?' Her legs weak, she sat down on the couch by the window.

'I...' he started. 'So much to say. May I sit down beside you?'

'Of course.' She shifted over to the other side of the couch.

He sat down beside her and took her hand. 'Maddy, why did you just hang up like that? Why didn't you give me a chance to respond?'

She shrugged. 'I knew what you would say. I knew you wouldn't want to change your plans for anyone.'

'But you're not anyone. You're *you*, Maddy, the woman I love.'

'Yes, but you looked so cold and angry. I thought…'

'I was just a little shaken up. You made me realise there had to be two people in this, two points of view and that we'd have to meet somewhere in the middle. Until then it was all me, me, me and that was wrong, I realise now. It was a hell of a wake-up call for me.'

'Oh.' She stared at him not knowing quite what to say. She hadn't expected this at all. 'Maybe I should have told you all this from the start.'

'Maybe you should have. But better late than never.' He took her other hand and kissed it. 'You know, when you got all uppity and angry yesterday, I think that was the moment I truly fell in love with you. I wished we could have been together in real life so we could have a rip-roaring row, throw things at each other and then fall into bed and make love. I'm not used to people saying no and I loved that.'

Maddy smiled. 'That's mad.'

He laughed. 'Isn't it? Totally mad. And that's what I want us to be. We have to dare get angry and lose it with each other and be honest and never hide our feelings, if we're to continue this… this thing we have.' He took her in his arms. 'Please listen. I know you and everyone else will think it's crazy to talk of love so soon. But at my age, it begins to dawn on you how very short life is and that you have to grasp every chance of happiness. Carpe diem, as the saying goes. And I intend to carpe the hell out of every diem I have left. With you.'

'Oh, Erik,' Maddy whispered, tears welling up in her eyes. 'That makes me so happy.'

He squeezed her tighter still. 'Is that a yes-I-want-to-make-up? Or…'

She pressed her face to his chest, breathing in the special lemon and verbena scent, so unique to him 'It's yes,' she mumbled. 'But only if we – you – can budge a little to suit us both.' She looked up at him. 'Can you?'

'I can, sweetheart. I haven't told you this yet, but I also had a little chat with Leanne on the phone just now, during which she gave me hell for being so rigid and for risking losing you by being selfish. She hung up on me too. But she sounded weirdly happy.'

'Ah, that'll be to do with the man in her life.'

'A man?'

'You'll love him. Responsible, kind, considerate.'

He pulled away and looked at her. 'Is it Carlo you're talking about?'

'No. Carlo and she… didn't quite click in the end. I'm talking about Tony. Lucilla's cousin. A doctor and—' She stopped and laughed. 'I'll let you make your own mind up when you meet him.'

'That doesn't sound like the kind of man I thought Leanne would fancy. Isn't she usually after the wild and free ones?'

'That's what I thought, too. But it appears we're both wrong. I'm very happy for her.'

'In that case, so am I.' He kissed the top of her head. 'Maybe we could discuss this further when I've rested? I don't have a room yet, so maybe you'd let me lie down?'

'Of course.' She got up and went over to the bed, folded the cover down and fluffed up the pillows. She walked to the window and started to close the curtains but he stopped her.

'I want to look at you.' He came closer and slid the straps of her dress off her shoulders, lifting her hair and kissing the back of her neck. 'You're wearing the perfume I made for you.'

His warm lips on her skin made her shiver. 'I wear it every day.'

'Come to bed, will you?'

She turned and put her arms around him while he slid her dress to her waist. She opened his shirt and pressed herself against him, before they took off the rest of their clothes and lay down, kissing, touching and whispering things that couldn't be said out loud. They made love quietly, lovingly, perfectly in tune with each other.

They showered together and then got back into bed and started to talk. Erik told her how he had lain awake all night thinking about what she had said. 'What a fool I must have seemed to you. Arrogant and selfish. I don't blame you for getting angry. And I also realised how silly I've been, thinking the little farm was such a paradise, which it is – in the spring and summer. I spoke to a few locals up there and they confirmed what you said. The winters up there are harsh.' He put a hand to his head. 'What was I thinking?'

She took his hand. 'It was a lovely dream, and it still could be – in the warmer months.'

He rolled over and looked at her. 'Exactly. And this is what I was thinking; we'd lock it up in the autumn and spend the winter at the house in Vence. And we'll go to Nice for shopping and the theatre and concerts. I'm going to appoint an assistant to manage things at the firm when I'm away. But you must come and go as you please and see your children and friends in Ireland. You should really have a little flat in Dublin too.'

Maddy laughed. 'I might. Later. But I think you should slow down. Let's just live for the moment and not plan anything further than Christmas – which I will spend somewhere you won't have thought of. And you can come with me if you like.'

'Christmas? Where?'

'Australia. Perth, to be precise. My daughter lives there and she appears to have a new boyfriend called Chris and I want to meet him.'

'Australia?' Erik said. He ran his finger from her neck all the way down to her stomach. 'Why not? You know my daughter, and now I want to get to know yours. What's her name?'

'Sophie.'

'Nice name. I bet she's a nice girl too. Will she like me?'

'I'm sure she will. If you behave.'

'I'll do my very best.' He closed his eyes. 'And now I think I'll sleep for a bit. Will you wake me up in time for dinner?'

'I will,' she promised, snuggling up to him. Closing her eyes, she wondered if it had all been a dream. She touched his shoulder to reassure herself. It was true and she couldn't be happier.

Chapter Thirty-Two

Early that evening, Tony waited for Leanne on the boat. When she arrived by taxi at the marina, he helped her with her bag while she carried Bridget, who whined and wagged her tail, trying to lick Tony's face.

'She loves you already,' Leanne said.

He patted her head. 'I love her too. As long as she doesn't pee on the boat or chew on the ropes.'

'She won't. She's a lady.'

Tony laughed and helped Leanne on board. 'So what did Maddy say when you told her you'd be going back to Trogir with me?'

'She was completely gobsmacked.' Leanne laughed at the memory. 'She thought I 'd spent the night with Carlo, so she started to rant about how awful he is and how I was making a big mistake that I'd regret for the rest of my life. Then she told me she had broken up with Dad, and that we were one and the same – rigid, selfish and pig-headed, or words to that effect. I finally managed to get a word in and tell her about us, and then she looked like she'd been hit by a brick wall. She'd never imagined in her wildest dreams you and I could fancy each other.'

'Neither did you,' Tony remarked drily. 'Even though I'd been drooling over you ever since you stepped onto that terrace in Florence.'

'You drooled so discreetly.'

'But I was secretly panting for you.'

'And then it happened for me too. When we were out sailing together. And then, when you took my hand in the restaurant, it was like an epiphany.'

Tony burst out laughing. 'You're a delight, my sweet.' He kissed her, jumped into the cockpit and held out his hand. 'Give me Bridget. I have some Guinness in the fridge and I got us some food. The others will be here for a drink and a bite before we head off.'

Leanne handed him the dog and jumped into the cockpit. 'I didn't tell you the rest. Dad arrived earlier and now he and Maddy have made up. They'll be going back to Trogir on the yacht and Claudia's flying to Florence early in the morning. So the yacht will turn into the love boat with two romantic couples on board. Poor old Nico will be the fifth wheel.'

'We should give him ear plugs.'

Leanne rolled her eyes. 'Oh, please. I don't even want to think about it. It's my dad, after all.'

'I know. But parents do have sex lives you know. Mine do. Very loudly. When they're not throwing things at each other. That Irish-Italian passion is wild. I can't wait for you to meet them.' He winked.

'You're having me on.'

'Yes.'

Leanne laughed, but it dawned on her that she had never asked about Tony's family. She knew he had a sister and a brother but not much else. 'You haven't told me much about them,' she said. 'What do they do? And where do they live?'

'My dad's a doctor but now he's retired and writes medical books. My mother is a piano teacher. They live in the hills above Florence. A lovely villa with a huge garden they bought when Dad retired. I'll take you to meet them when we get to Florence.'

'I'd love that,' Leanne said with a happy feeling. He wanted her to meet his family. This was getting serious and she liked it.

'My dad will be delighted to meet you. He's secretly yearning for me to have an Irish girlfriend.'

'What about your mum?' Leanne asked with a pang of nerves.

'She's Claudia's sister and Lucilla's aunt. Very much cut from the same cloth. But she has her own quirks and charms.' Tony suddenly laughed. 'Can't wait to pitch the two of you against each other.'

'Can't be scarier than mine,' Leanne countered. 'I can't wait for you to meet the Irish mammy from hell.'

'There's no way she could be scarier than my mum,' Tony said, putting Bridget down.

'Ha, just you wait.' Leanne grabbed her bag. 'But in the meantime, I'm going to enjoy our sailing trip. Where do I put this?'

'In the smallest cabin. That's where I put all my stuff. We'll sleep in the other, bigger one. More space that way. This isn't a five-star yacht, so you'll have to get used to slumming it.'

'Slumming it?' Leanne laughed as she looked around the small but comfortable saloon with its gleaming mahogany panelling and swish galley. The large cabin she was going to share with Tony had a comfortable double bed, mahogany panelling and a porthole trimmed with brass. This boat was a little gem and she knew they'd be cosy and happy.

The sound of footsteps on the jetty and voices calling them interrupted her thoughts. She stuffed her bag into the small cabin and closed the door just before Erik and Maddy peered into the saloon. Bridget rushed at Maddy, wagging her tail, trying to jump up.

'Hi, Dad,' Leanne exclaimed and gave him a hug. Smiling, she looked up at him. 'You look happy.'

Erik hugged her back. 'Yes. And a little shorter after Maddy cut me down to size.'

Leanne laughed. 'Good for her. So it's all okay between you, then?'

'For the moment,' he said. 'But you never know what the future will bring.'

Leanne stared at him and burst out laughing. 'This is not the dad I remember.'

'Oh, him.' Erik shrugged. 'That old arrogant bastard is gone forever. Meet the new me, all soft and amenable and a real pushover.'

Leanne glanced at Maddy. 'Jesus, what did you do to him?'

Maddy laughed and picked Bridget up. 'I think I scared him when I showed him my claws.'

'But never mind that,' Erik interrupted. 'What about the new man in your life, eh? A doctor and all. Your mother will be so happy.'

Leanne giggled. 'I know. Mam will be beside herself. I'd say she'll even break out the Belleek china that's been in the cupboard since my first communion.'

'Come up here, Leanne,' Tony called from the cockpit. 'The others are here and Claudia has brought champagne and a picnic for us to have later. Get some of the snacks and we'll have a deck party.'

'I'll give you a hand,' Maddy said, handing a wriggling Bridget to Erik. 'Here. You go up on deck and say hi to everyone. Tony will introduce you.'

'Yes, my love,' Erik said and climbed back up to the cockpit.

'What have you done to him?' Leanne asked.

Maddy giggled. 'It's an act. He's pretending to be Mr Nice Guy just to make me laugh.'

Leanne hugged her. 'I'm thrilled to see you two so happy together.'

'And you,' Maddy said, hugging her back. 'Tony looks years younger too. I think he and Erik like each other already.'

Leanne made a funny face. 'Jesus, all this sweetness and light is making me sick. But hey, let's enjoy it while it lasts.' She opened the cupboard and pulled out packets of crisps and nuts and two large jars of olives. 'Let's get these out and join the party. Then we'll be off into the sunset. Literally.'

'You're going to sail in the dark?'

Leanne poured the crisps into a wooden bowl. 'Yes. We're going to navigate by the stars. Tony's done it before. Can't wait to experience it.'

'Sounds incredible.' Maddy opened the jars of olives and started up the steps, Leanne following.

Up on deck, Claudia was holding court and serving champagne in paper cups. 'Not quite correct but I've learned to compromise during the trip. I've even done some housework,' she said, looking proud of herself.

'That was very brave of you,' Lucilla said with a laugh.

'Thank you. It's a farewell party until we meet again,' Claudia announced. 'Leanne and Maddy, grab a cup and I'll pour you some champagne.'

Leanne put the bowls down on a small table and picked up a cup. She smiled at Lucilla standing beside Claudia. 'Hi, Lucilla.'

Lucilla smiled back with surprising warmth. 'Hello, Leanne.'

'Sorry about the outburst earlier.'

Lucilla shrugged. 'No problem. You were right anyway. We're working on something different for the client. They were delighted with the way you kickstarted their campaign. It'll go very well now, I think. They have nearly more orders than they can cope with. They said you can keep any of the clothes you modelled and they'll give you a cut of the profit of the sales of the summer collection.'

Leanne relaxed. 'Oh, brilliant. Thank you. I'm donating it all to Doctors Without Borders. And, hey, sorry about acting the bitch.'

Lucilla laughed. 'It was hot and we were all tired. It's okay.'

Leanne looked around. 'Where's Carlo?'

'Back at the hotel. He had some work to do, setting up an Instagram account for Risorse Naturali and a few other things. He said to tell you bon voyage and see you on the ferry in Split for the trip back to Ancona.'

Leanne nodded. 'Oh, okay. Thanks. Tell him I said hi.' She looked at Erik and Maddy. 'How are you getting back to Nice, Dad?'

'We'll be going back to Trogir on the yacht,' Maddy replied. 'Then Erik's catching a flight back to Nice from Split and I'll join you for the ferry trip to Ancona and the drive back to Florence, where we'll pick up our car.'

'Oh?' Claudia cut in. 'So you won't be joining me in Florence?'

'No,' Maddy replied. 'So sorry, should have told you before. I guess I got a bit swept away in all the drama.'

Claudia laughed, waving her hand. 'Don't worry. I saw your… uh… the tall Viking god, and put two and two together.' She beamed at Erik. 'But I hope you will both come and visit me in Florence soon.'

'Thanks,' Maddy replied. 'Of course we will. Right, Erik?'

'It would be a pleasure,' Erik said and bowed to Claudia, who laughed and winked at him.

'Now might be the right time to ask you something.' Leanne sipped some champagne, looking at Maddy over the rim of her cup. 'I was wondering… I mean Tony and I thought…'

'What?' Maddy asked.

Tony stepped next to Leanne and draped an arm around her shoulder. 'How would you feel about another passenger in that amazing car?'

Maddy blinked. 'You mean you want to come with us? All the way to Ireland?'

Tony nodded. 'Yes. But if that's not okay with you, I'll get back some other way. I just thought you might like a little company.'

Maddy glanced at Erik. 'I haven't even thought about the trip back to Ireland. I was just looking forward to getting back to Nice. I'd like to stay with Erik until the end of the summer, but…'

Leanne noticed the conflict in her eyes. Maddy obviously wanted to spend more time with Erik, just as she needed to be with Tony. 'We'll sort something out,' she said.

'Hey, cut the dancing around and get to the point,' Claudia interrupted. 'Why don't you fly back from Split to Nice with Erik, Maddy? Spend the rest of the summer there. Then Tony and Leanne can pick up the car from Florence and drive back to Ireland together.'

Tony laughed. 'What would we do without you, Claudia? You sort everyone out better than we do ourselves.'

'But then the big escape will come to an end,' Erik cut in. 'I'm sure that'll be a bit of a wrench for you both.'

Leanne and Maddy looked at each other. Leanne felt a sudden pang of sadness. Was this the end of their adventure, their close friendship and the fun of escaping from their dreary everyday lives? What a long way they had come since that day in June when they had taken off from Maddy's house. Both their lives had changed beyond recognition and now, maybe it was time to part. For the time being anyway. 'I don't know what to say,' Leanne mumbled. 'What do you think, Mads?'

Maddy took Leanne's hand. 'I'll be sad to end our adventure. But it doesn't mean an end to us. Just a slight shift. We can't drive around in a red sports car forever, like the *Flying Dutchman*. We have to finally land and get on with our lives. But it's not the end of our friendship, it's the beginning of the rest of our lives. And we'll always be close. Nothing can change that.'

'No,' Leanne said, enveloping Maddy in a warm hug. 'Nothing can. Thank you for everything and for looking out for me. We'll do as Claudia suggested. It's a brilliant plan.'

'Bravo,' Claudia said and held up a brimming paper cup. 'And now a toast. To love and friendship and new beginnings.'

'Amen,' Tony said, downing his champagne in one go. 'Time to get out of here.'

'Don't forget to take the food I brought for your picnic,' Claudia said, handing Leanne a basket filled with lobster, salads, bread, cheese and a chocolate tart. 'And a bottle of wine. Italian,' she added with a cheeky smile. 'That Croatian wine has a strange effect on people.'

'It sure does.' Leanne took the bag. 'Thank you, Claudia, that's very kind.'

'Thought you might forget about food,' Claudia said with a cheeky grin.

'Spot-on as usual,' Tony laughed. He held up his empty paper cup. 'Cheers to you, Claudia, even if the champagne is all gone. And now, dear friends, the sails are ready, the wind is perfect, the sun is setting and we have to leave. I wish you all a good night. And get the hell off our boat so we can cast off!'

They all laughed, everyone hugging each other and bidding one another farewell. Erik, Maddy, Claudia and Lucilla stepped onto the marina, waving as Tony and Leanne pushed off, setting sail and gliding out to sea in the golden glow of the setting sun.

As the sun slowly sank behind the islands in the west, stars glinted overhead in the deep-blue sky. With night falling, Leanne and Tony made their way with slack winds through the black water, the only sound in the still night the soft clucking of the waves against the hull and the click of the rigging as the sail moved. Leanne looked up and saw the Milky Way stretching across the heavens like a wide, diamond-studded path, its millions of stars glimmering and twinkling against the navy backdrop. Staring up, she suddenly realised how tiny she was and how little her life mattered in the vast space of the universe. 'Less than a speck of dust,' she said softly. 'Our planet is only one of billions in the galaxy. And we are like tiny molecules.'

Tony looked up at the sky from his position at the wheel. 'Very humbling, isn't it?'

'But incredibly spiritual at the same time.'

'Yes, it is. Makes you wonder what it's all about, doesn't it? All our conflicts and wars and arguments. All our plotting and scheming and falling in and out of love. They're but tiny whispers in the universe.'

'Or even less than that.' Leanne sighed and put her sweater across her shoulders, as the night breeze brushed past her. She yawned. 'And now I'm going act like a five-year-old and ask: are we there yet?'

'Funny you should say that. I've just noticed we've almost reached the island where I planned to stop.'

'Thank God for that,' Leanne sighed. 'I'm starving. And sleepy.'

'I'll just check our position.' Tony picked up the sextant he had been using.

Leanne went to stand beside him. 'How do you navigate by the stars?'

Tony pointed at the sky. 'See that constellation?'

'Yes. That's the Little Bear, you told me.'

'Or Ursa Minor. And the brightest of its stars is Polaris, the North Star. You have to determine the angle in degrees between Polaris' position and the northern horizon. The most accurate way to do this is with a sextant, which lets you read the angle off its curved section.'

'Oh,' Leanne said, leaning her head against his shoulder. 'How come you know all this stuff?'

'My dad taught me. We used to sail off the west coast, north of Rome in the summers. We always had clear skies, so it was easy. I loved it.'

'I love it too. It's like we're the only people left on the planet.' Leanne yawned again. 'Sorry,' she said, laughing. 'It's way past my bedtime.'

'We're nearly there.' Tony pointed at a dark shape ahead. 'We'll have a midnight feast and then go to bed. Why don't you go and get the hamper Claudia gave us? I'll drop the anchor when we're in the shelter of the bay.'

'Perfect.' Leanne went below to prepare the picnic. Then she had an idea. When Tony climbed into the saloon, Leanne called him, sitting up in bed holding a glass of wine.

He peered into the cabin and grinned. 'Ah. There you are.'

'How about dinner in bed?' she asked.

'Oh, yes.' Tony sighed and stretched. 'Sounds good to me.' He got undressed, climbing into bed beside her, taking the glass of wine and the plate of lobster salad Leanne handed him and kissed her bare shoulder. 'What a lovely end to a perfect night.'

Leanne finished her food, drained her glass and handed it to Tony. She lay down, snuggling under the blanket, Bridget curled up at her feet. 'Can't keep my eyes open,' she mumbled. 'Sorry for not being romantic. I can't seem to stay awake. G'night, sweetie.'

'Very sleepy myself,' Tony said, joining her under the blanket and putting his arms around her. 'And isn't this as romantic as it gets; us here together in a boat, the waves rocking us to sleep?'

'Mmm...' Leanne mumbled. 'S'lovely.'

'Night, my Irish colleen,' Tony whispered.

They were asleep in seconds, arms entwined around each other, until the first rays of the morning sun poked through the porthole, waking them up to a new day and the journey they were about to begin. Together.

Farewell, dear friends and followers.

Have your hankies ready, because this is going to be a little sad… Today is the day when Maddy and I depart in different directions. It's also the last day of our great Euroscape. Oh what a fantastic, fabulous, incredible roller coaster ride it's been! Since we set off from Dublin a month ago, we have had the most amazing adventures, met incredible people and most importantly of all, had some truly life-changing experiences. Neither Maddy or I are the same women who got into that gorgeous car and drove off into the wild blue yonder. During our trip, we've had some hair-raising adventures, caught up with people from our past, made new friends and found true love with the most unlikely but wonderful men. I can't speak for Maddy, who doesn't want her love life splashed all over the Internet, but I certainly want to shout it from every rooftop I can climb onto. I have to confess that I have kissed a lot of frogs in my quest to find my prince. This wasn't a totally unpleasant experience and I had a lot of fun with a lot of frogs, some of them really cute. But then – wham! – there he was, Mr-oh-so Right, hovering in the background while I was busy flirting with Mr Wrong. But then my vison cleared, the clouds scattered and I saw him… Yes, you might have guessed, it's the cute doctor. That's all I'm going to say for now, because this is about Maddy and me. And she deserves a huge round of applause and hugs and kisses for being such a true-blue friend in all kinds of weathers. Gorgeous, fun, smart, kind, everything you would wish your future stepmother to be. Oops, did I reveal something there? Ah, well, sorry, Mads, it's out there now. And in any case the secret will be out soon. I will say no more, except that my dear dad is a lucky man...

So, darling friends, as I sail into the sunset with the cute doctor, I will think of you and wish you all the best. And don't think you'll have seen the last of me! I'm planning a blog of my very own, but haven't set it up yet. If you follow my Instagram account, I'll keep you posted there.

What will we do now, you might wonder. Well, we have to go back to our teaching jobs for one more school year, which will give us a chance to plan the next chapter in our lives. Funny how we now need to take a break from this champagne lifestyle! But I have to tell you, lads, luxury living takes a lot of work! Looking good, staying slim, and being polite all the time is EXHAUSTING! Not to mention all the painful spa treatments – ouch! Now I'm looking forward to lying on the couch in my pyjamas eating burritos and watching a box set of Game of Thrones. True bliss.

And Bridget? She will be taking up residence with me in my new flat in Dublin and will be all mine, except Maddy gets to have her on Sundays.

So this is cheerio for now, but not goodbye. Thank you from the bottom of our hearts for your support and all the fun, cheery comments to our posts. We love you! Hugs and kisses from us both,

Maddy, Leanne and, of course Bridget, who waves her cute little paw at you.

A Letter from Susanne

Thank you so much for reading *A Holiday to Remember*. I hope you enjoyed reading this story just as much as I did writing it. If you want to keep up to date with my new releases, please click on the link below to sign up for my newsletter. I will only contact you with news of a new book and never share your email address with anyone else.

www.bookouture.com/susanne-oleary

I love hearing from my readers and would be very interested to get your reactions to the story. Did it make you smile or even cry at times? Did something in the life stories of Maddy and Leanne feel familiar to you? And did you love the settings as much as I did when I visited the locations in real life? I would love to hear your thoughts on the book in a short review. Getting feedback from readers is hugely helpful to authors, as it might help new readers pick up one of my books. I will continue writing and hope you will keep reading my stories!

While you're waiting for my next book, you might like to try one of my earlier releases, which you will find on my website.

Thanks,
Susanne

www.susanne-oleary.com

authoroleary

@susl

Acknowledgements

Again, huge thanks to my amazing editor Christina Demosthenous for her support and terrific feedback that always hits the right notes, the terrific team at Bookouture, and the gang in 'the lounge'! Also my Italian friends Patricia and Luigi, who brought us on that sailing trip in the Dalmatian islands, which gave me so much inspiration for this book. That was truly a holiday to remember! Many thanks also to my family and friends, many of whom actually read my books!

Made in the USA
Coppell, TX
17 September 2021